JOY COMETH WITH THE MOURNING

DAVE FREER

JOY COMETH WITH THE MOURNING Copyright © 2014
Dave Freer
Cover art: Tasmanian Church © Anne Davis
Title page art: Early spring landscape © Torky
Interior art: Wild duck spring © Ard 001 Dreamstime.com
Proof reading by Periwinkle Proofs
Printed by Createspace
All rights reserved.
ISBN-13: 978-0-9925490-2-2

A Magic Isle Press Imprint

DEDICATION

**This book is dedicated to the memory of
Johanna Alida Freer 1916-2009
Until we meet again, mother.**

Other books by Dave Freer
Morningstar
A Mankind Witch
Dragon's Ring
Dog and Dragon
Cuttlefish
The Steam Mole
Stardogs

By Dave Freer and Eric Flint
Rats, Bats & Vats
The Rats, the Bats & the Ugly
Pyramid Scheme
Pyramid Power
Slow Train to Arcturus
Sorceress of Karres

By Dave Freer, Eric Flint & Mercedes Lackey
The Shadow of the Lion
This Rough Magic
Much Fall of Blood
Burdens of the Dead
Wizard of Karres

More books are only available on Kindle at this point.

Author's Note

This is a work of fiction. Any resemblance to real people or places is pure coincidence. My thanks go to my first reader, Barbara, and to Rosemary A, Anne Davis, Meredith Loudon, Mel Telfer, Melissa Siah, Christine Dorsett and Tania Shipman for reading and commenting for me, to Bill and Maria La Grue for various bits of technical advice on mechanical and art matters. I also need to thank Dr Alex John, and Sergeant Russ Judges for their advice on matters of unexpected death. Any errors are mine, not theirs.

I have donated the print and electronic rights (and the proceeds from that) for this book to the Anglican Parish of the Furneaux Islands for the next ten years. It is a tiny, isolated parish, and my family's church, serving a small community in remote Australia. Like many small parishes in far-flung places we struggle to make ends meet. Right now, we can't afford a priest, and that means while we have an excellent and dedicated ministry team, there is no regular communion service. My mother always said: 'God helps those who help themselves,' and this is my attempt to do just that. I'm a writer, not a millionaire, so what I have to help it with is words and a story.

CHAPTER 1

"I've, um never really... er grasped the country life," said Reverend Joy Norton, hoping her voice and her face didn't betray her dismay.

The Bishop peered at her over the top of his half spectacles. Looked down at her neat blue shoes. And at their heels. Joy felt herself flush, slightly. She was only 5'3". Heels weren't vanity. She corrected herself. Not entirely vanity.

A small smile twitched at the corner of the bishop's mouth. "You'll get over the mud, Joy. Buy a pair of gumboots. They make nice flowery ones now."

"It's... not the mud. Not just the mud, anyway. I'm not really sure that I am ready to... I don't know how I'll cope with... It's a lot more responsibility. I've always been part of... well, had other clergy to turn to." She knew that she was floundering. But it was true. Since she graduated from the seminary she'd been a junior part of two large city parishes. That was where she came from. It was safe and familiar.

The Bishop was smiling openly now. "And that's why you need to go, Joy. My wife thinks the experience will give you a certain gravitas. She's usually right, and if that means putting on weight, she'll be right about that too. The last time I went there I had so many cream cakes I put on three kilos before I got home. Besides there is a telephone, and the internet, and you'll find that they have a well-run parish council, and a very organized warden who chairs it. And there is always God. Even out beyond the black stump."

"I, er, try to avoid too much saturated fat. It's not good for one's health."

1

The Bishop shook his head. "You won't be able to avoid it without offending the locals. I wouldn't tell your parishioners about the health part either: most of the bakers are twice your age. Mind you, it might be what killed Peter Hallam. Look, Joy, it'll probably just be for a few months. The church and the community there need you. Having the vicar drop dead was hard enough for them, and the coroner's verdict has really upset people, I gather. And you won't have to do the funeral service. I'll be down to do that myself, and Dean Leahy and I will be there to introduce you to the church elders. You'll enjoy the place, it's a lovely little old town, with some nice walks. But I would buy the gumboots."

Of course, that wasn't quite the way it worked out. But she had bought the gumboots.

Sometimes choosing to drive the scenic route will do that to you, reflected Joy as she nudged her way along through the pelting rain. At least it stopped her worrying about meeting the parishioners who were apparently going to be waiting for her with a bring-and-share supper. God moved in mysterious ways to answer prayer, she thought wryly. When she'd asked for help in coping, she'd thought of things like self-confidence, not about having to concentrate intensely on the road instead of worrying. The route, no matter what it had said in the map-book, certainly wasn't scenic right now. It was also not so much driving as feeling her way along, because she couldn't see very far ahead, but she was so late already, she didn't want to stop. Besides if she did, she wasn't sure that her little Micra would get going again. When the psalmist had written about the mountains running like wax he probably hadn't meant across the road, in a thin slippery slurry, but it seemed very accurate now. She had no idea how much further she had to go, the nearest thing she'd seen to a sign-post had been some large stone gate posts a kilometer or so back. She should have been concentrating entirely on the road, but her mind kept turning to the situation she was heading into. The Reverend Peter

Hallam had been found dead in the aisle of his own church. That was bad enough. And then the fact that they couldn't bury him, because the coroner would not release the body, had not helped matters at all.

The back end of a huge tractor was suddenly there, right in front of her. Joy swerved and braked. Inevitably the car slithered, and ended up, after a heart-stopping moment, with two wheels in the muddy ditch, the engine stalled. The tractor cheerfully thundered off into the gloom, leaving her shaking, clinging to the steering wheel, and sitting at a very odd angle. The rain came down steadily.

She hadn't seen a vehicle for half an hour, and then it had merely been lights coming towards her. It took her seconds to realize that those were car lights shining through the rear window... and as she frantically tried to wave, but she had been too slow to wind down the window, or think of flashing her lights. It raced on past.

Too late she thought of putting the car's hazard lights on. Trying to restart the car had got her nowhere. A nasty click sound, and then something worse, no sound at all.

Taking a deep breath, and wishing that her new gumboots had not been packed into that unreachable odd corner under her boxes of books in the boot, Joy opened her door. Black slithery mud stood waiting for her neat blue half-boots. The little car was deep in it. Well, there was nothing for it. She got out into the rain, just as the headlights of yet another a car came around the corner.

She waved hopefully, and got a shower of muddy water as the large maroon Land Cruiser SUV rushed past, leaving her looking at the disappearing tail lights and thinking very uncharitable thoughts. She barely noticed the fact that a second vehicle had drawn up quietly, sidling up next to her. It was a muddy white ute, and the driver leaned over and opened the passenger door: "Hullo love. Are you a duck, or would you like to get in out of the rain?"

"Duck?" she said, bobbing her head down... and then opening the door fully, before being suddenly struck by doubt.

"Well, it is nice weather for you then," said the driver. "Hop in, while I have a look-and-see if your little car can be pulled out or if you'll need a tow-truck."

She did. It was better than standing in the rain. The driver roughly cleared space for her on the cluttered seat. He was a weather-beaten fellow of middle years, with bright eyes, a large nose, hair like white thatch and a small clipped beard of more or less the same shade. He edged the vehicle forward, putting his hazards on too. As he did this he asked "So what happened, love?"

Joy was about to point out that actually she wasn't his love, or a duck, when it occurred to her that her Samaritan was at least not driving past. And she was already wet, and really didn't want to get wetter. "I braked for a tractor."

"Always wise. But next time stay on the road too," he said with a cheerful lack of sympathy, and started rooting around at her feet. She pulled them aside in alarm, and he pulled out a section of chain, and a length of stout, oily rope, and an elderly torch from under the seat. "Sit tight. I'll go and have a look."

He got out into the rain, but he was wearing muddy gumboots and an elderly Drizabone oilskin, and seemed unworried by the downpour. She sat there and shivered slightly, partly from the shock and partly from being soaked just in those few minutes. It was at least warm in the cab. The engine was running, and the heater was on.

Her rescuer came back, dripping, with mud on his knees. "Back into the rain and mud for you, I'm afraid. I have got the shackle on your little car's towing loop, but you'll have to steer and apply brakes when we get her out. Do you want my jacket? I'm afraid it is pretty wet already."

"Oh, no. I'm also wet already. Thank you, but I'd just wet the inside of it. I have dry clothes in the car, and, er, and we can't be that far from Felixtown?

"About five miles. Now try and start but don't drive forward until you see me wave out of the window. You'll just dig in."

"Um, I did try to start the car again... and she didn't want to."

"That's the problem with making cars female," he said, cheerfully treading feminism beneath his muddy heel. "They do what they want and not what they have to. The worst comes to the worst, I'll tow you to my shed. It'll be better than working on it in the rain. Then I can see if you need more than a farm mechanic. If it won't start, put it in neutral. You probably have power assisted brakes to add to your joys. Well, off you go then."

So she went. If anything, it was raining harder, and darkness was closing in now, even if it wasn't four o' clock yet. Joy got out of the warm security reluctantly, and squelched and slithered her way back into the Micra. She tried starting it again, failed, put it in neutral and then found herself moving steadily forward. The steering was heavy, and brakes... well, when she popped out of the ditch and back onto the road she thought she was going to hit his towbar. The car did stop, and so did her rescuer. He got out again. "Not going, is she?"

"Um. No. I think her feelings are hurt."

He laughed. "I'll tow her to the shed where she can fraternize with a manly tractor and a dashing quad."

"I'm having trouble braking."

"It's mostly uphill from here, and I'll take it slowly."

Joy was always a nervous driver, and he could have been pulling her through the gates of hell, or Jerusalem, for all she saw of the rainy surroundings. But she did manage to stop, hands white-knuckled on the steering wheel, in the shed. It was huge, dim, and full of farm machinery.

5

He got out of his ute and turned the shed lights on as she was still damply unfolding herself from the seat of the Micra. It was plain that, besides being the home of the workaday tractor and quad bike, she'd arrived at the place where old machines came to die, or at least to be dismembered.

"I'm a bit of a junk man," he said apologetically, taking in her startled look. "I hate seeing something useable being thrown away. You look wet and frozen. Do you want take your dry clothes through there" – he pointed at a door – "and get changed and warm. I'll fiddle with your car."

"Oh, yes. I'll just have to get my bag out of the boot. Look, I could just 'phone the AA or, or the local garage. I don't want to take up any more of your time."

"Oh, it's no trouble," he said. "You've saved me a trip into town to meet the new minister they've sent us. My sister pestered me into going, and now I have the perfect excuse. Mud on my knees and I only have one pair of smart trousers. Can't meet the priesthood like that."

"Um, that would be me," said Joy. "And even with mud on your knees I would say that being a good Samaritan was a better reason for not going in to town."

He looked at her, askance, and then started laughing. "Ah, not only a duck, but a mallard duck," said he, shoulders shaking.

Joy wondered briefly if she'd fallen in with a lunatic. "What?" she asked warily.

"They have clerical collars around their necks," he explained. "At least the males do! So they've sent us a woman minister? Well, now that's going to be interesting in this district. I can't wait to see Major Ambleside-Smith's face." He thrust out a hand, and then pulled it back and hastily wiped it on his trousers, before sticking it out again. "Tom Truman. Nice to meet you."

A punster. Possibly worse than a lunatic, if less dangerous, she thought to herself. What else could she do but take the hand. "Joy Norton. You would get on well with my Bishop. He shares your sense of humor."

"And you're not sure you do," he said, as if he was rather used to that. "I try to avoid Bishops. Now, you'd better come inside and call my sister. They have a welcoming committee waiting for you. If you want to get your dry clothes out, I'll get the kettle boiling." He sighed. "I daresay I'll have Mary here in ten minutes to rescue you from my clutches, and demanding tea at the same time."

"Mary Truman is your sister?" asked Joy, as she opened her car boot. Mary Truman was the person the Bishop had said would be so helpful.

He threw out his hands and smiled. "For my sins, yes. She is a typical older spinster sister. Interferes in my life endlessly. She's the chair of the Parish Council. I wish you luck. It's easier to go along with her than to resist, as your predecessor told me, and after nearly fifty years of it, I had to agree with him. Only women are allowed to even voice dissent, and so I'm out of luck there."

"You're not married then?" she asked, taking the top case out, wishing she'd packed more systematically, rather than assuming she would unpack it all into a cupboard.

He shook his head, for the first time, not smiling or saying anything. Just taking her case, and leading the way through a doorway, down a passage to the house, where he kicked his boots off with the ease of long practice. He obviously saw her start to bend down. "Don't worry about your shoes. Years of habit in my case."

"But they're very muddy," she said, parting with them. Her stockings were rather poor protection from the concrete floor. She was glad to go through the next door and into the kitchen of his house. It was delightfully warm, with a wood-burning stove in the corner. "Basket, Belle," he said patting the head of the Border Collie who greeted him with an adoring tail-wag. The dog was instantly obedient, although obviously curious about the visitor. "I'd best call Mary," he said, picking up the phone from a cradle just inside the door. "She'll be getting her n...herself upset. And then she'll take it out on all of us."

As he was dialing Joy had a few moments to look around in the room, while the Border Collie, from the basket in front of the fire, watched her with unblinking eyes. It was obvious that Mr. Truman spent most of his indoor time here – there was an armchair, a TV on a bracket, a newspaper on the wooden table... and very little else showing signs of use, apart from a coffee mug in the drying rack. He might be a bachelor, but he was a Spartan one. The window above the sink had pink floral curtains, lace trimmed, and there was a small potted begonia...

"Yes, actually I do know that I am late, but so is your new minister," said her rescuer. "Which is my fault, of course."

Joy could understand why he held the receiver away from his ear. She could hardly avoid eavesdropping without leaving the room, or possibly the house. "Thomas, I was relying on you. I am so disappointed," said the booming voice down the telephone. "Anyway, we've just heard that the Menham Bridge has been closed so they won't be able to make it."

Her rescuer winked at Joy. "I've been waiting for years to tell you that you're wrong, Mary. And now I can. I've got your new priest here at the farm."

"What?" demanded the voice down the 'phone at full volume.

"Rescued from a ditch, one wet, miserable little lady-priest. She came over Hangman's pass, and ended up going off the road just on Pascoe's corner. I am going to see if I can sort her car out while she gets into some dry clothes and warms up."

"My goodness. Dear Lord! I'll be there in two minutes! Does she need a Doctor?"

"I'd guess he'd prescribe dry clothes and a cup of tea. Take it easy on the road. I've done my share of rescues for one day."

"Well, see that she gets that tea, and a warm bath immediately. We'll be there soon. Good-bye, Thomas."

He put the 'phone down. "The irresistible force. I didn't think of a hot bath. Would you..."

"No thank you. Just some dry clothes, and a cup of tea, would be wonderful."

He nodded, and picked up her case. "Follow me." He led her out of the kitchen down a short passage. Stopped at a cupboard. "You could probably use a towel." He took one out of the linen store, and handed it to her, before leading her on to the next door. "In here. I'll go and ginger up the fire a bit, and put another kettle on. Mary will probably whisk you away, but she may demand more tea first. She's good at that."

One of the things that life before entering the Ministry had done for Joy, was to make her good at noticing details. She had always been quite fussy about them, and working as a museum illustrator had honed those habits. She didn't need to be that observant to realize this was a girl's room. The three fluffy ponies on the bed, the heart shaped little pillow, the little dressing table, the knick-knacks among the horse-riding trophies on the shelf, and the rosettes and ribbons pinned on the edge told that story. The table was slightly dusty, and the air had a faint mustiness to it. He put the case on the bed, waved at it and walked out, closing the door. She wondered about her rescuer. Divorced? Widowed? Plainly sensitive ground, whatever it was. She opened her case, and, naturally, the top items were an alb and a cassock. That might be a little too much! She found her blouse with a clerical collar, some slacks and a warm, navy cabled cardigan with a broad collar and large buttons. Not her first choice for meeting her new parish council, but acceptable. The only problem was shoes – either rather wet or somewhere in the depths of the car boot.

She dressed, tidied her hair as best as she could, and then considered putting the wet clothes in the case. She settled on folding them instead, and carried them, and her case, back to the kitchen.

"You could have left that for me," he said.

"I'm quite capable of carrying my own luggage."

"Yes, but I come from an era when it was considered polite, as was calling a woman a lady. And now I am too old to change," he said cheerfully. "And I have no intention of trying. Now, tea? Coffee? Hot chocolate... er, I think I have some. And only ordinary tea I'm afraid. I don't do chamomile or mint or whatever."

Somehow she would have been surprised if he did. "Just tea would be wonderful."

"Do have the chair," he said, waving at the slightly worn leather recliner, with a folded old tartan rug on the arm. "I'd take you through to the lounge but I haven't got the wood-heater burning in there. It takes a while to warm up."

"But I can't take your chair," she protested.

"Why not? I won't be using it. Pop your case down. Sit, and I'll make a pot of tea."

She chose instead to sit at the kitchen table. The black-and-white sheepdog slipped out of her basket, sniffed tentatively at Joy's legs, and lay down at her feet. She patted the silky head.

Her host noticed. "Oh you are favored. I hope you don't mind."

"She's lovely. Very well behaved," said Joy who had met some rather boisterous dogs in her work in the city.

"She's a timid girl, is my Belle. But a very good working dog."

"So tell me about my new congregation?" she asked, as he busied himself making tea.

"Me? Oh you'll get it all from Mary. I suppose it is a typical country parish. Rather conservative about most things. Too many old folk, too many women... I suppose from my point of view anyway. Your predecessor was doing a good job to change things, I think or at least he was trying. He joined the local gun club, and was in with the local fly-fishermen."

"Oh dear. I think I may fall short on that... I'm not very familiar with the country."

He laughed. "Neither was Peter Hallam. He couldn't shoot or catch fish, poor fellow, but people took the will for the deed. He joined everything, even the local art group for a bit. They thought his efforts cartoonish. His death was a bit of a shock." He raised his eyebrows at her. "You do know they're saying that he was murdered?"

"I'd heard the coroner had reserved judgment."

He snorted. "In a country district that's as good as saying 'we found the axe embedded in his head, he'd been shot fifteen times at long range... we think it might be suicide.' They all know that he was murdered, and the details get even more lurid and inventive by the day."

In spite of herself, Joy asked, "But was he?" as her host brought a tray with a teapot, mugs and a sugar bowl across to the table, and sat down.

He shrugged. "Probably not. But that doesn't stop the old tabbies gossiping. There's not much on TV. And he had rather fed it, I'm afraid. He said to me someone was out to get him, and he had also separately spoken of it to Mary, and I gather to a few other people, by the stories. Who knows? Maybe he was right. The fact is: he thought he was going to die, and then he did."

It was, she rationalized, her job to hear these rumors and scotch them. "Who did he think was trying to kill him?"

"Ah." said Tom, turning the teapot round three times before pouring the tea. "That's where it gets really complicated. It seems he changed his mind, depending on who he was talking to, and the day. He suspected everyone from the local pagan to my sister. But he did believe it was going to happen. He had a new will made up about a week before his death. I was one of the witnesses. And, no, he wasn't killed for his fortune, because he didn't have one. More than that I won't say."

"He sounds, well, paranoid."

"Sometimes he seemed a little that way. But he was not a bad fellow, really."

"So who would have wanted to kill him?"

"Oh, not more than three-quarters of the village," he said, he said with a wry smile.

"But I thought you said he was doing a good job and was not a bad fellow?"

"I said he was trying. But why does that change anything? You know, the trouble with a small community is you can't avoid each other like you can in the city. There are only just so many people, and it doesn't matter if Henry is a Green or Jenny an atheist... you can't live in separate worlds as you could do in a larger place. They'll be on at least one committee with you, go into town and you'll meet them. And sometimes the small gets very large out here. Sugar?"

"No thank you. I don't want to get very large out here too."

"Ah, but a bit of sugar might sweeten you up. Give you energy. And I think you're going need it. Honestly, the suspicion is worse than having a known felon in our midst."

"I can imagine. So, why don't you actually tell me what happened? All I know from the Bishop is that the poor man was found dead in the church, presumed dead of natural causes, and then there was an issue with the coroner."

"Well, yes, that's the story in a nutshell... but the devil is in the details."

"And those details are?"

"My sister turned up to collect a hymn book for the service she was preparing. She found him sprawled in the aisle, she checked to see if he was breathing, and when he wasn't, she rushed out to call the Ambos. They arrived as she got to the gate, they tried CPR, loaded him into the ambulance, whisked him off to the hospital, where he was pronounced dead."

"Your ambulance service is very fast."

"Aha. Detail number one. Actually, she never got to her mobile, which was in her purse in the car. The Ambos were there already, called from the rectory 'phone, by persons unknown. The front doors to the church were locked, but the back one was ajar. And, as you'll find out, the local doctor who was initially disposed to sign the death certificate... changed his mind and asked for a full post-mortem examination. More I don't actually know. I don't think anyone does. But you will doubtless be told some interesting variations!"

"Can't you just ask the Doctor?"

"Not this one, no," said Tom, pouring her more tea. She hadn't realized she'd drunk all of it, but plainly she had. At least she was feeling warmer now. "He's a reasonably good doctor, but he believes in patient confidentiality. And he's one of the people Peter Hallam said was trying to kill him."

At this point there was a loud knocking from across the house, and a sudden cold breeze blew through.

"Close the door! We're in the kitchen," shouted Tom, getting up.

Moments later they were greeted by the irresistible force, or rather, his sister, bustling in. She was as large as he was spare, and trailing two other women in her wake. "Reverend Norton," she said, grasping both of Joy's hands, "How good to have you here. I'm Mary Truman, and this is Isabella Da Freitas," she waved at the dark-haired oriental-looking woman, who gave Joy a broad smile "and Lindsey McCassil," – a faded blonde, who didn't. "We're part of your parish council. Tom, how can you entertain our new Pastor in the kitchen?!"

"So nice to meet you all," said Joy. "Really, Ms. Truman, he has been so kind, stopping and rescuing me, and towing the car here."

"Mary, Mary, everyone calls me Mary, Reverend Norton," said the large affable woman. "And Tom has no manners."

"Everyone calls her Mary, except those who call her 'Contrary'," said her brother, calmly. "The kitchen is warm, and she was wet and cold. The rest of the house is on the chilly side, but you're welcome to go and sit there while I go and fiddle with the car."

"And you haven't given her anything to eat!" said his sister, ignoring his comments, as she was plainly used to doing.

"The only biscuits I have are for Belle. If I have people-biscuits, I eat them. So I don't buy them," he said, moving to the door in unhurried strides, with the sheepdog suddenly pressed hard against his knee. She wasn't staying with strangers! "Now, I'll leave you to the women folk and go and see what I can do about that car. You can stay in the kitchen and be warm, or go into the lounge and be cold. I'll be off to the quiet of the shed!"

"He's impossible," said his sister, shaking her head at the closing door. "Shall we go and sit in the lounge?"

It was a command, really. But Joy felt she would have to establish herself in the parish, and now was as good a time to start as any. Besides, she felt Tom Truman had not really wanted anyone in the rest of his house, and she did owe him a debt of gratitude. "If you don't mind, I would rather stay here in the kitchen. I did get rather wet and cold, and I am appreciating the heat."

"Is much nicer here," said the still smiling Isabella. "Such a good brother you have, Mayree. "

"And it is rather lovely in a farm kitchen," said the faded blonde. "So homely. A country welcome."

Mary Truman sniffed. "A country welcome has food. Tom never does. And the place looks like a barracks. At least Alice always had it suitably decorated! Anyway, we've got almost everything all ready for you in the rectory. You'll have to forgive us. We had to put poor Father Hallam's possessions in boxes in the spare room. I was hoping to ask the Bishop about what we must do with them. But this isn't the country welcome we wanted to show you."

"Really," said Joy, "Being able to get warm and dry, a cup of tea, and help when I needed it, seemed very welcoming to me! Though I must admit that until your brother came to my rescue, I thought I had blundered into Psalm 107, you know: 'I wandered in the wilderness in a solitary way; I found no city to dwell in'."

"Sounds like a good thing to do," said Tom Truman coming back in. "Considering cities. How times change, once they were good places to live in. I've sorted your car's problem out, by the way. The coil lead had come off with the bump. She's not built for your wilderness wandering or ditch-driving."

"Oh thank you! You've been so kind," exclaimed Joy, relieved.

"A regular good Samaritan," said Tom, with a skew smile. "So, now that I've met you, I'll let them take you off into town and talk holes in your head. I've still got mud on my knees. I can't go."

"I'll come in with you, Reverend Norton," said Mary, "To show you the way and to keep you company."

"Oh no you won't," said Lindsey. "Isabella or I can, I'm not driving that tank of yours."

"Um, the passenger front seat is rather cluttered," said Joy, looking to head off battle royal. "I wasn't expecting a passenger."

"Is no problem, I go!" said Isabella, with one of those smiles that said it really wasn't a problem to her. "I am small. I help. I put on my lap. Is not far."

Joy decided she was probably going to like Isabella. Her English was quite accented, but if a face ever said 'good-natured, and kindly' without speaking, it was hers. "I could clear..."

"Nice hair." Isabella said, taking Joy's arm, and leading her towards the door. "I cut the hair here."

That was it. Sooner or later, hairdressers heard everything. If healing the schisms in this community required her finding out who killed Peter Hallam... this woman would hear. And sooner or later she'd also need her hair done too. "I am sure I can clear enough space for you." She turned back to her rescuer, who was looking at his sister's chagrin with a finger to his lips, and a decidedly unholy smile on his face. "Thank you so much, again. I can't tell you how much I appreciate it."

"It's a pleasure," he said. "Always good to help someone suffering from a Mallardy."

"What malady?" asked his sister.

"Donald's!" grinned a man who would plainly pun, and play on words for hours if he got the chance.

Joy acknowledged that play in the time honored fashion of a groan, and shaking her head. The punster beamed at her.

"Thomas, I wish you'd talk sense! Donald is doing quite well," said Mary Truman. "Well, I will see you at the rectory," and she made a sweeping exit, followed by Lindsey.

Joy found herself ushered to her car. Their host came out with them, bearing her case. He plainly considered packing a favorite form of puzzle, as he managed to get all the bits and pieces from the front seat into the boot or the foot-well, leaving Isabella a small amount of foot-room. "I spent too long at sea. No space shall be wasted!" he announced.

They drove out along the muddy track, and onto the main road again. Joy, always a nervous driver, was even more so now, and she was not really inclined to chat, but rather to concentrate. Her companion seemed completely at ease, and made up for her silence for her. "A very nice man Tom. Is so kind. He cut down the pear tree for me. Is so sad about his wife. I never think it!"

Before Joy could ask what she never thought, Isabella was off on another tangent. "So sad the Reverend Peter. He was a very nice man. He like my flowers. He like the boy scouts."

Why those two should go together was a mystery that the wet road stopped her thinking about too much. "So have you been here long?"

"Fifteen year now. Is a very nice place. So friendly. You like it. Look, that where Mr Donald live. You know him?"

Joy didn't look – she kept her eyes on the road. "Um, no."

"Oh, he is nice man. Very clever. He is pharmacist in town."

Joy was beginning to wonder if anyone wasn't a very nice man. But the tone suggested a distinction between nice and very nice. "Is he one of our congregation?"

"Oh no!" she sounded slightly shocked. "He is... atheist. He fight with Reverend Peter. Shouting. Shouting."

"Oh. Did Peter Hallam have lots of fights with people?"

For the first time there was a silence from her companion. Eventually Isabella said: "Some. Sometimes he... he was not like usual. He said to me one time I am trying to kill him! He cough and cough and cough from the product I use on his hair. Allergic. I did not know! He never say. And no-one else ever was allergic. It say hypo-allergic. I ask Mr. Donald he say is a good product, very safe. Just some people react to funny things. He say was not product, was maybe the coating on the protection. He laugh a lot. I don't understand. Ah. You turn here!"

So Joy did, and followed Isabella's simple directions to the neat red-brick house next door to the chocolate-box little white church with stone corners, and a small steeple. "It is a lovely church! I do flowers, Mrs. Smithson do flowers, Mary do flowers, and we have roster to clean silver and brass and windows."

"I'm looking forward to seeing it, to meeting all of you."

The rectory fortunately had a carport to let them park in the dry and unload. They each took a case. "Everybody come fetch as soon as they know you are here. Come, come," said Isabella. There were several other cars already parked there, a large station wagon, and a maroon Land Cruiser...

Joy had to wonder if the car that had so studiously ignored her, stuck in a ditch, was driven by one of the people she was about to meet... or had met.

Inside the door was a little hallway, which was ornamented with a pair of large wellingtons and several dripping umbrellas, ranging from a utilitarian large black one to a frilly edged purple one, and a dripping raincoat. The smell of fresh baking and something deliciously tomato scented had seeped into the hallway, as did the sound of loud voices. A lower pitched one, and a loud high pitched voice: "I don't care! It's not fair that she shouldn't be told! I mean..."

Isabella opened the door, "Hello! We are come!"

That silenced the voices within, so Joy went inside to meet them. They were a rather varied group, but she did understand why Tom Truman had been happy to have an excuse not to be there. Of the welcoming committee, only one was male, and he was on the elderly side of very elderly, and appeared completely unaware of her entry. The white-haired woman next to him gave him a prod with her elbow, and he looked up, and hastily fiddled with his ear. Then there was a welter of introductions, and, as was usual with such meetings, it was very hard to keep track of who was who. Luckily, they didn't seem to realize that she had no real idea who they were yet. It was intimidating, but she'd sort them out as time went on. The trouble was that she was deathly tired, after the drive, and after the accident, and all the stress.

Fortunately, the organized Mary must have noticed. There were some advantages to that sort of personality in a crowd, in that she banished everyone quite effectively and, for a church group, fast. It couldn't have taken more than an hour, and in the process the dishes had been washed and various casserole pots taken away. Joy regretted only the departing lasagna, but at least she had a loaf of home-made sourdough for company.

It must have been noisy sourdough, because, tired as she was, she lay in her new bed, unsleeping. Thinking about the day, and thinking about the people she'd met. Thinking about her task here. A resolution to the question of what had happened to Father Hallam – any resolution, would be welcome. "If a kingdom be divided against itself, that kingdom cannot stand."

Who had called the ambulance? Why had it not been considered a natural death?

CHAPTER 2

It was a good thing, Joy reflected, as she donned her vestments, that even out beyond the black stump, God was still here to be talked to directly, because if she'd been relying on the internet, or the telephone, or even motor transport to get hold of him, she'd have been out of luck right now. There was certainly no earthly help on hand, as the landline was down, and the mobile 'phone tower had been damaged by the storm. The bridge was still underwater, so, at least in the human sense, she was alone with her new flock. It was a flock in which the lambs were few, some of the ewes were as curmudgeonly as rams were supposed to be, and one of the rams had impressive horns, or at least the curling horns of a moustache of impressive proportions. He felt it gave him a license to make dry comments at what he thought was a less than audible level.

The little church was quite full, despite the rain. It had never been built to hold many, but according to the parish register, thirty-five people would be an exceptional crowd. By her quick count there were thirty-seven here for this Sunday service. Curiosity had brought them in despite the rain.

It was very intimidating. She'd never been good at talking to people. Joy turned to look at the beautifully polished cross. She knew, in the logical part of her mind, that God would listen no matter where you were looking, but, well, not all of anyone was ever logical. She just couldn't do this on her own. What if I stammer? What if I forget or lose my place? What if I trip and fall or faint?

I was a man. I understand. I walked that long road under a much heavier load. And when my body failed, my father saw to it that someone else carried my cross for a while. Do you think he would do less for you if your body was falling? Get up and walk. You will have the strength, or someone will carry your load for you.

So she walked. And the words came. They were familiar, practiced, repeated often with familiar friends and support back in the city. They were the same words here too, with the same message, just with different ears to hear them. "We are the body of Christ." "We who are many are one body, because we all partake of the one bread." Except... was part of that body diseased? It was dividing them, she saw, even after the brief unity of the sacrament. When the peace was shared, there was an unease... not the usual this-goes-on-too-long greeting and gossip that she'd been told about in country parishes. It was a problem that she felt would be welcome right now. She prayed that it would prove to be someone outside the congregation, if it turned out to have been murder.

At the end of the service she waited to greet them, as they trickled out of the church. The fellow with the vast moustache was first... well, just after Isabella who scuttled past her with a hasty smile, "I go turn up the urn!"

"Not a bad sermon, Vicar. Better than that other feller. But I prefer the old service. I'm Ambleside-Smith. Major. British Army, retired. This is my wife Penelope."

The woman in the print skirt, and the fur tippet was one of the ladies from last night's welcome. She was quite a bit younger than the Major, still on the other side of sixty, Joy decided. She had a small prim mouth, and looked as if she disapproved of smiling, but was still making the effort. It wasn't very successful.

"And this here is our son, Arthur. Doesn't come to church often enough," grumbled the Major.

Arthur had a receding hairline, was clean shaven, and wore an expression of worry that had set into permanent lines around his eyes and mouth. He was somewhat smaller than his father, had slightly stooped shoulders and looked, right now, as if he'd rather be on a death march across Borneo. Joy did her best to give him a welcoming, encouraging smile, as she shook his wet, limpid hand. Her reward was a look worthy of a rabbit facing a large Dobermann. As she was only 5'3", it was not a look Joy saw very often. His "good morning" was so inarticulately muttered that it might possibly have also been 'green Przwalski' but she took it as she assumed it was meant, and gave him a second smile, before he scampered off after his father.

The next person was Tom, but she had no idea what he said, because his words were drowned in a roar of over-revved motorbike exhaust noise, as a rider in black leathers on an off-road bike did a donut, and then got the bike up onto one wheel for a good fifty yards past the church.

"Mad MAD," said Tom Truman, cheerfully when the noise stopped echoing around the church. "You're getting a broad introduction to the local wildlife."

"Well, I wouldn't have gone that far. Just some boy playing the fool," said Joy as the thunder of the bike faded into the distance.

"No, that was Mad M.A.D., also known as Madeleine Anne Denton, being a hooligan and getting up our Major's nose. It's a family tradition of sorts."

Indeed, the mustachioed Major was shaking his fist at the departed motorcyclist. His wife was fussing around him like some overprotective mother hen, patting at his shoulder. The son was looking woefully down the road.

Tom Truman looked amused by it all. "Maddy was in my daughter's class. And inevitably when you call a child Madeleine, her name gets shortened. And when her initials are MAD too, she either has to go along with it or turn into a mouse."

"I see, Mad squared." *So he'd had a daughter, had he?* thought Joy. *Well the room she'd changed in had said that.*

He chuckled. "Oh, she's anything but square. Her parents are old hippies, and did their best to raise a carbon copy. She's actually a nice kid, when she's not play-acting. Any small community like this has its share of odd folk. You might want to steer clear of the Chamomile Natural Foods Café and People's Store on the main street though. That's mummy. She takes it all to a new level. Daddy's mostly harmless. Catches fish and smokes dope, not always in that order."

"I wonder why I left the excitement of the inner city. Hello Mrs. McCassil."

"I'm not married, actually," said the faded blonde of last night.

"Oh, I am sorry."

"Not to worry. It happens all the time."

It did not sound as if her thoughts concurred with the words.

The line of people continued and Joy did her best to fix names to people, before going to the tea laid out in the little church hall, where she tried to do the same, assisted by cream sponges. They seemed to be doing their very best as a congregation to keep the dairy industry afloat, at least in this district. That was real butter in the shortbread, real butter and real cream on the scones, with real strawberry jam. Could one make false strawberries to go in jam, Joy wondered? Obviously, not here, though. They'd drum you out of the congregation, if not the town.

After the congregation left, the last of the faithful zealously cleaning the floor after washing and drying cups, Joy was left alone, to return to the rectory. The sun was coming back to Felixtown, peeping through the scurrying clouds. So was telephonic communication, by the ringing sound from the rectory. It was the backup support team, now that they were no longer needed. She knew, now, that the Bishop had been right, and that she could do this, without their help. She had been given more than they could offer.

23

"And how was your cream?" asked his assistant, calling on the crackly line from civilization. Obviously the reputation of the place had spread far and wide, especially wide.

"Creamy and plentiful, Dean Mellors. I was going to take a long walk to try and work some of it off."

"It's a pretty area, and I enjoyed a lovely walk along the coast when Linda and I went there on holiday. Of course I am a bit old for that now. And how was your introduction to the congregation? I'm sorry we couldn't be there, but I'm sure you managed fine."

"I think the service went off reasonably well. But I must say the Bishop was right: it's a house divided at the moment."

"I spoke to one of my friends in the police. He says given the lack of evidence it'll probably be put down to natural causes eventually. Once they're through investigating witnesses. It's a low priority matter, apparently."

"I don't think that'll actually help. If anything it might make matters quite a bit worse. I would guess most of them believe he was murdered."

"Well, then, I suppose it is part of your mission to persuade them that he wasn't."

It was casually said, but, thinking about it later, as she walked down the street towards the sea, perhaps it was just what she had to do. Or she had to, at least, help them to forgive.

The church and the rectory were just on the edge of the town proper, which was barely two streets of commercial district, leading down to the sea, and not more than three blocks long, in which nothing went above two stories high. The architecture spoke too much of the sixties to make it beautiful. It did make it square and slightly weather-beaten, however. The town was one of the earliest settlements on the coast, but apparently most of the original buildings had been destroyed in a fire in the fifties. The church on the very edge of town was one of the few places to have survived that fire.

Still, the town had everything that a farming district could want... a farmers' Co-operative on the main street, two car dealerships with utes and tractors, a small supermarket, a post office, two banks and a pharmacy. They were all closed on a Sunday, bar the supermarket, which had a 'Sunday open from 10 AM – 3 PM' sign. There were a few cars parked outside it, but Joy had the street to herself, except for two kids riding their scooters along the pavement, and a wild-haired guy drifting a swaying path along the road. He looked under-washed, but, by the standards of the city, comfortably plump for someone under the influence at two on a Sunday afternoon. He was singing tunelessly to himself, and didn't even appear to see her as he wandered past.

Joy was accustomed to using her nose to work out just what the possible substance abuse was – inner city work among the homeless had taught her that knowing what the problem was, was part of finding the solution, or at least the best way to help. Cannibis, alcohol, the smell heroin gave to their sweat... One smelled the unwashed, and closed one's mind to its unpleasantness, just the way that nurses did to vomit, picking up the other clues. In this case... Joy had to conclude his problem might be fish, or something that smelled that way.

At the point where the town met the sea, the road bent along it to the breakwater. There were a couple of boats at the quay, a slipway, and facing them, the parts of the town which obviously relied on tourism, and made some attempt not to look quite as ordinary and unbeautiful as the rest of the place. The enterprise on the corner was an example of how this could be taken a bit further than was appealing... it was painted to look like a tropical forest, well, at least painted with lots of jade green leaves, and biologically unlikely mauve flowers. The artwork continued onto the little pillars and portico set up around the chairs and tables on the pavement.

The sign swaying in the breeze told her that she'd found the Chamomile Natural Foods Café and Peoples' Organic food store.

Despite the weather, a couple of people were bravely sitting at the tables, being waited on by a Christmas tree... Or at least by a woman whose layers of costume jewelry, bangles, pendants, brooches, scattered over a garment made of emerald green flounces and tucks made her look like one – if you could have a Christmas tree with a Mohawk hairstyle and an expression of complete disgust on the face it wore. "Another bloody priest. And there I thought we'd killed off the last of you parasites," said the Mohawk-Christmas tree-woman. "But they're harder to get rid of than roaches or flies. And it's female. I hope it can't breed." She shook her fist at Joy. "Bugger off. We don't need your kind in Felixtown. You're a traitor to womankind."

It was hard to know just which cheek to turn. "Actually, I was hoping to buy some tofu," said Joy.

By the look on the face of the Christmas tree woman, that was the last reply she'd expected. It made the customers pack up laughing, whereas a minute ago they'd been looking embarrassed. "Well, Zenobia, you've just been telling us you wished someone in this town would try the vegetarian option, and that tofu was so much better for us," said the woman customer.

The green-clad woman closed her mouth with an audible snap. Then narrowed her eyes and stared at Joy. "You're having me on, aren't you?" she said, thrusting her head forward... now she looked more like a snapping turtle than a Christmas tree.

"No, I really was hoping to buy some Tofu. I was hoping for some of the soft tofu, the unprocessed kind," said Joy, innocently.

"You're not a vegan are you?" the woman asked, still with a sharp edge to her voice.

"No, but I do like to watch my diet, and Tofu is a good source of calcium, or it can be, depending on how it is made."

"She's been listening to your spiel, Zenobia," said the other customer, with an unholy look of delight in his dark eyes. He was a sharp-faced man with greying temples and hair just creeping onto his collar.

"Huh. Her kind are always throwing your words back at you. They can't think of their own. Madeleine! Here, you come help this corpse-crow. She says she wants some Tofu."

"I'm feeling sick," said a sulky voice from inside. "And I'm trying to study. Can't you help her?"

"Get off your lazy butt, girl. I've got customers," she yelled back jangling her vast array of bangles and bracelets, as she waved her podgy arms around. "I know you're just reading that trash, and pretending to work." There was a voluminous sigh from inside the shop. "Go in, my daughter will help you," said Zenobia. She rolled her eyes. "Anything to help you on a quest for better health," she said sarcastically.

The incense in the shop was enough to remind Joy how little she liked that aspect of a high church service. It made her eyes water and her nose itch. The little shop had to have tables outside – there was no room inside. The walls were full of shelves holding all sorts of seeds, dried fruit, mushrooms and gluten free products. The dream-catchers that hung from the roof made it a shopping experience for the short of stature, or those prepared to be permanently ducking their heads. The counter – or bric-a-brac stand, had a glass front, partitioned, which was just as well because one half held fish, shell-fish and a pink and curly-tentacled octopus, and the other had everything from olives to halloumi. Normally, it would be a place Joy would have loved to browse, without always being brave enough to try the strange things there, but now, with the incense, she just wanted to get out of the shop.

The young woman behind the counter put aside the file she was holding. Joy caught a glimpse, as it closed, of the paperback stashed inside it. Zenobia's daughter had very red hair, and a purple-dyed fringe, and if she didn't have the bracelets of her mother, she had had an entire colander made out of her ears, and had filled the holes with an array of studs. Most of them seemed to be skull shaped, some complete with cross-bones. Her facial expression actually didn't go with the hair or ear-ornaments though.

Joy had some years of counselling behind her. The girl's face, when she looked up at her, had held a mixture of fear, defiance, and outright misery -- something Joy had seen often enough before. And either the incense also made the girl's eyes water, or she had been crying. But hastily she'd masked the expression, and tried to look shop-assistant-professional. "Tofu," said the young woman. "We have silken tofu, douhua and nigari. There's also some processed stuff in the fridge over there, and we've got some almond tofu, only it's not real tofu."

"Goodness me. My friend Alia always bought it for me, so I'm not that sure exactly what I want. She showed me how to make a sort of dessert with palm sugar..."

"Aha. You want douhua. Was your friend Malaysian?"

"Why yes. Chinese, but from Malaysia. She was very brave. It was not easy for her to be Christian, let alone to enter the Ministry. If I could have about 300 grams please? And could I get some palm sugar here too? I love that."

"On that shelf behind you," said the girl, pointing.

"Thank you. That's wonderful. I didn't expect to find this kind of food here." Joy smiled, and almost got a smile back, before the girl lapsed into the sullen-defiant expression. She peered out of the door to where Zenobia was in loud, animated conversation, accompanied by bangle castanets, and grimaced slightly. "Mother buys it. We mostly end up eating it."

"The seafood looks fresh and wonderful!"

"Yeah. That moves. Keeps us afloat in winter. That'll be five dollars thirty."

Joy paid, took her change and left before she actually started sneezing. Zenobia studiously ignored her, as she threaded her way out, onto the pavement again, carrying her little paper packet. Joy walked on, down towards the small dock, looking at the wheeling seagulls, and the sea-spray flying up above the breakwater.

That was a very unhappy young woman, presumably the motorcyclist of this morning. She'd still been wearing the leather jacket.

There was an art gallery two doors along, and Joy walked over to their window, thinking that the poor shop-keeper must spend his or her entire life trying to clean the sea-spume off it. There was enough spume on the inside too, but most of that was painted onto the pictures. It seemed that a sea-side art gallery had to sell seascapes. The prices, thought Joy, looking at them with a professional eye, were enough to make one's eyes water even if the salt spray didn't.

"Ah. Does an interest in art go with the clerical collar?" asked someone from behind her, nearly making her drop her tofu and jump into the plate glass window. She turned to see who it was. It was the woman who had been at the table outside the café. "I'm Amabelle Tilton. The chairperson of the local artist group. Can we interest you in joining us? Do you paint? Your predecessor came on several of our outings."

Now here was an opportunity to mix with the locals. But something, perhaps in the woman's tone when she'd commented on the tofu to Zenobia set warning bells ringing. Joy had had a professional training in art, and knew herself to be a reasonably competent museum-class illustrator, which meant precise drawing and colors. There were several slim volumes of flower guides, and one of birds of prey, and a fish identification manual, out there to prove that she had been good at it. Joy settled for hedging. It would be wrong to lie, but there was no harm in not saying too much. "I've only just got here. I really don't know how much opportunity I will get. Did Reverend Hallam join you often?

"For a few sessions, yes. But honestly he just couldn't grasp watercolor. His pictures were ludicrous. He just wasn't getting it right. He got quite angry when I told him so and offered to teach him. He could be a little strange."

"Oh, I am sorry. People have very different ideas about art, of course. And it is difficult when you're starting anything new."

"We have a lot of beginners. I make sure they get the basic skills right! You'd be fine, as long as you can take instruction."

Joy wondered just how closely she would be required to follow those instructions to be 'fine'. "Perhaps I should just hold off for a while. It's very difficult to follow directly in someone's footsteps without being compared to them." To change the subject she pointed at the pictures in the window. "Some of these are lovely."

"That's one of mine, said Amabelle, pointing to a slightly out of perspective fishing-boat on a turquoise sea. "That is Zenobia's partner's boat. One of my better pictures, but no buyers yet. What do you think of it?"

Rather than have to say '*You've got the shading on the boat going in two different directions, and the man's proportions are wrong*' Joy said: "Oh. Is that her husband?" She pointed at the bearded man pictured hauling at the rope.

That got a snort of laughter. "Zenobia? Husband? You must be joking. She regards marriage as a form of female bondage, and one step away from the evils of the church. Possibly even a step down. Don't ever get her started on the subject. Joe is the father of her child though, and does bring in the fish. The café is the only place to get fresh seafood around here, unless you catch it yourself."

"I might have to try that. Is she always so... pleasant to customers?"

"That's her on her mild setting. People are used to it," said Amabelle.

"Goodness me!"

30

The artist shrugged. "There's not a lot of competition. And actually, her food is very good. And she has the prime position for the tourists in summer. Anyway, I must be running along. I'm behind with my schedule. Cheerio. If you want to join us, just ask Isabella about the times."

"Oh, does she paint with your group?" asked Joy.

That got another bark of laughter. "She belongs to everything. She's no good of course, likes all of those garish colors, but she still comes along. Cheerio."

And with that she turned and walked off, across the road to her car, got in and drove off down the road, leaving Joy to solitude and the wind again.

The next shop along sold curios and tourist tat, and the one after that shell jewelry. So Joy turned up the next road and made her way back to the rectory with her tofu.

CHAPTER 3

The next morning Joy got a half a brick thrown through her window.

As the window was open at the time, and the brick landed on the carpet, it was somewhat less serious than it might have been. The brick was also gift-wrapped. Well, a piece of paper had been tied around it with string. Joy peered out of the window – cautiously in case the other half brick followed. It was still early – she had just got up to make coffee, before starting to try and make sense of her parish duties, and to make a start at packing up Peter Hallam's remaining property. The street was silent except for the racket the birds were making. In the distance a truck rumbled away. Somewhere in a house down the road a young child was announcing to its parents that sleep was for other people, in the traditional way. A dog barked a couple of houses away. But of the brick-thrower there was no sign. The loudest noise was the wind slamming her own lounge door.

There was a cross on the wall, and it seemed to Joy a good idea to say a few words of thanks about where she'd been standing before her morning had had half a brick added to it.

And a few seconds later she saw someone move the curtain. A hand reached in the window. She screamed.

The hand pulled back hastily, and there was a sound of running feet. After a moment of fear-paralysis, Joy ran to the window. The dog barked again, and she caught a glimpse of the back of a tousled dark head, as the person ran past the gap in the hedge.

Whoever it had been, they had not been very large. That hadn't been a very big hand. That didn't stop her from shaking a lot, and wanting to sit down. After a few minutes she got up and fetched her mobile, staying away from the windows, and from the brick. Perhaps she should have screamed louder, because no one had come to her rescue. Who should she call? The police, obviously.

Or maybe not. A still voice within her said. *If they'd had wanted to hurt you, they would have thrown it at you, or at one of the closed windows. Not the one you'd just opened wide to let in some fresh air, before wandering off into the kitchen to put the kettle on, whilst whistling 'Morning has broken.'* "They could just have knocked, or slipped a note under the door," she muttered crossly. "Instead of frightening me out of a year's growth."

She looked down at the half brick still resting on the carpet. At the piece of paper around it. Years of experience with expensive art materials said to her: that is not just a sheet of A4 from the printer. It was too thick, and, now that she looked carefully at it, she could see that the one edge had plainly been torn out of a wire binding – typical of an artist's sketch pad. She went over to it, knowing she shouldn't touch it, from the law's point of view. She knelt next to it and looked at it. Sometimes being a priest had to take precedence on the letter of the law, or even common sense, she reassured herself. Besides, the brick-tosser had tied the string with a neat little bow. She pulled it undone, unrolled the paper. It was indeed art paper. Arches 300 gsm, cotton, unless she was much mistaken. The note, signed with a skull and crossbones, said 'Homofobes go home'. It was written in a rather rounded hand, and, at a guess, with a 4 B pencil. The skull and crossbones, however, had been drawn using at least two different hardnesses of pencil, and was... professional-looking, unlike the spelling. And it was odd in some way. Joy knew she'd seen precisely that design, somewhere.

Her next step was to call in for advice to Dean Mellors. To express her doubts that it had been intended to hurt her. And to hear rather what she'd expected to hear. "I'm sorry Joy, but you've really got to report it. This time wasn't serious. Next time could be."

"I suppose so. I'll get onto it," she said, wishing it unnecessary.

"Do you need someone to come and give you some support? One of the ladies from the Parish..."

"Oh no. I'll be fine. I'll get the police to have a look at it. Was Peter Hallam known to be very anti-homosexual?" *Did someone kill him for that?* She thought, but didn't say.

"Not that I know of. He was a pretty standard old-fashioned doctrine priest, from what I recall. Not a firebrand, but with not a stain on his character as far as I know," answered Dean Mellors. "He was quite good friends with my predecessor, Dean Werthe, for some reason. But I hardly knew him, I'm afraid."

So Joy was left to call the police, who, in the shape of a big sergeant, came around remarkably promptly. She said so. He smiled. "Country district, Monday morning, Reverend Norton. This isn't the big city. We don't have a lot of crime, really. We do get very upset when people tell us we have nothing to do, but honestly, there isn't much. And with the death of the previous bloke, well, anything happening here will have to be referred to the investigating officer. He may come and see you too."

"Well, I can't tell him very much. Someone chucked a brick in through my window, stuck their hand in, and then ran away when I screamed. I'm afraid I looked at the note on the brick."

"Natural thing to do," said the Sergeant. "I'll bag it up and take it with me."

"It's written on art-paper, and has a very well executed skull and crossbones, but not great spelling skills," said Joy, showing him.

"A kid I reckon," said the sergeant looking at it. "We had a rash of skulls about five months ago. Kids got into graffiti – until I caught one of them." He gave a wry smile. "One of your parishioner's grand-daughters actually. I'll do a little follow up on that."

"Ah. Who?"

"I shouldn't have said that much. Now let's go and have a look in the garden."

The garden outside of the rectory was not overly large, and had plainly seen a sudden rash of extra work just recently. There was a huge hydrangea much in need of pruning just a few yards from the window, and a few seconds examination showed that someone had pressed into the foliage, and broken a few of the pom-poms on the side away from the window.

"That's where they stood. Not much of a long-range throw. My eight year old could have done it," said the policeman. They went back inside, finished writing the statement, and he left.

Before the kettle could boil the first of the reaction arrived, knocking at her door.

It was Mary Truman. "Hello. Can I offer you a cup of tea?" asked Joy.

"Er, the police. Have they found out who murdered dear Peter Hallam?" asked Mary Truman, ignoring the offer of tea.

"No, nothing like that. Just my criminal past catching up on me," said Joy cheerfully. And then, seeing the look on Mary's face. "That's probably not the kind of joke I should be making, is it? It was only something trivial. I would have just have left it be, only Dean Mellors seemed to think I ought to report it. Come in, if you have the time? I need to establish what else belonged to Reverend Peter. It appears he has no next of kin, and according to Dean Mellors, that means all his belongings will go to whoever he has named in his will. Your brother said something about witnessing a will, so there must be one."

"He did?" said Mary. "He never told me." She came inside. "Honestly. That man! I never know quite what is going on in his head."

"Was he a friend of Peter Hallam's?" asked Joy.

Mary shook her head. "Not really. He took him trout fishing a few times. My brother's a very odd sort of Christian. Ex-navy. He has some very strange ideas," she said, disapprovingly, busying herself with the kettle and tea things, as if she lived here... and then suddenly realized what she was doing. She guiltily started away from the kettle, blushed. "I, I am sorry. I used to make tea here quite a lot. Peter was, was so unhandy. A typical man. But so very kind."

"And you were very fond of him. Look, go ahead. I really don't mind someone else making the tea. I'm still finding my way about the kitchen."

"I was very fond of him." She'd stopped making tea. A small tear trickled down one cheek. "But not like people think. I was always very careful... in a small place like this..."

Where they know the copper has been around to see you before the dust from his footsteps has settled, thought Joy. But she didn't say that. She simply offered a box of tissues from the bench. "He's in the best of all hands now, Mary," she said.

That provoked tears in earnest. "Oh, I know. But I, we, miss him terribly," she said as she wiped her eyes. There was a knock on the door. Mary stood up hastily from the stool she'd put herself down on, and said "I'll go and effect repairs," and dashed towards the bathroom. She plainly knew the way.

"Coming, coming," Joy called, and walked slowly to the door. It was, inevitably, the next person wanting to find out just why the police had been to call. "No, actually it was nothing to do with Peter Hallam. Would you like to come in, Lindsey?" That seemed safer than the 'Ms or Miss' choice with this sensitive woman. "I was just going to have some tea."

The faded blonde came in twisting her hands together. "I can't bear this, Reverend Norton."

"Call me Joy. And tell me about it. That's partly what the priesthood is about. Listening."

"Oh. I'd... never thought of it like that. I don't think I can tell you. But it's not true."

"What isn't?" asked Joy.

"What they're saying behind her back about Peter Hallam. He wasn't having an affair with Isabella. You mustn't believe them."

As Joy hadn't actually even heard this story, it was not hard to say she hadn't. "I've heard nothing about his relationships, Lindsey."

"Oh, we all knew he was seeing someone. He... I mean several times I came around to see him and he, he, took a long time to come to the door. And then he didn't invite me in, whereas normally he did. But Isabella? It's not true. I've talked to her. I thought it was Mary... she was after him all the time."

Joy was painfully aware of the fact that Mary Truman was in the house, quite possibly in earshot. "I don't think it really matters. The poor man is dead, and let's not talk anyone down. I hadn't heard any rumors and I won't believe hearsay, don't worry. I'm more interested in our strengths as a congregation."

"But someone murdered him."

"We don't even know that. And let's not think ill of people who probably were... and still would be friends, otherwise," said Joy.

The phone rang. It was yet another link in the gossip chain. Another parishioner. "Milly told me the police had been there. Are you all right, have they found out anything?"

Joy decided that she might as well let it out. "I'm fine. Someone tossed a half-brick through an open window this morning. Nothing to get excited about, no harm done, nothing to do with Reverend Hallam's death."

"Oh... how nasty. Things like that don't happen in Felixtown. Well, they didn't used to. I put it down to modern schools, and no discipline, and all the violence on TV. I mean we even had graffiti on the walls not long ago. A bunch of the kids suddenly started it out of nowhere. Anyway, I'm so glad to hear you weren't hurt."

"Yes, a blessing. Now I'm going to try and visit everyone in the next while. When would be a good time for me to call on you, Mrs. Jenkins?"

She saw how Lindsey rolled her eyes, and mouthed 'talk, talk, talk' and waved, and left. Joy could only be glad because it avoided the possibility of a scene, and, yes, Mrs. Jenkins liked to talk. She had grandchildren. It was important that everyone should know all about them, in great detail. It was part of being a priest, too, but it was difficult when she didn't actually have children of her own.

It took her a good ten minutes to get Mrs. Jenkins off the telephone and go and liberate Mary Truman from the bathroom.

It was obviously not a very soundproof room. Mary sighed. "She used to be my best friend, you know." She didn't need to explain. She bit her lip and looked downcast. And then blurted: "But I wasn't having a secret relationship with him. Why should I? He told us all he wasn't married. I'm not married. Isabella is."

"Is she?"

"Yes. Husband is RC. Won't agree to a divorce. She... Donald – the pharmacist, tried to date her, but it never went anywhere, because she can't get divorced and doesn't believe in a relationship without marriage. It's a pity because his son really needs a bit of mothering, poor boy."

"Then why would she do so, with Peter Hallam?" asked Joy, gently.

That gave a pause. "Oh. I suppose... well. I suppose it also depends on how much you like someone."

There was no gain in arguing the point. Joy settled for having planted a seed of doubt about it. She suspected that Lindsey might have incidentally been right, and that what she was seeing was projection, not truth. Still, even the harshest rumors did come down to a grain of truth, somewhere. It was always difficult to find out quite what that was, though. It wasn't always what anyone thought, either. "I still don't think it is worth breaking up friendships for," she said firmly. "The man is dead. We need to live with and love each other. And make tea."

Mary Truman guiltily looked at the teapot. "I'd better start again. The Bishop did us a favor sending us someone as calm and sensible as you are."

"Oh, I am not either of those. And I was terrified coming out here. I've never really been out of the suburbs, and I'm used to city life, and I'm used to having other senior clergy to support me... But I was told everything would be fine, because Mary Truman would help me."

"Really?" Mary stood slightly straighter.

"Yes, really. The Bishop seems to think you're very organized and would even know where the coffee was kept. I found a grinder, but no coffee, but there was fresh coffee when I arrived on Saturday night. Yet I couldn't find it in the morning. I'll need to go shopping."

"Reverend Peter insisted on keeping his coffee in the freezer. He said it stayed fresh for longer. That's why he had the fancy coffee grinder."

"I gathered from the Bishop that most of the furnishings actually belong to the rectory. I'm sorry. I didn't mean to use his things. I have a few pieces of my own arriving sometime during the week. I only used to have a small flat."

"I hadn't even thought of kitchen things. I don't know... the rectory was fairly well furnished before Reverend

Peter came. And... well, he wasn't fussy. Just a typical man, he had no idea about décor, or that kind of thing. They don't."

Joy decided that now would not be the tactful moment to mention that one of the wardens in her last church had been an interior decorator, and a man. Mary might be the soul of organizing and could be a great support, or not, but Joy had realized by now that she was rather set in her ideas. And she would probably benefit from being kept busy. "I'm going to need to set up a list of all of the congregation, with their 'phone numbers and other contact details. I'd like to try and visit all of them."

Mary nodded. "I'll see to that. We've got a list from the parish roll, but some of the numbers may be out of date. And we have lost a few people." The tea was made, and they each took a cup. "Now, shopping. Obviously, there's the IGA supermarket down the road, Felixtown Butchery's meat is good, better than at the IGA, and Mellons sells some dry goods, crockery and plastics. They're also the newsagent." She pulled a face. "I'm afraid, the only place you can get fresh fish is that Zenobia Parks's place at the end of High street. She can be quite unpleasant, but the seafood is fresh."

"I had a little run in with her on Sunday afternoon. She was... abrasive."

That drew a little laughter. "You should hear her and Major Ambleside-Smith squabble. The Major's on the local council and so is she. Apparently they argue about everything, to the point that the other councilors are talking about giving it away if they get voted in again. He's very popular with the bowling club and she gets the... I suppose the protest vote. He owns the building next to her café. He doesn't think she should be allowed to fill the pavement with her tables and chairs. Honestly they've even had the police called when the two of them have been arguing in the street. Poor Reverend Peter tried to make peace between them."

That was enough to make her sniffle a bit again, so Joy tried turning her mind in a different direction. "The brick. It had a note tied onto it. It said... well it implied that I am expected to... to have conflict with homosexuals. Um. Has it been a big issue here? I'd just like to know."

Mary blinked. "I wouldn't have thought so. Um. There are a gay couple out toward Cape Campbell. They're musicians, with a little orchard. But they're, well, very popular around here. Everyone was a bit iffy at first, but they're so... so, nice. Matthew helps out with the oldies bus, and Garth does the volunteer ambulance, and does the lights and music for all the town functions. They both do a lot with the annual show and if there is ever a community affair they always help out or donate prizes. Matthew always gives me some pots of marmalade for our stall... There was another young man, but he went off to the city... and the only lesbian here was Tom's ex-wife."

"Oh." That did explain a few things. Joy could imagine he wouldn't have taken it well. "That must have been awkward."

"Poor Thomas. He had no idea. He was away at sea a lot. He suddenly got a message that she'd met up with an old girlfriend, and had decided she was tired of living a lie, and wanted a divorce. He was really, really bitter about it all, but he seems to be getting over it. She moved away, and doesn't come back very often, thankfully. For some reason their daughter, my niece, blames him for it all."

"It must have been very difficult for him to deal with," sympathized Joy.

"Oh it was. Awful for everyone. And of course he came home from sea then and settled on the farm, but well, a bit late." Obviously the word was a mental trigger because she looked at her watch, gave a panicky look at the wall-clock, and scrambled to her feet, "Oh my! I'm going to be late for work. I'll do my best to drop round an updated list this evening. In the meantime there is one in the office."

Joy puttered around tidying up for a little, trying to learn where things lived, and thinking about her morning as

41

she worked. The parish was more complex and the task harder than she'd imagined it would be. She eventually went and 'phoned poor Dean Mellors again. "Now, about Reverend Hallam's possessions..."

"I did talk to Mary Truman about that. We're trying to track down any relatives as he died intestate."

"It appears that he didn't. One of the parishioners, Tom Truman, told me that he was a witness to Peter Hallam's will, quite recently."

"Well, that would simplify things a little. I wonder why it hasn't been brought to our attention," said the Dean Mellors, sounding faintly annoyed.

"I assume everyone thought you knew. With your permission I'll try and find out a little more."

"Of course. I'd give this witness a call, ask him if he can tell you any more about it. At least it may lead us to his relations. The next of kin listed on his paperwork with the diocese has been dead for some years, and was also an unmarried priest."

So Joy 'phoned Tom Truman. She found the number on the list in the office, and called. It just rang. Well, he was a farmer, and it was a landline number. She went shopping instead, and bought some basic supplies, and some of the necessities of life, like instant coffee. It was all very well having a fancy coffee machine, but in the early morning she wanted coffee – or at least something vaguely like it, in a hurry. It was interesting to discover that the woman at the checkout counter knew exactly who she was, asked how she was settling in, and said how shocked she was about the brick.

Small country town dynamics were going to take some getting used to. "It was just a silly prank," she said, with a degree of calmness she could not yet feel about it all.

"It's not something we get happening here! Mind you, Sergeant Grogan will get to the bottom of it. He knows what's going on around here," said the woman confidently.

So, it seemed, did everyone else. Walking back down the road she saw Tom Truman loading sacks into his ute, just outside the co-op, which explained why she'd got no reply to her telephone call. He waved. "Did your little car not survive its wetting, or do you like to walk?" he asked.

"I like to walk, but I'm regretting it. I bought too much."

"I didn't know he was for sale! Good thing you got there before me, or I might have had him loaded in the ute before you could snap him up," he said grinning.

"We ducks never snap. That is reserved for turtles."

He laughed. "I'm never going to be allowed to forget that, am I? Why don't you put the bags on the ute seat, and I'll drop them around when I've finished loading up. I shouldn't be more than five minutes. Then you can tell me what mallards do, instead of snapping."

"A tricky question," she said, gratefully offloading the bags onto the seat. "Ducks dabble, but Mallards... I have a question for you, but I will ask it when you drop off my shopping," she said, noticing he'd already picked up another bag. "Perhaps I can repay the tea. And I have biscuits. Bought ones, but still."

He shook his head. "I'll stand you a tea, or a coffee, at the infamous Zenobia's establishment. So you can know what to avoid except on Mondays."

"Er. I had that experience yesterday."

"You missed the key word," he grunted lifting the next sack. "Monday." He dropped the bag in the tray. "That's her day off."

Joy stepped over to the pile of feed sacks, and took hold of one side of the next bag. "Right. Then let's get these done."

He looked at her, and smiled, but took the other side. "You really are determined to get them talking, aren't you," he said as they swung the bag up, together.

There were only another four bags to go, which was quite a relief.

"Better... talking... than ignoring the church," she said as they hefted yet another bag on the ute.

"Oh they can do both around here," he said cheerfully. "And give me a hard time about it. Hello Marcus."

"Shame on you, Tom. Getting old?" said the new arrival, who looked about seventy plus, but tough as old whipcord. "Let me, little lady."

Joy defiantly held on to her end of the bag. "You can relieve Tom. He did all of these by himself. You should be ashamed of yourselves not lending a hand."

Tom Truman plainly enjoyed the expression on the newcomer's face. "Exactly. And it's not as if they were my bags of pig-pellets, and I ever do it myself normally either. Marcus, this is our new priest, Reverend Duck. Now get on with it. I'll supervise."

"I'd shake your hand, but I know it's a trick to get me to let go of the bag," said Joy. "I'm Joy Norton, not duck. I've come to replace Peter Hallam."

Marcus was grinning now, displaying big snaggled teeth beneath his white moustache. He took the other side of the bag. "Right. A one, two, three."

And they lifted the remaining three bags between them, by which stage Joy was wishing she had been less obstinate, or maybe just carried her own bags home. But Marcus was impressed. "Churchmen... sorry, ladies, getting a bit more gutsy these days, Tom." He said as he wiped his hand on his trousers. Held it out to her. "Marcus McGregor. First parson's hand I'll have shaken for forty years I reckon. I come to fix the forklift, but I don't think I'll bother now. They can just nip up to the rectory if there's a pallet of something that needs shifting."

Joy wiped her own hand and shook the callused hand held out to her, squeezing with all her strength to match some of the casual firmness in the handshake. "Only if they want to kill me," she said slightly breathlessly. "They're heavier than I realized."

"Oh well, we've killed enough priests," said Tom. "You better fix their forklift, Marcus. I'm off for a coffee at La Zenobia's with our new priest, unless you want to join us."

"Huh. No, shaking a priest's hand is enough for one day," said Marcus. "I'll see you on the river, Tom. You got any good fish lately?"

"Nothing worth writing home to mum about. Looking at the water-level it should be getting better over the next few days if we don't get more rain."

"Sure to, before the weekend. Well, I'll be seeing you. Nice meeting you, Reverend Duck."

Joy realized she was likely to be stuck with that one. Protesting would only make it worse. So she just smiled: "Call me Joy."

"Oh we ain't on first name terms with the parson until he... or she's buried us, around here."

"I'll do my best to put it off then, Mr McGregor, Sir."

"Heh. Reverend Joy then," he said, acknowledging the hit and walking into the store.

CHAPTER 4

"Does any of the stuff you've bought need to go into the fridge or freezer?" asked Tom Truman, after the exchange with McGregor, once his shoulders had stopped shaking, and still trying to smother a grin. "You give as good as you get... Reverend Joy."

"Isn't that what do unto others is all about? If it is thought about the other way around, anyway. Yes, I am afraid I have ice-cream in there, and milk. I'll just walk it, really."

"I've got steering and brakes, and even an engine that works," said Tom opening the door for her. "I can stop, and turn around, and that's something to be shown off. You can go and put your ice-cream and milk in the fridge while I show the admiring people of Felixtown that I can turn around."

"They do seem to spend enough time peering out of their windows at vehicles, and then telling each other about it," said Joy, not fighting the tide, but getting into the ute.

"Which is why a single man visiting you on his own would just not be clever, while they're still trying to decide if they approve of a lady priest," explained Tom. "Of course there are quite a few who would approve, or not worry, but they're not the ones you need to watch out for."

"It's not that bad surely?"

"No, not really. But this place can be a bit silly at times. As you'll find out."

"I did this morning," said Joy ruefully.

"What happened?" he asked.

"I think you should try that stopping, and showing off your turning off skills. You've just gone past the rectory," she said, as they drove past the church.

"Oops. Ute on autopilot, going home. Good thing I never did that with a ship. They're harder to stop and turn around."

He did a U-turn, just managing it, as the vehicle plainly had a huge turning circle, and then came to halt outside the rectory.

Joy ran in, disposed of the things that needed keeping cold, and ran out again. Tom was already chatting to a young woman with a stroller. He introduced yet another new person to Joy, and she made appropriate cooing noises at the baby. They drove off a few minutes later, Tom shaking his head. "They're all so determined to be nice to me."

What he wasn't saying was 'Because they feel sorry for me,' but it was there in his voice and manner. "Would you prefer it if they weren't?" she asked.

"I'd prefer it if they weren't making such a deliberate effort," he said, with a snort.

"But that says good things about them, and that they think you're worth it."

"I can see why you went into the priesthood," said Tom.

"I was very doubtful about it, but..."

"Well, I think you just put a hand into the wound where they pushed the spear with old Marcus. He was barely polite to Peter, and he couldn't stand the fellow who was here before that. Anyway, you were saying about your morning?"

"I'll tell you when you're not driving on autopilot, because I value the lives of pedestrians, and I don't want to end up in the bay," said Joy, who was an even more nervous passenger than she was a driver.

"No need to worry. I automatically turn left at the end of high street, and park. Every Monday at 9.30. The pedestrians get a warning note in their post boxes," he said, parking in a convenient slot just past the café.

"I need to go and find the Post Office! I knew I'd forgotten something."

"Explains why you didn't get your note," said the ever-inventive Tom, as they got out.

"Well, I'm sure my presence here will be well reported too. Probably in notes in post boxes for those not on the telephone."

"Oh it will be. But it is public, and will be seen as you taking on the anti-Christ. And anyway, there really is nowhere else," he said pulling out a seat for her. There were another couple of folk just standing up after their coffee, but otherwise the place was unpopulated. "After breakfast and before tea," said Tom. "Suits me. Now tell me about this difficult morning?"

So she did. All of it, including the awkward part about his sister. No one came and took an order, and, out here in the wind it seemed quite private. "Well," he said. "I did warn you about the gossip. I thought a couple of last-chance tabbies had a fancy for Peter Hallam, including my sister. For what it's worth, he wasn't, as far as I know, interested. The bit about the homophobes gets me a bit. He certainly never preached anything about it. People get ideas though. I'd have said Zenobia, and a few others would be loudly pro-gay marriage and anti-church. I wouldn't have thought brick throwing was their thing, though. She talks the talk, but that's about it really."

"I thought she thought marriage was a form of feminine bondage?"

He grinned. "You've had the speech have you? But you've got it wrong, it is repressive patriarchal slavery. But she's very much in favor of homosexuals being allowed to do so, in church."

"Ah. Cognitive dissonance. Do you think we should go and see if there is anyone here?"

He got up. "Maddy will be reading. She always is. I'll go and disturb her." He stuck his head into the shop. "One, two, three, where's my coffee!" he called.

"Hello Commander Tom," came a voice from inside. "The usual?"

"Good book is it? I'll have my usual, but I've got another customer for you."

"I'll be out."

She was wearing the leather jacket – and an apron, which looked decidedly odd together, and seemed faintly surprised to see Joy, but was entirely professional about dealing with the customer. "How was the tofu?" she asked.

"I haven't eaten it yet. I've had a bit of a disturbed morning. I'm going to be really ordinary this morning and have tea."

"What kind would you like? There's a list," said Maddy, pointing.

"And some people don't just have normal old tea," said Tom, "But not many."

"I'll have the Darjeeling," said Joy.

"I think she's trying to prove a point," said her companion with a fair degree of accuracy. "And to eat? The cakes are actually very good, and the lemon meringue is exceptional."

"He always has that. I got into such trouble for not having made it once," said Maddy.

"Well, even if I shouldn't, I will too," said Joy.

"The tarts and cakes are good," said Tom. "And, so of all things, is the steak, kidney and oyster pie."

"I wouldn't have thought of that mixture," said Joy.

"It's that or buy them from the supermarket," said Tom.

Maddy nodded. "Yes. My mother won't have pies, because she says they're not healthy, but I get away with doing those, because it's kind of retro. I mean we do them the way they were made in the 18th century, with oysters. Oysters were cheap back then, and they used to put them in so they didn't have to use too much meat. It's really popular, one of the signature meals at the café."

49

She sounded rather proud of it. "Um. I still think I'll have the lemon meringue," said Joy. "I've got a sweet tooth, I'm afraid. I will try a pie some day though."

"Do," said Tom.

When Maddy had gone back into the shop Tom said: "Do tell her it is good. She does a lot of the cooking. All the sweet things. Zenobia wants everyone to eat salad, which is a tough sell, around here!"

After the tea, coffee, and wedges of lemon meringue arrived, Joy asked about the will. "It's just that we're trying to sort out what do with his things. The Dean has been under the impression that he'd died intestate."

"Well, he did it all properly," said Tom, adding sugar to his coffee. "He had one of those standard templates, and he initialed every page. He asked Wiley and I to witness it. Look, it's got to be around in the house somewhere. And no, I don't think it was a motive for murder. I didn't read enough of it to tell you anything much and even if I had, I don't think it is right for me to disclose details. But he was a parish priest, not a millionaire. He said as much when we were signing it. He said he was just tidying things up, when I asked what the sudden urge to do a will was. He didn't sound worried, and I doubt if it could even possibly be grounds to kill him. It's like all the other rumors: ridiculous."

"You have such material to start a whole new thread of gossip going here! I'm disappointed in you," she said with a wry smile.

"Well, it would be better than the lurid tales of cat-fights among middle-aged women over the parish priest anyway. How on earth do they suppose that resulted in his death, and not that of the woman who had snatched him from her rivals? A spurned lover did him in, perhaps? Hell hath no fury? And Isabella of all people! She does favors for everyone, takes part in everything. Helps out at all sorts of functions and always seems to be doing the dishes, or sweeping or all the important jobs that important people just don't get to. She's close to a saint, in my opinion. It's all a bit silly, really," he said, stirring his coffee.

"That's true, but it isn't any less upsetting to the people involved."

"I know. It's still daft," he said and applied himself to his lemon meringue tart. A little later he said: "From the point of view of making matters easier for the function of the church and its new priest. He told me that he had specified that all his personal possessions were to be used by the parish or sold if they were of no use to them, with the proceeds donated to St Andrews Children's home. He was an orphan, and had disappointingly warm memories of the institution."

"Disappointing?"

Tom waved a cake fork. "It's sort of de rigueur to have been abused and miserable as an orphan. All he ever said about that was the abused and miserable part was before he got to St. Andrews."

"We tend to let the bad overshadow the good, I suppose," said Joy.

"One part bad always outvotes nine or ninety or ninety-nine parts good. Anyway, 10 to 1 he'll have put the will in an obvious place."

"Which means it may never be found," said Joy, who had done this often enough herself.

"Exactly!" said Tom cheerfully. "Isn't that a natural law of the universe?"

"Well, I will have to do my best. Who did you say was the other witness?"

"Jeff Wiley. He happened to be out at my place, to go fishing. He's the assistant postmaster. Lindsey McCassil is his boss."

"Now I understand how the warning notices about the farmer on autopilot arrive in the post-boxes. Well, I shall go to the post office."

He grinned. "Good luck. Jeff turns to jelly the moment a woman even speaks to him. Must be his dragon boss."

They ate, drank their tea and their coffee, talked about the local weather, farming prospects and fishing. All of which were matters Joy knew nothing about. She did realize they would become essentials to understand and acquire a knowledge of, if she was going to be able to do her work here. It was a temporary situation, probably, and not what she was naturally suited to, but no good ever came of burying that talent in the ground. After a brief argument about paying for tea, which ended in a draw, and some compliments about what really had been a good piece of tart, Joy refused the offer of a lift back to the rectory, and set out armed with his directions to find the Post Office. It wasn't that complicated; it wasn't that big a town. There was a rather mousy-looking, slightly plump balding man behind the counter. He gave her a very tentative half smile and said: "Good morning," as if this was a rather daring bar-room pick-up line he'd been talked into trying by his friends.

"It is turning into rather a good morning," said Joy smiling encouragingly. He didn't quite back off all the way until he was up against the racks of parcels, but he did retreat slightly. "I'm the new priest, Reverend Joy Norton. I'm afraid I didn't know the rectory address, so I asked people to use this as my *post restante* address for now. And I have ordered some books, and wondered if they'd arrived."

"Er. Nothing in for you yet, I'm afraid, ma'am... uh, Reverend." He looked as if he would stick a finger into his collar at any moment. He had plainly had been savagely bitten by some woman somewhere.

"And I imagine there will be post for the Church, and possibly Reverend Hallam. I suppose I'd better collect that. And I don't know if there are any formalities for the Post Office box, with me now being the incumbent."

He nodded so fast she was quite scared that his head might come off. "There's a parcel for him, came in this morning's post. But... well I'd better get Ms. McCassil, she's just sorting at the back. I... I'll just call her." He dashed off like a coursing hare, escaping through a door at the back of the racks.

It was going to be very difficult to get any information about the will out of him, Joy concluded. A minute later Lindsey McCassil came bustling out of the back, with the unfortunate hare two paces back. She smiled, seeing Joy, but there was a subtle change in her demeanor: this was her domain, and she happy and confident in it. She plainly hadn't been that in the rectory, or when they'd met the night Joy arrived. Seeing her now in her own environment, that was obvious. "Hello, Reverend Joy. Mr. Wiley said you wanted to know if there are any formalities you have to go through. Well, the box is held by the Parish, so no. It just continues as normal, and you don't have to worry about it. Reverend Hallam was issued two keys for the box, and I am sure they must be in the rectory somewhere. I'd ask Mary. She boxed his things with Isabella and Sarah Porter."

She picked up on Joy's expression. "The little lady with the hearing aid. Tends to make rather loud comments in church." Joy knew exactly who she was talking about, immediately, even if hearing aids were not that rare in the congregation. "Of course you can just ask at the counter for your mail, anyway. We know who you are! As for the parcel, you may as well take it, and see what should be done with it. It doesn't require a signature, and we need the space."

"I can see that. I'm amazed."

"Internet shopping," said Lindsey. "It's made life busier out here, hasn't it, Mr. Wiley?"

He nodded. "Our incoming parcel traffic is up nine percent so far this year." He sounded a great deal more at ease now that his boss was present. Obviously she wasn't the source of his terror, but more of a buttress.

"Yes, but hard on the local businesses, though," said Joy. "If I could see what one of the keys looks like, I would be grateful. It would make recognizing it much easier."

"Mr. Wiley, could you get us one?" asked Lindsey.

"Certainly, Ms. McCassil," he said, heading back through the door, but in far less of a panic. The stilted formality struck Joy as odd, but, by the way it was said, it was not so to either of them.

"They're quite recognizable," said Lindsey. "I just hope it won't be necessary to replace the keys. They're expensive. The parish really can't afford to waste money."

"I'm sure it will be somewhere. So is it just the two of you who work here?"

"Yes, Mr. Wiley came about four years back, as a relief. He arrived about the same time as Reverend Hallam, actually. I'd hurt my back and with the parcel volume, well, I didn't know what it was going to be like, but I was finding it difficult. Before that it was just me."

Her assistant had come back through, and produced a key. He was actually managing a tentative smile, thought Joy. Amazing. The key had quite a distinctive back, and Joy was sure she'd recognize one if she saw it. He then brought the parcel to her, and Joy walked back to the Rectory, mentally mapping the various stores, including one labelled "Junk and Mechanical Repairs". Honesty in advertising made her turn from her path into it.

"I don't need any feed-sacks moved, Reverend Joy," said the proprietor, from a work bench against the wall, where he was busy turning one piece of oily machinery into enough pieces to make three, all bigger than the original. "What can I do for you? If it's not bust, it doesn't need fixing. I don't do improvements, just telling you in advance."

"Actually, I came to see if there was any junk I needed. I loved the sign," she said.

"Heh," he chuckled. "Gets me a lot of business. Look around. I'm in the crucial stages of surgery here. The patient may not survive. Oh, and if it's for sale, it works. I don't know for how long it'll go on working for, and I don't offer no guarantees."

The shop was one of those places Joy knew she'd spend far too much time browsing in, and probably end up buying all sorts of things she didn't need. It had everything from a mechanical peach peeler, to an outboard motor that looked as if it was the same vintage as a paddle-steamer. It didn't have an outer cowling and you could see all the works. "They don't make 'em like that anymore," said Old Marcus, looking up from his delicate operation with a hammer and a punch. "One of the few things I haven't had to work on. Ran perfect, started first pull – mind you, you needed to be a bull to pull it. Belonged to old man Denton, used ter fish here in the 40's. He was cleaning his shed out, and asked me if I wanted it. You could fit it on that wee car of yours, and next time you go into a wet ditch, you could just drive yourself out."

It was interesting that the story had got this far, as Tom hadn't had much of a chance to tell him. Country towns only needed newspapers for out-of-town news, she decided. "Would that be any relation to the girl at the café?"

"Granddaughter," he said, continuing his tapping, while swearing gently at the obdurate screw, probably quite unaware that he was speaking to it, thought Joy. "Aha... it's bloody moving at last. People always think you get there by belting the thing, but a light tap around the edges can get the oil in. Now if you want anything, now's the moment, because I'm going to have springs and retaining clips and a gear assembly to keep from blooming going their own way in a moment or two. Otherwise come back later. I'm going to put the 'closed' sign up."

"I'll come back. I'm not sure about the outboard on the Micra. Maybe a paddlewheel would be better."

"I've got one out the back. It came off a water-mill mind you," he said as she walked to the door, and he came across to close it, and hung up the 'closed' sign.

She learned later that he closed whenever he felt like it. On the other hand he could, apparently, fix almost anything.

CHAPTER 5

Back at the rectory Joy decided that having to go through other people's possessions and papers was an excellent motivation for disposing of her own before she died. Although Mary and her helpers had done a hasty job of clearing up, that had largely been done by simply putting everything into cardboard boxes, and putting those in the spare room, which also doubled as an office. It was a store for the various requisites of the rural priesthood – boxes of paper, pamphlets from Anglicare and various other organizations. Attempting to order the desk so she could at least work it, she had found they had somehow missed emptying the drawers.

There could surely be no more likely place for a will.

After a while she realized there could be many more likely places. It appeared the Reverend Peter Hallam, whatever his strengths might have been, had not been terribly organized. There were pieces of old sermons, telephone bills, pamphlets, seed catalogues, letters... and the empty envelopes which had been written on. A torch. A magnifying glass. A book on how to tie your own flies. And that was just the first drawer. She was wary about throwing anything out, just in case it proved to have the will inside it, or perhaps was important to somebody. This definitely came under the 'best to make someone else's problem' heading, she thought. She decided her efforts called for tea, perhaps lunch, and perhaps opening the parcel she'd put down in the hall on coming in, or seeing if it had a return address.

It did. But it was in China. And as it was from a Gold Fish Smiling Products in Urumqi, Xingjiang Uyghur

Autonomous Region, Joy was fairly certain the item had been paid for in advance, and was not a personal gift. The box had been opened for quarantine inspection and bore the re-sealing tape of the Border and Quarantine Inspection, which might be why it had taken so long to get there. She opened it.

There was a large bag of dark red flakes inside. The label on the packet said '800 gram Superior Quality freeze dried Goji flakes'.

Joy had no idea what they were, or why Reverend Hallam should be ordering them from China. But she did have her laptop, and internet access. She soon knew that they were a part of Chinese cuisine, and traditional medicine, and that they might help for cardiovascular or immune system diseases, as well as vision related ailments. None of the medical side seemed supported by much science, but it was certainly produced in large volumes.

It didn't leave her a lot wiser. No one had mentioned that Reverend Hallam was keen on unusual Chinese dishes. She had some lunch, and was about to return to her task when someone knocked. It was Mary, looking very red-eyed and rather downcast. "I've taken time off from work. I... I need to talk to you, Reverend Joy. I don't think I can serve on the parish council any more. In fact... I won't be coming to church here anymore. And I just wanted to let you know, it's... it's not you."

"If it is not me," said Joy who had a fairly good idea what it had to be, "Then you should come in, and let us actually talk about it. And I've never had a talk that didn't go better with tea." She put the kettle on, and, to help Mary settle, talked calmly as she did it. "I've done my first lot of shopping. Things are a little more expensive here than back in the city. Even the milk and vegetables. That was a bit of a surprise."

"It's the transport. And of course the shops are taking a bit of a profit from a captive audience, I suppose. But because of the health-and-safety rules, the supermarket can't just sell local produce. So most of it goes into town, and then gets processed and comes back. Even the milk from Tom's place."

"Sometimes I think we go too far with all the regulations," said Joy.

Mary nodded. "Tom's theory is they should have an 'It-has-to-be-more-likely-than-being-stung-to-death-by-bees' cut off on what they should be able to make laws about. He has some odd ideas."

"That's a new one! How does it work?" said Joy, encouraged. When people were too deep in their misery to rescue easily, they answered in monosyllables. And everything related to their issue.

"Well, Tom likes numbers. So do I... It's a family failing I suppose."

"A strength, if you ask me, and one I wish I was better at. So tell me about the theory. Maybe I can use it for a sermon," she said, as she set the mugs on the tray with the teapot, sugar and milk jug, and walked over to the table. "Shall we sit here? There's a shortage of comfy chairs."

"Oh. Yes. We were meaning to do something about it..." She trailed off. That meant this was close to whatever was bothering her.

"So the theory and the numbers?" prompted Joy. That seemed a safe subject.

"Oh, just that there is a probability for everything in life, including the chance of being stung to death by bees. There's not a very high chance of that, but it happens, but we can't destroy, ban or really control bees. We just avoid them, are careful around them, and occasionally deal with individual problem hives. So: If that is reasonable behavior, then we shouldn't try and ban things that are even more unlikely. He's got a list of less likely things, all of which we have rules and laws about."

"I don't see that as an odd idea, but I bet the politicians do," said Joy with a smile. "Why, Mary, they'd be out of a job! Will you be mother, please? The tea will be strong enough for me by now, but I don't yet know how you like it."

"Strong," answered Mary. "But it'll get that way faster if I take your cup out of it."

She poured, and Joy waited until she had her tea too, before saying: "Well, if the problem is not with me, then... is it with God?"

"Goodness! No. I didn't mean it that way. No, just... well um..."

"If it is not with God, then we can deal with anything else. You're upset because of what you heard your friend say. And it's been gnawing away at you like a worm in an apple, and now you just don't know how to face her, or how to deal with this. So you're trying to leave it all behind. But... you have a conscience, and you didn't want to hurt me."

"You put it all into words very well," said Mary after a brief pause.

"I had help," said Joy. "And by the fact that you didn't just not come to church, so did you. Look, we all react like this. We're human, Mary, not perfect. And God understands that perfectly. That's why so much of the advice in the Bible is about humans dealing with other humans. It's good advice, which is why it acts as a framework and foundation to so much in our world, even for the people who'd never set foot in a church. And Colossians 3:12-13 puts it better than I can ...'compassionate hearts, kindness, humility, meekness, and patience, bearing with one another and, if one has a complaint against another, forgiving each other; as the Lord has forgiven you, so you also must forgive.' You have a compassionate heart. And... I do think you need to remember that she is your friend, and one of us. I think she will be very ashamed and embarrassed too, when she finds out, as she must in this kind of a community, that you're avoiding her."

"Uh." Mary bit her lip, but the expression on her face said she was not ready to go that far, just yet.

"Imagine something for me. Please. Let me try to show you things slightly differently."

"Er. What?"

"Let us imagine that you were not the first person to come to see me this morning. Other than the policeman, that is," said Joy.

"Wasn't I?"

"Let's just imagine Isabella Da Freitas got here before you, and was in the office-spare-room. It's not sound-proof either."

"She didn't really, though. She lives out toward Cape Campbell."

"She came in early to join the painters. They'd done a dawn beach scene, and had just got back to town."

"Oh. You're just making this up, aren't you? She is part of the painting crowd and they...You're making this up aren't you?" Mary asked again, flushing as Joy kept a straight face.

After a moment of looking the woman in the eye, Joy nodded. "Yes. I asked you to imagine. But you just felt as I'm sure Lindsey McCassil will. And you have done to someone else precisely what she did to you. And how you feel is how you will make her feel. Ashamed. Probably a bit angry that you were hidden away."

"For heaven's sake, don't tell Lindsey! I wasn't hiding to eavesdrop."

"I won't, unless you ask me to. But she's not stupid. If you don't show up in church, she'll ask why? And, as you worked out when you came to see me, and to tell me, she'll blame me, as will the rest of the congregation. You wanted me to know it wasn't my fault, which I understand. And you wanted help, which I think we should pray about."

She hadn't expected Mary to get down on her knees, then and there, and then to leap to her feet, saying "Ouch!"

"What's wrong?" asked Joy, coming around the table in haste.

"I've got a fishhook in my knee. It must have been lying on the carpet. Ah! It's out. Thank heavens it wasn't as far in as the barb." She held up a tiny bronzed hook.

"Oh, I am so sorry. Do you need me to take you to the doctor?" asked Joy, who did not like blood, even in tiny amounts.

"Oh no. It's nothing more than a big pin-prick, and heaven knows, I do that often enough sewing," said Mary, dismissively.

"It is bleeding slightly. You'll need an anti-tetanus shot."

"I had one last year. They last a few years, these days. Tom and I got more than our share as children on the farm," she said, practically, pressing a clean tissue on to the wound. "It'll stop."

"Let me see if I can find a Band Aid. I always kept some in my bathroom cupboard," said Joy, running off to look. She really did not handle blood well, she knew. Her mother had wanted her to be a nurse. Nothing could have appealed to her less!

The drawers under the basin had been emptied, but the mirror-fronted medicine cupboard in the bathroom proved to be another place the hasty house-clearers had overlooked. Joy was aware that Mary had followed her into the bathroom, saying, behind her: "Really, you needn't worry. It's nothing," as the door opened revealing an entire pharmacopeia's worth, with Band Aids right in the front.

"Oh. We must have missed that. Well, I'd love a Band Aid."

Joy gave her one, and she applied it to her knee. "There. All better now, as mother would have said."

"Yes," said Joy, with a smile. "Perhaps God is telling you to get off your knees. He forgives you."

"Get off my knees and help you clean out the place properly. I'm sorry. There were a few of us doing it, and I think a few places... I assumed someone else had done it. And I was still too upset to be methodical. I usually am thorough."

"If and when you have the time, I'd appreciate a hand. I'm going through the desk drawers right now."

"Did we miss those too?" asked Mary. "Oh dear. I do apologize. We wanted to have everything ready, but, well we didn't really know quite what had to be done with things."

"Your brother says there definitely was a will, and it would make life much simpler for the Dean if we could find it. The desk drawers seemed the likeliest place, but so far all I have found is a lot of papers and old bills and... things I have no idea if I should throw away or not. It's the kind of decision easiest taken together, so, when you have some time..."

"Well, I have taken the day off, and caused a panic because I haven't done so in ten years. So I may as well help you with it now, if that suits you, Reverend Joy?"

"Very well, but have you had something to eat?" asked Joy.

That got a smile and a nod. "You're starting to sound just like one of us. Food in all crises. Yes, I had a sandwich to try and calm myself down. I was... letting it get to me. Silly really. Gossip is like breathing around here, I don't know why I should have got so upset."

"Along with tea, that seems a good recipe for coping with anything. I drink too much tea – even without that excuse," said Joy.

"Er. Me too," admitted Mary.

They collected their tea, and went to the office-spare room. "We were hoping to give this a proper repaint and get a new computer and... but Lindsey says there's no spare money. She's our treasurer. I'll have to work with her on the parish council..."

"You'll have to talk with her, and the sooner the better in my opinion," said Joy, firmly. "You said she used to be your best friend. What has changed, really? Other than the fact that she said something today she shouldn't have, and, I would guess, also possibly cherished deeper feelings for Reverend Hallam."

That caused a pause. Mary nodded slowly. "She probably did. I never thought of it quite like that. Around here... well if you're over a certain age, you're past last prayers, and any men of a suitable age are either married or interested in younger models. Peter didn't seem to be."

Joy had opened the second drawer and out came... feathers. A shower of them billowing up, along with a scampering mouse, which zig-zagged frantically across the floor and out of the room.

Whatever other problems Mary Truman had, a fear of mice and ineffectual behavior were not her flaws. She raced after it, snatching up a broom from the corner.

Joy felt she'd done her bit, by screaming. Anyway, however fast and effective Mary was, the mouse was faster still. It hurtled into the living-room and dived into a crack behind the sofa. "I'll pull the sofa away, you can get him," said Mary, offering the broom to Joy – who was standing well behind her.

"Er. I'd rather pull the sofa. I don't like mice much."

So they did it that way.

But of the mouse there was no sign.

"It might have gone down that crack between the floor and the skirting board. Or it might have gone out the other side," said Mary.

They spent the next ten minutes moving furniture, exposing dust and a fifty cent piece, but no mice, or evidence of their presence. "It must have gone. I'll ask Tom if he can do something about the gap. He's our Church fixit man, poor Tom. It's him or the Major or Arthur, really. The others are too old to ask to crawl around or climb ladders, not that they won't. The Major wouldn't and Arthur couldn't," said Mary. "So Tom gets landed with it. He doesn't seem to mind though."

"I am quite good at practical things. Just not mice," said Joy. "Or... whatever those feathers came from."

"We'd better go and have a look. And I think some traps would be a good idea. I'd suggest poison, but they always die in the most unreachable places and smell. I'd leave the sofa pulled away from the wall until Tom can get to it. Mice like coming out under cover."

The drawer, which Joy had populated in her mind with the maggot-crawling remains of dead birds being devoured by mice... proved to have nothing more dangerous or unpleasant than the feathers. Most of the feathers were in neat little bags, plainly unopened, and labelled with museum-like preciseness, barring one plastic packet that had been somewhat more roughly done... even before the mouse got into it. Joy wondered what the ladies would have made of the feather collection.

"Fly-tying stuff," said Mary, answering the unvoiced question. "Reverend Peter said he wanted to try his hand at it. He thought it might help with the men. As you might notice there are a shortage of them in church. It looks like someone gave him a bunch of pheasant feathers besides the ones he bought, and the mouse was in them."

"I'm guessing he didn't get on very far with it, by the looks of the packets. There was a book about it in the top drawer."

"It's quite hard, I gather," said Mary, taking out more packets of feathers and colored wool, "Takes a lot of patience and an eye for detail."

There was already quite a mound of packets on the bed, besides the pheasant feather packet that had been consigned to the bin. "What are we going to do with it all?" asked Joy.

"Put it with the rest of his stuff, I suppose. It's one of those hobbies where the materials cost an arm and a leg, but no-one really wants to buy used stuff. We might be able to give it to one of the fly-tying people. You'd have to ask Tom. I think he's done a little of it, and he knows all the local fly-fishermen."

The drawer proved to have all the other accoutrements of fly tying: a vice, colored cotton, various delicate little brass tools, and several boxes of little hooks. "Those look like the one you were kind enough to find with your knee," said Joy. "I deduce that he tried his hand at this at the table, and dropped a hook on the carpet. Once it was hooked through a couple of fibers of carpet not even a vacuum cleaner would shift it."

"It could be. The vice does screw onto a table as I remember, and the light is better out there," said Mary. "I did nag him about getting a new prescription for his glasses. He said it wasn't worth it. We, um, had quite an argument. I so wish I hadn't pushed the issue."

"I know. And so does he. There is something to be said for not letting the sun go down on your anger, but we all slip up, sometimes," said Joy, soothingly.

They went on to the next drawer, which proved to hold nothing but old bills, some of which were personal – everything from an invoice from an art-supply shop to a dry-cleaner's receipt, and some possibly related to the business of the parish. Each had to be looked at and a decision reached. Some were quite clear. Some quite mystifying. Joy was glad to have help with it. "Wheat germ oil?" He did seem to have ordered some odd things.

"Supposed to be good for your skin, I think. He had very sensitive skin. Always wore a big hat, and seemed very prone to rashes," said Mary, rather sadly. "I blamed it on his diet. He was very much old-fashioned Australian cookery, meat, potatoes and two boiled veg." She sighed. "His favorite food of all was just a plain old steak-and-kidney pie, and he avoided salad like it was dangerous. He thought lasagna was *avant-garde*. He was very allergic to shellfish, and we all had to be so careful about anything that had even a hint of seafood."

Well, that did open questions about what he wanted to do with Goji flakes. It obviously wasn't for adventurous cooking though. "And you? What sort of food do you like?"

"Oh I would be in trouble with my mother. I love playing with my food," said Mary, with the first real sign of the sense of humor that characterized her brother. "Some of the odder offerings on Sundays are mine, so be warned. I should have given you a run-down on the food earlier, only it's a... touchy area. There are a few offerings you want to be... careful about, unless you like ending up with the collywobbles. Old Mrs. Pike doesn't see too well, and her cakes can be... interesting. Mrs. Jenkins can't see her hand in front of her face, but hers are a dream. Penelope Ambleside-Smith's cakes are survivable, but for heaven's sake avoid her casseroles and vegetables. I think that's why Arthur is so scrawny, poor little man. He always eat twice as much as anyone else at tea. And Reverend Hallam would never eat Isabella's offerings, even the cakes. They were a bit too exotic for him."

"Fortunately I have a cast-iron stomach. But I just have to look at food and it goes to my hips."

"As you can see," said Mary with a grimace. "It's not just my hips it goes to."

By the time the drawers had been unpacked, and the merits of various regimes of diet and exercise had been discussed, Mary seemed to have recovered her tone of mind and also her intent to bring Joy a list of parishioners and their phone numbers and addresses, with notes on when they were home, and if they'd like visiting.

CHAPTER 6

Joy awoke to the midnight skritchy-skritchy noise of the mouse. She really did not enjoy small rodents. Not even drawing them. It took great determination to get out of her bed. Still, she knew that there was nothing for it but to take action, and to be as swift, silent and effective as possible – or she'd spend the rest of the night awake, waiting for it to return. But there was no way she was going to face the might of the mouse, unarmed.

Fortunately she knew that the broom was still leaning against the wall, at the foot of the stairs from the failed search under the sofa. It was also not particularly dark, an almost full moon was shining down. She hadn't drawn the curtains, so that she could enjoy the clear sky and star-scape from her bed. Most of the other buildings were single story, and she was not overlooked. Besides, if someone had wanted to be a peeping Tom, with her in her very respectable flannel pajamas and old dressing-gown, well, they were considerably less revealing than what most people wore shopping, let alone on the beach.

The beam of moonlight shone neatly down the stairs, but the lounge beyond that was far darker, as she'd closed the curtains down there. Joy was just recomposing her strategy hastily -- she had no desire whatsoever, with a broom or without, to go to war with a mouse in the dark – when she realized that the noise wasn't coming from the gap under the skirting, or from anywhere in the house, but was actually coming from the window. And it didn't sound very mouse-like any more.

Armed with the broom she tiptoed closer to the window. What could it be out here in the wilds? A bird? A bat? A cat? A wallaby eating the hydrangeas? Did wallaby eat hydrangeas? Did they come into town – if you could call this a town? It sounded a little metallic for a wallaby. She whipped the curtain aside.

With a startled gasp the balaclava-clad would-be burglar turned and fled, leaving the piece of wire he'd been trying to work up to the catch, and making odd maybe-mouse noises with, stuck in the window.

Now, Joy knew that common sense dictated a really good scream. But two things held her back – firstly she'd plainly given the person far more of a fright than they'd given her. That retreat was an out-and-out panicky sprint that would get the runner into the Olympics. And secondly, it had been a fairly small fleeing figure. Smaller than her, she'd guess.

That didn't stop her from being very wide awake, and wondering if she should call the police. She was fairly sure that that was what Dean Mellors would tell her to do, if she disturbed his sleep. On the other hand, a 1 AM call from the local policeman... was bound to be noticed, and after the last time... Also what did she have to show him? A piece of wire. Wire was wire, surely. She opened the window slightly and brought it inside, and then closed the window, looking around for some way to stop anyone from succeeding at that kind of window opening. She found there was actually a locking clip on the window-catch, so she put that down, and felt a great deal more secure.

She looked at the cross on the wall, and thought about it all. There really was no point in calling the police right now, there was nothing for them to catch or see. She was still quite shaken up about it. Why would anyone want to try and rob... or otherwise molest her? Surely there were better or easier targets?

Well, she wasn't calling the police, directly, but... what if the burglar came back and she was asleep next time? There had been a spool of fishing line in the study. She fetched it and set about devising an alarm system. The clatter of falling pots, a counter stool, and a brass tray should wake the dead, let alone a relatively light sleeper. And in the dark, they'd not see the fishing line trip-wires. She finished up with some eight strands of line across the lowest step as that had an ornamental pillar against the wall, which gave her a little gap to push the line through and the poles to the stair-rail. After she'd set it all up, she retreated up the stairs, with the piece of wire, and the broom. Turning the other cheek was all very well, but she'd rather stop it being done at all. Anyway perhaps this would be a case of doing unto others what they were trying to do to you?

In her bedroom, Joy set her mobile up so she only had to hit 'call' to dial 000, then she closed her curtains and got back into her bed.

Where she simply could not drop off. She tossed, and turned, played through the events of the last few days. She tried hard to turn her mind to the sermon for next Sunday, and considered going downstairs again to make herself a cup of hot chocolate, but couldn't be bothered to, with the thought of un-setting and resetting her makeshift burglar alarm system. She heard all sorts of noises in the night, but nothing more threatening than a cat, yowling. It wasn't that she was afraid, just awake.

Somewhere around dawn, when the birds had started singing and the rest of the world was waking, she'd tried prayer, too tired to do more than recite familiar words long since embedded in her memory, and she had fallen into a deep sleep.

She was woken from a complicated dream by the walls of Jericho crashing down. It took her sleep-muzzy mind a few seconds to work out that it wasn't so much Jericho as a brass tray and several pots and a kitchen stool tumbling to the floor. It seemed to make about the same tumult as the collapsing walls, and was mixed with shouting. She blundered out of bed grabbing the broom, hauling open her door to have a look, before her planned retreat to the 'phone. In retrospect that wasn't sensible, but in her half-woken state it seemed like a good idea.

What she didn't expect in the dim downstairs was a recognizable male voice shouting "Reverend Joy? Are you all right?" and sunlight shining in through her open door. There was someone on the floor too. With horror Joy realized that it was Arthur Ambleside-Smith. She rushed down the stairs, completely forgetting her last failsafe and found herself – and the broom -- going flying as she tripped over the fishing line. She landed in a sprawl at Tom Truman's feet, just as he had helped the hapless Arthur to get up.

He gave her a hand as she tried to stand up, and apologize at the same time. "I am so sorry!" she said, aghast at the effect of her trap.

Tom shook his head "What would my mother say, me picking up a fallen woman, and at this time of morning too. What's going on here, Reverend Joy? Are you all right? Or are you in shock from Arthur's outcry of delight when everything including him fell over when he walked in?"

"Oh, I am really so sorry!" repeated Joy ignoring the jokes to concentrate on the victim of her trap. "Arthur, are you all right?" she asked anxiously. "It's all my fault. I really am so terribly sorry. Did you get hurt?"

Arthur shook his head. "Um no. Just tripped, and er, must have knocked a lot of things over."

Tom had found the light switch, was looking at the scene, feeling the strand of fishing line. "What on earth is going on in here?" he asked, plainly struggling to suppress a smile. "Is this normal church practice, or a new liturgy you're working on? I'm sorry we interrupted it. We came with strict instructions to fix a mouse hole and set traps."

"Oh... oh no. It's just I had a burglar last night. I thought it was the mouse and chased whoever it was off. So... well, I was scared I wouldn't hear them if they came back, so I er, made sure I would!"

She could see that at least Arthur was looking at her as if she was possibly a dangerous lunatic. Of course Tom was laughing. "I now understand the meaning of 'build a better mousetrap, and they will come'," he said, looking at the fallen pots and pans, and the chair and brass tray. "Did you really think Felixtown was crime central, Reverend Joy?"

"It did happen!" she protested, indignantly. "Wait."

She ran upstairs with as much dignity as possible, and re-emerged having put her dressing gown on, with the piece of wire. She handed it to them. "This wire was being pushed through the window gap... here." She walked over to the window, nearly tripping over the remains of her home-made alarm system. "Look, you can even see a few scratches on the paint. And there is a bit of black mud here. It wasn't my imagination!"

"Aluminum MIG welder wire," said Tom, thoughtfully. "Wouldn't have been my first choice. Too soft."

"Did you call the police?" asked Arthur. "We, um, don't have many break-ins... or anything like that here. Someone took a car outside the Pub for a joyride last year though." He sounded almost... relieved they had that much of a problem to cite.

"Well, no. After the last performance with the brick... and they didn't actually get in," said Joy. "But... I was rather nervous. I was scared they might come back and I would wake too late to call for help. So, uh, I set this up."

"Very ingenious," said Tom. "And wise, considering that you must be a rock-solid sleeper. We've been knocking for ages and then I remembered I happened to have a key from when we were clearing the place up. I thought you might... well, be in trouble, or be an early riser and have gone out, and we could do the repair work and set the traps quickly before you got in. I'm sorry we disturbed the death-trap, but it was the one time that Arthur and I could both make it."

"I'm just sorry Arthur fell. I... struggled to sleep after that, and I must have fallen into a really deep sleep when I finally did. I normally get up early -- around half-past six, for morning prayer, and I'm quite a light sleeper. Just not this morning, I am so sorry."

"Heh. Early is relative. For dairy farmers like me, this is mid-day. For Arthur, this is predawn. And God will probably forgive you for being late with the prayers," said Tom.

"I am sure he will. But actually I meant sorry for Arthur being ambushed by my burglar alarm. And for not waking up. And for arriving in my pajamas with a broom," said Joy, assuming dignity. "So I hope you weren't hurt, Arthur, and that you will forgive me for being so silly."

"Really, I um didn't get hurt," the younger man said, smiling sheepishly. For all that he had obviously started balding very early in life, he wasn't a bad-looking young man – in his early thirties perhaps – Joy guessed, when he wasn't looking like a terrified rabbit.

"Or even say words that must have led our poor new pastor to think she'd been attacked by drunken sailormen" said Tom, laughing again. "I'm impressed, Arthur. I hadn't heard you being quite that expressive before. I haven't heard anything as descriptive since I left the Navy. Is that what you've learned at those conferences you keep going to? I'm sure you've given Reverend Joy material for at least three sermons. Now, come on, let's get on before you have to get back to work, and I have to get back to meet the dairy truck. If we can have a look at this mouse-hole, and measure up, I've got a new length of skirting board in the ute. We can cut it out there and avoid making a mess in the house."

"Well, I do have a broom to sweep up with," said Joy, waving it, and wincing as some new falling-down-the-stairs bruises made themselves known.

"I did wonder about closet witchcraft when you came flying down the stairs with that. But Zenobia told me that's blatant nonsense and that all witches are just innocent naturalists, like her."

Joy happened to be looking at Arthur's face as Tom made this crack. His mildly miserable expression suddenly pursed itself into a look of intent hatred, before he hastily looked away. It wasn't just his father who didn't like Zenobia, Joy thought.

Her own wince had obviously been noticed too. "Are you sure you're all right after that little tumble, Reverend?" asked Tom.

"Just a bit bruised I think. It serves me right."

"You should go and see Dr. Hammond, just in case," said Arthur. "I know someone who broke her collarbone and thought it was just a bruise."

"Maddie," said Tom. "She was at the pool, with my daughter. They never would tell me quite what they were up to."

"They were playing rocket-ships into the pool, you know, where one of you lies on your back and pulls their legs up against your chest, and the other one sits on the feet, and gets boosted through the air. Katie launched Madeleine so hard she hit the other side," said Arthur. "They didn't dare tell you because apparently your wife, um, ex-wife, had forbidden them to do it."

"Ah, that explains the evasion. It wouldn't have worried me, but they always believed we were in collusion. I didn't know you knew Madeleine and Kathleen. They must have been seven or eight years behind you at school."

"Oh, er, I heard it somewhere," said Arthur, earnestly peering at the gap which could be a mouse hole. "I'll go and put a trap or two in the crawl-space. Have you got any peanut butter, Reverend Joy? Although it seems a waste on a trap, it's the best bait, I'm told."

"Um. I don't think so. I could offer the bread to go under the peanut-butter, but not the peanut butter."

"Are you sure they wouldn't like marmalade instead?" asked Tom. "I have heard many people like marmalade instead."

"I had no idea you were an Alderney, Mr. Truman," said Joy, recognizing the quote.

"Can't be. The Alderney are extinct as a pure breed." He grinned at the expression on Arthur's face. "Winnie the Pooh. The King's Breakfast. The mice will just have to be a little less fussy and have a piece of bread. And it reminds me: I have marmalade from my sister, and eggs, and some home-cured bacon from my pigs in the ute for you, Reverend Joy."

"You had to say that after I had Weet-Bix for breakfast," said Arthur, far more human now that he was away from his parents. "Mother won't have bacon in the house. 'Too much salt and fat, bad for your father's blood pressure. Are you trying to kill him?' So we don't, ever," he said in remarkably good mimicry of manner and voice.

"She means well," said Tom.

"You don't have to live with it," he said, resignedly. "Some bread will have to do."

Joy gave him a slice, which he tore in fragments and baited the mouse-traps with, while Tom calmly took a well-used pen-knife from his pocket and cut the fishing line before kneeling to measure the skirting board. Joy put the kettle on to boil and retreated upstairs to change out of her night-clothes. Really, what would the good people of Felixtown think!

Coming back down, as the kettle whistled, she heard a brief terrible shriek outside. It took her a few frightened seconds to realize that it was a power-saw. Moments later Tom returned, with Arthur, carrying a new skirting board, and a basket – with eggs, a vacuum-pack of bacon slices, a jar of marmalade, a hammer and a bag of nails.

"I was sure the eggs would survive close proximity to my hammer, but the two had better be separated or they might start to bicker," said Tom. "The relationship is not what it was cracked up to be."

Joy relieved his arm of the basket, and took the hammer and nails out of it.

"Actually, I want the basket back, you can keep the eggs, bacon and marmalade. It's handy for putting the old nails in."

The two men worked well together. Joy had expected Tom Truman to be handy with tools, but Arthur was not the sort that she would have assumed would be good with his hands. Which all went to show, Joy thought, how stupid it was to judge people by appearances. She could hover and try to help, or make coffee. The latter, she decided would help her, and them, most.

So she asked if they'd like some, got an assent, and busied herself with that. They had the old, gnawed skirting out and the new nailed in before she'd finished. "If you can live with the smell of varnish, I'll give it a first coat right now. It's a smell best countered by the scent of frying bacon," said Tom.

"Before I joined ministry I used to work in a museum. No little bit of varnish can compete with the smells in the back rooms of museums. I am not going to cook bacon for myself while you work. Would my reputation in Felixtown survive my offering you both breakfast?"

"Yes," said Arthur, nodding his head eagerly. "Bacon!"

But as it turned out, she varnished and they cooked. Watching Tom with tape and paper had been too much to bear. "I have taped a lot of things, and, um, painted a lot of things. Do you mind if I help?" she asked after a few seconds of watching the fumbling.

"Delighted," said Tom trying to detach a piece of tape from one finger and attaching it to his thumb. "I'll fry the bacon and supervise from the stove."

Joy discovered that what she'd been told about Arthur and food was all too accurate. He would cheerfully have eaten all of the food. He did get through six slices of toast, butter and marmalade. "Douglas Adams was wrong. The answer to life the universe and everything may be bacon, not 42," he said, contentedly.

He might not have read or remember Winnie-the-Pooh, but he obviously had read the Hitch-Hikers Guide to the Galaxy. "I think I have to professionally disagree about the answer to life," said Joy, "But I'm not Marvin. This is the best bacon I've ever tasted."

Arthur looked at her in some surprise. And then gave one of his rare smiles. "Even a paranoid android would have to enjoy it."

"What are you two talking about?" asked Tom.

"Science Fiction."

"Ah. Arthur has been to several conferences about it," said Tom, getting up, collecting plates and heading for the sink as if this was a habit. "I'll pass."

"You also won't do the washing up," said Joy, getting up, and wincing.

They both noticed.

"What is wrong?" asked Tom.

"My ankle is a bit sore," she admitted.

"You'd better see the Doctor."

Some argument – in the nicest sense of the word -- ended in Joy agreeing to book an appointment with the town's only doctor and for them to leave her to the smell of varnish and bacon and to the washing up.

CHAPTER 7

Joy got someone's cancelled appointment, for three o'clock, and felt her disturbed night, and relatively early morning entitled her to sit with her sore ankle up and try to prepare the message for Sunday. It was perhaps not the best position for doing so, and it was just as well she'd set an alarm on her mobile to remind her that she had an appointment, or she'd have slept through it. She drove hastily to the surgery and parked next to the maroon Land Cruiser. Honestly, was she being haunted by it?

It was interesting to notice that the receptionist was the woman with the pram whose baby she'd admired with Tom Truman. That was still the feature of this small country town that she was struggling to deal with most. Now the mother, in a crisp uniform blouse with a headset on, looked rather more harassed and professional. Did the two go together? She still had time for a bright smile, and to give Joy a new-patient form on a clip-board, and point her at the waiting room area. The room already had several occupants, one of whom was Major Ambleside-Smith. He looked mildly discomforted to see her there, but greeted her politely enough. "Afternoon, Reverend Norton. I won't ask how you are, because if you're here, the answer is obviously not well."

"Actually," said Joy, "I'm feeling fine. I... um tripped on the stairs and was persuaded that I ought to see the Doctor. I do need to register as a patient anyway, and so, here I am. I am feeling much better and rather like a fraud for being here. But I did ask and the receptionist said she couldn't fill this slot anyway."

"Hmph. If it wasn't for the fact that two thirds of us are too old, he couldn't fill half his slots. Ah."

The 'ah' was aimed at the Nurse who was beckoning to him. He got up and waved a farewell to Joy, ignoring the rest of the waiting room. The other woman in the room was trying hard to stop her spotty little boy from destroying the furniture, so she didn't pay him any attention either. Joy filled in the form and returned it to the front desk.

"Thank you, I'll enter that right away. He's only one behind at the moment. And how are you finding Felixtown, Reverend Norton?" the receptionist asked, typing as she spoke. "Mum says she was ever so surprised at having a woman priest. She's a bit old-fashioned."

Joy resisted the urge to say that she was still looking for Felixtown, but was sure she'd find it any moment now. "And your mother is?"

"Oh, Lorna Smithson. We're so used to everyone knowing everyone else here. Can I have your Medicare card please?"

Joy produced it. "Yes, I'm still finding that quite strange. I'm not used to seeing my parishioners and their families everywhere. I suppose it is part of country life. I saw your mother heading into the IGA and I just saw Major Ambleside-Smith here."

"His wife has him in here every few days," said the receptionist with just a slight shake of her head. She handed the card back. "Yes, it's like that here. Doctor will call you in a few minutes, Reverend Norton."

So she returned to the waiting room, well stocked with piles of the magazines no-one wanted, unless they were keen on improving their golf swing or into the Celebrity gossip of ten years earlier, neither of which really held much interest for Joy. The Doctor came out and called Ms. Clemens and Dylan, before Dylan could rip any more pages out of anything. Joy got another wave from the Major as he walked to reception, where the next patient was trying to find out when she could have another appointment, and the receptionist was dealing with one phone call, being interrupted by a second caller that she'd had to tell that she'd 'be right with in a moment'. The poor receptionist was also looking for travel forms, and trying to get a signature on another document. Otherwise it was quiet.

Shortly Ms. Clemens and a now howling-his-lungs-out Dylan came down the passage, and added more happiness to the poor receptionist's day, just as Joy was called in.

Dr. Hammond had probably, Joy decided at first look, and first handshake, played Rugby Union at University. He had a broken nose and a stocky muscular build that was now turning into a paunch. It could have been the copper rugby-ball paperweight on his desk or the picture of the university team on the wall, just as much as his appearance, however. "And what can I do for you this afternoon?" he asked, motioning her towards a chair, while returning to his own.

"I tripped and fell down the stairs. I don't think there is anything wrong with me, but I did end up promising two of my new parishioners I'd come and see you."

He nodded, slowly. "So you must be the new priest. The unfortunate Peter Hallam's replacement. Well, I'd better have a look at the injuries, once I have taken a proper history."

"Yes," said Joy, trying the direct approach. "It's been very difficult for the congregation. What did he die of?"

"I'm afraid that crosses the line of patient confidentiality," he said, with the sort of stolid assurance that told Joy she'd get precious little out of him. "Now, you have no allergies listed here?"

"That's because I am not allergic to anything, or not that I know of."

"That'll be easier, anyway," he said.

"Easier than what?" she asked. After all, Mary had said Peter Hallam suffered from allergies.

He smiled and shook his head, "Now, I see you had rheumatic fever?"

"Yes, my mother always said that was why I was so small. Nothing to do with her being five foot two. My heart is as sound as bell, I had an ECG when I moved to Dr. Virthanan's practice two years ago."

"Well, if you could fill in the paperwork with Jenny on your way out, we can get your records here. I assume you'll be here for a while?"

"I'm afraid that crosses the line of Church confidentiality," she said with a twinkle, trying for humor.

It struck no chord. "Well, we'd better examine you then."

Looking at the bruises and flexing the ankle he asked calmly. "You really did fall down the stairs, and not get beaten up by someone?"

"I have two witnesses who were rather surprised to see me land in a heap at their feet," she said tartly. "Why do you ask? Do they beat up the priest here, regularly?"

"You did collect a few impressive bruises in the process," he said, ignoring the lure. "In my opinion, however, nothing is broken. Unfortunately we don't have a radiographer here. It's the ankle that is troubling you most, is it? I'd settle for giving it a few days' rest and elevation, and if it is still troubling you, we can send you back to the city for X-rays." He scribbled a script. "Here. There is a pharmacy just up the street."

"What are you prescribing? I don't need painkillers. It's fine if I am not walking on it, or if you aren't twisting or prodding it."

That got the first sign of approval he'd given her, in the shape of a slight smile. "Unless it is chronic, pain is a warning." He crumpled the script. "Most patients seem to think that the only reason for seeing a doctor is to collect scripts for painkillers and antibiotics." He stood up, plainly a signal that it was time for her to leave.

"I do have a couple of further matters, which don't relate to my ankle," she said, remaining seated. "Firstly, I need to know what to do with Reverend Hallam's medicines. The prescription ones have your name on them."

"Take them to the pharmacy. They will dispose of them according to the regulations. And what else?"

"When I worked in the city, there was a fairly well established set of procedures, and contacts for dealing with... problems, family violence, drugs, alcohol particularly, but ill-health and age issues too. Um, we had several friendly medical and police and social work contacts we could turn to for advice, because as priests we're not always sure what we're seeing. And sometimes they would reverse the situation, particularly with the elderly and let us know when we should visit someone. I wanted you to know that I am available to do that, and to ask who to best to talk to about other issues."

"We've got a district nurse, Grogan for police matters, and a psychiatrist visits every two weeks. I don't foresee myself needing your help, but I'll remember the offer. Now I really must see my next patient. Don't forget to fill in the paperwork to get your records transferred."

So Joy limped out, and the Doctor called his next patient – who was the only one in the waiting room. The receptionist was looking considerably less harassed now, but was still busy on the headset phone, while filing some papers and, seemingly in the gaps, typing information on the computer. "Well, that's all, thank you, Mrs. Jenkins. Three o'clock tomorrow. I've booked him a double session. And please ask him not to be late again, and congratulations on the new job."

She disengaged from the chatty Mrs. Jenkins with a skill that Joy could only admire. She smiled at Joy. "Sorry. Her hubby has a new FIFO job in WA and she's in a mess about it. I shouldn't tell you that, but you'll hear about it in church anyway. I expect I've got to do a records transfer request for you?"

Joy nodded. She suspected that the receptionist did half of what the doctor was supposed to do, in treating his patients: she listened to them. And did all the rest of her job, kept his patients sweet, and didn't get paid his salary for it either. It might make more sense to set up a communication channel here, than in the Doctor's room. Of course it could be awkward for the young woman, with confidentiality issues. "The only Jenkins I think I have met so far is rather elderly."

"Her son. If you could sign here and here please."

Joy did. "Ah yes. I noticed that the children become invisible when there are grandchildren around. She's got quite a few."

"Isn't that true. They all go goo and gah over my Amber, and talk to her not me," said the receptionist with a happy laugh. "But those are mostly old Joan's daughters' children. The son, Will, only has the one daughter. They've been away for the last couple of weeks. He's been between jobs, and they went to stay with some cousin in the city to look for something. But now this has come up, so Jeannie Jenkins says they're staying. You'll meet her at your church, though Will won't go."

Still thinking that she was sure 'Will won't go' had been a chorus for a pop song, Joy limped out to her car, and drove herself home. Fortunately it didn't hurt to drive. There, she emptied out the medicine cabinet. Because she was a careful soul, who had worked in a Museum of Natural History, she carefully wrote down the names of the pills and ointments, and then dropped them into a carrier bag. Temptation was just to let it wait another day, to put her foot up and rest, but instead she went out to the car and drove to the pharmacy. It seemed quite wrong to drive such a short distance – in town she could have covered more distance walking between a car park and the shops – and country folk said that the townies were lazy, but it seemed everyone drove here. She'd seen several shoppers get into their vehicles at the IGA to drive sixty yards down the road, and park directly outside the establishment they were going into. Perhaps it was that they could park so easily that led to the habit. Today Joy was glad of it, as even with the little rail, the few steps up into the Pharmacy were uncomfortable.

It took her a while, and if she'd not found it an effort, she might have retreated again, because even through the glass door she could hear someone inside getting a loud peal rung over them – and fighting back. "...Like it's not like I failed it!"

"At sixty-four percent you might as well have failed it! You're never going to get into a decent university unless you pull up socks. You can do better, a lot better, and you're going to have to, Cam. This is just not good enough, and you know it, or you wouldn't have tried to hide it from me!"

"You just don't even listen to me."

"Unfortunately, I can't avoid hearing your execrable taste in music! Now go and do some work on it. And don't just sit there and doodle on the margins of your book for hours. Get in there and concentrate, son."

"I don't want to!"

A door at the back slammed as Joy pushed open the glass door, and the white-coated man at the back dispensing counter adjusted his expression from one of fury, still looking at the vibrating door next to him, to a faux welcome-to-a-customer expression. He recognized who, or rather what the customer was, and his expression shifted again. Joy recognized him too as the small sharp-faced man who had delighted in the discomfort of Zenobia... actually, probably not that so much, as in having a ring side seat in what he'd assumed would be a nasty fight, thought Joy, reassessing. The pharmacy was relatively small, with not all of the shelves full. To her mild amusement, there was a small book-display rack of field guides on the counter – and a copy of the book that had her wild flowers illustrations in it.

The ubiquitous assistants she was so used to in city pharmacies were nowhere to be seen. "Afternoon," the man said, his voice carefully neutral. "What can I do for you?"

"Are you the pharmacist? Mr. er... Donald?" asked Joy. "I'm Joy Norton, Reverend Peter Hallam's replacement. I've just emptied out his medicine cabinet and Dr. Hammond said this would be the right place to bring his medicines to."

He looked a little taken aback, but then nodded. "Yes. I am the pharmacist, and yes we do handle the disposal of medication. My name is actually Donald van den Vaestermark, which no-one can spell or pronounce, so I tend to be called Donald." He took the carrier bag and emptied it out onto the counter. "My. I didn't realize what a lot of business I was depriving myself of. I didn't see much of Hallam in here."

"Oh. Is there another pharmacy I should rather have taken it to?"

"No. It doesn't matter. There isn't another in town. We just had words about his stupid sky fairies and he obviously decided to buy online instead." He glanced at the bottles and ointments, picking up one and looking at it, and then at a second tube of ointment. "Still mostly corticosteroids, anti-allergenic stuff, by the looks of it." He shoved it back in the bag. "I'll dispose of it for you, Ms. Norton."

As he did that, Joy glanced around the shop. And then her eyes caught, on an upper glass-fronted and locked cabinet behind the pharmacist, several bottles with a symbol she recognized, placed and, with shock realized where she'd last seen. The skull and crossbones used to mark poisons was not the same as the typical pirate flag... it was very stylized and always the same. And absolutely identical to the one drawn on the piece of paper that had disguised the brick thrown through her window.

The last time she'd seen this particular man, he had been having coffee with the local artist. And he was not a very large man, and dark haired. Had she just handed him the reason he'd been trying to break into the rectory? She couldn't exactly snatch the bag back. And he was looking at her. An assessing, curious look. Not entirely pleasant.

She did her best to smile graciously, to camouflage her roil of emotions, and indeed her fear. "Thank you," she said, praying that her voice would be steady. It was.

"Anything else I can do for you?" asked the Pharmacist.

"Perhaps if you have some arnica ointment. I fell and bruised my ankle." It was a supreme effort at keeping a calm tone, and a level and relatively disinterested voice, quite out of synch with her racing heart.

He found some for her and rang it up. Joy was rather surprised at how much he charged, but said nothing. And although he pointedly referred to her as Ms. Norton, the town's atheist and a possible murderer and burglar... gave her no reason to scream and run as fast as she could hobble. She left, and walked as calmly as she could down the few steps to the road.

As she got to the foot of the stair, she looked back and saw that he had emptied out the carrier bag again, and was carefully examining the contents.

She got into her car, wondering if she should drive straight to Sergeant Grogan. But what would she say to him? The Pharmacist has the same skull-and-crossbones on his bottles of poisons as on the note the brick had been wrapped in? The man was friendly with an artist? She might just have given him the very thing he had tried to break in for?

She turned out of the parking space and got a loud hoot from a passing ute that she had been too distracted to notice coming up behind. Thoroughly rattled, she drove home very carefully.

Tea, and few minutes of prayer, and then looking out of the window at the red sky of evening settling over the trees, leaving them black and silhouetted in its grandeur brought Matthew 16 to her mind... 'When it is evening, you say, 'It will be fair weather, for the sky is red...' thinking on the rest of that passage, she realized that she wasn't even very good at interpreting the signs of weather in the sky out here, let alone the signs that might point to murder. She got up, had a twinge from her ankle, and collected the list of medications and her laptop, and set about looking them up.

It was a confusing occupation. And the irritating half-remembered tune playing in her head didn't help. Still, none of the first seven medications gave a pharmacist any reason to need to recover the pills... unless he'd substituted them for something toxic? But so far they seemed to be treatments for arthritic pain, and allergies... Steroids, relatively cheap and not high-schedule drugs. Even the one that turned into an osteo-painkiller was nothing exceptional. He'd obviously been very allergic to something, because even she had recognised the epi-pen, but the rest had to be looked up. Some of them were homeopathic. The oddest was the anti-malarial treatment. But he might have gone to some tropical place, she supposed. And also it was used for some arthritic conditions, she saw, reading through the turgid medical terminology. She was quite glad when the 'phone rang.

It was Mary. "I heard from Tom that you took a fall this morning. Do you need me to bring over a casserole?"

"If I said yes, it would be pure laziness. I have a slightly sore ankle. It won't stop me cooking."

Naturally, Mary Truman wanted all the details. Joy was not prepared to give all of them. Felixtown had enough speculation and gossip, and some instinct told her to not to mention her suspicions about the Pharmacist. So she turned the discussion to the other people she'd met at the Doctor's rooms. She learned a fair bit about Kylie Clemens, and Dylan, and the fact that her older child had a different father. And of Major Ambleside-Smith. "Checking his blood pressure again. Honestly, why he or Penelope can't do it at home? He had a minor heart problem a few years ago, but you'd think it was a triple bypass by the fuss she makes. It's her fuss, but he likes it, or least puts up with it with good grace, and he doesn't about anything he doesn't like."

It wasn't very Christian, but it seemed probable that it was not an inaccurate assessment of the situation, Joy thought. But she still urged Mary toward charity on the subject. "At least she cares, and loves him. That has to be a good thing, Mary."

Mary was not ready to let her opinions go on this subject. "If you ask me she does it just to bully Arthur into doing exactly what she tells him. But I suppose you'll say that is uncharitable too."

"We're complex people, we all do things for complex reasons we don't fully understand. And it is quite possible to be genuinely worried and to um, use that as a lever. Now, do you know anything about medications?"

"Not a thing. I'm usually very healthy, and find it hard to be sympathetic with people who quack themselves. Of course there are some really sick people. Why do you ask? Donald's the person to ask about medicines. He's very knowledgeable, much more than Dr Hammond – he actually has a Doctorate in Pharmacy. We're very lucky to have him here."

"I was just looking up Peter Hallam's medications online, and then I was having to look up what the terms meant. I think I'll just work on my message instead."

"Take them into Donald. Pay no attention to his comments about 'God-bothering'. He just does it to get a reaction. Poor Reverend Peter was fine with him until the day he snapped and they had a shouting match. It was the first time I saw him really angry, but you're... so much more sensible. Now, about visiting your parishioners: there are quite a few who live out of town, some down roads your little car won't do for. And not all of them are that easy to find. I could take some more time off..."

Joy had decided by now, well-meaning though Mary undoubtedly was, that those visits needed to be done without her, to give the parishioners a chance to get a word in, to express their own opinions and feelings. "I think I'll put those ones off until my ankle feels better," she said firmly. "I'll look into getting myself out to those places then. I think it something that I need to do on my own, Mary. It's very much a part of my mission here. Tomorrow I have the Danyards to see."

Mary seemed to take that well enough. All she said was: "Take antacids!"

A few minutes later, just as she was wrestling with a difficult phrase for her message, and having that dratted tune pop into her head instead, the phone rang again. Perhaps that put an unintended bit of snap into her tone, when she said: "Joy Norton listening."

"Ah. Well, it is Tom Truman speaking."

"I'm fine, really."

"I was pretty sure of that. The bush telegraph would have told me otherwise. But I actually called to apologize, and by the sounds of it I need to," he said, sounding amused. "So no mallardy. I'm afraid I did tell Mary you'd stumbled on the stairs, and she'll be bending your ear soon enough. I wouldn't tell her about your midnight adventure if I were you."

"She has called already, and I didn't."

"Oh. Sorry. Well, make sure you lock well. I would say a thread of fishing line across the window, attached to something would be more than adequate, if you must set death-traps. Much safer than across the stairs."

"I was just tired and nervous. I don't really believe it is possible to break in here quietly. Anyway, I think I know who it was, and I suspect I gave him the reason he was trying to break in. I am not sure I can do anything about it."

"Oh. Well, tell me. Perhaps I can figure out what to do about it. And other than very rare slips when grilled by my sister, I am quite good at confidentiality."

So she did.

There was silence when she'd finished. Then he said... "Hmm. Tell me, do you recall hearing any vehicles just after either incident?"

"The second one, definitely not. The first... let me think. I heard a heavy truck, but that was before they tried to climb in. It was early morning, in Felixtown."

"Ah. That pretty well rules out Donald van den Vaestermark. He can't fly even if he is a duck. He's got a gammy hip, which would make running unlikely. And he couldn't run home. He lives a couple of miles outside the town. You know, that rather run down hobby-farm you can see across the river on the way in from my place. And he drives a car with a very loud and recognizable noise to it. It's an old e-type Jag, about all he salvaged from his marriage break-up. It's not a noise that is easy to miss. A low-pitched deep 'lub-dub' sound. Go down to close to the shop around closing time, and you'll hear him leave, and you'll surely know if you've heard it before."

She sighed. "And there I thought I had the ideal suspect."

Tom Truman wasn't slow on the uptake. "No, not 'local atheist murders priest'. Anyway, I'd guess the town's sympathies probably lie with Donald. He's got a sharp tongue, but generally gives good advice. And the blow-up that Peter Hallam had with him was no help to the reputation of the church."

"You said – and I think Isabella said, Peter Hallam had had a few fights. Everyone else seems to imply he was a plaster saint. Is this a case of not speaking ill of the dead?"

"I suppose so. He was a gentle and quietly spoken bloke most of the time, Reverend Joy. He just, well every now and again something would trigger him. He even had a go at Jeff Wiley once, over fly-tying. And Jeff is as inoffensive as a mouse. Well, a mouse that's not breaking into your rectory, or eating my oats, and he's master craftsman at his fly-tying too. He apologized to Jeff, and that was that. He'd apologized to a couple of folk to my knowledge, but there were a few people – Donald, and Zenobia that wouldn't take it. Actually, if it came down to suspicion on the basis of overt dislike, I'd say Zenobia would be more likely. Except she'd have done him in with a block of tofu between the eyes or Odin's Yew log or something exotic and completely unsubtle."

"And I cannot image her doing anything quietly, and I would have noticed the castanets of bangles. Talking of noise, I have an earworm I am trying to place."

"Earworm? Is this in humans or in livestock? I think someone is having you on. Never heard of it in cows, sheep or pigs. There are quite a few hearing aids in your congregation. Someone could have dropped one and not noticed."

"No, I mean a song that won't get out of my head, that I can't place and can't remember properly. The receptionist at the Doctor's Rooms..."

"Jenny. Nice kid."

"Yes, well, she said something about 'Willie won't'... and it started the tune in my head but not the word's"

"You're probably too young for it. 'Little Willie, Willie, won't go home.' By The Sweet, if I remember right. Look it up on the internet, that what I always do with those bits of half-remembered song. And I bet it was Willie Jenkins she was talking about."

"Er yes."

"He's the size of a house," said Tom, with a laugh. "And he used to be about twice as much trouble as the character in the song. He settled down when he finally got married. He's been job hunting since the brickworks closed down, poor bloke. I've had Little Willie fencing out on my place a bit, but there's not enough spare work in the district to hold him. He's another one Peter had a clash with. What's up with him?"

"I am ahead of the local gossip chain there, but I'll leave you to find out for yourself," said Joy cheerfully.

"Oh I shall. He married Marcus's daughter. I'll get chapter and verse when the old guy comes out to fish."

"Everyone is related to everyone, in this place."

"And those that aren't are working on it. Well, cheerio, then."

She locked up carefully that night, and slept well, not hearing any nightly noises, or e-type Jaguar driving villains, or even mice. That was a relief to her sleep-debt anyway.

CHAPTER 8

The morning brought more flexibility to her ankle, and a call from Dean Mellors. "Joy, you obviously have Bishop Michael all stirred up. He asked me to investigate if there was anything odd about your parish records. He said that it was best if we found it, and dealt with it, rather than waiting for it to come and find us. So I've been looking through the correspondence and I'll be talking to our accountants on Monday. But you might want to look for the parish accounts for the last few years. There is something distinctly odd about them, for all that the accounts are signed off."

"Odd? Er. In what way?" asked Joy.

"Well, firstly I don't have them. That could have been my predecessor, Dean Werthe's filing skills. But I eventually found a record of the figures. They balance. Perfectly."

"I thought that was the idea," said Joy, puzzled.

He sighed. "I'm expressing myself badly. The chances that the amount of money coming in will precisely match the amount spent, to the last cent, are about as good as the chances of a flipped coin landing on edge. Sometimes parish councils will spend, carefully, getting the two quite close. Mostly they don't. There will be a little saved if they are prudent, and a little over-run if they're not. For a small congregation Felixtown appears to have done well. It has an endowment, which helps, of course. But there is something odd about them. I wouldn't make a noise about it, but see if those records are accessible."

"Oh dear me. I don't know... I'll look in the parish office. It will cause problems here," said Joy, feeling faintly sick at the thought of what it would do to her little flock.

Lindsey McCassil – the treasurer, already at odds with Mary, and a fair number of the others, by the sounds of it.

"If I am right about this, the treasurer and the accountant who signed it off, this... A. Ambleside-Smith will both have problems," said the Dean, grimly. "It's funny, I wouldn't have thought there was enough money in a little parish to make this sort of theft worthwhile. But it does have the endowment."

Joy had no time to look into it just then, because she had to go off on her pastoral visit, but it did distract her through that entire process. Was that why Arthur seemed so worried and unhappy? Why Lindsey McCassil had apparently kept telling Mary and the parish council there was no money for things like new chairs for the rectory? Lindsey and Arthur seemed the most unlikely pair of co-conspirators possible.

When she got back, feeling the advice on antacids might have been foresight for the wrong reason – the cookies she had been offered came from a packet courtesy of a baker called Arnott – she took herself into the little room called the parish office. It had a separate door from outside, a photocopier and an elderly PC as well as box files and miscellaneous pamphlets.

It was, compared to Peter Hallam's desk, very well organized and relatively easy to find things in, obviously a place someone else worked, presumably the parish secretary and the treasurer. As it happened, the files of the accounts for the last six years were easy to find, and what she started on first was the oldest. Rather fearing it would make no sense to her, she looked in to it. The summary statement on top of the mass of bills and the like, seemed the easiest.

Six years ago, the parish had had to dip into its savings account quite considerably to make ends meet.

Five years ago – just when Peter Hallam arrived, the parish expenses had over-run its income. The offertory was down. Not by a lot, but enough to force the church to dig further into its slender savings. The treasurer signing off had been Lorna Smithson. So Joy took out the next year's file. That showed a similar picture, except of course that expenses were higher. In fact without the income from the church fair they would have been in the red. As it was, barely in the black. Again it was Lorna as treasurer.

The next year... the income matched the outgoing to the last cent, despite a small upward creep in expenses. And the Treasurer was now Lindsey McCassil. She looked at the two years that followed... and saw the same pattern repeated.

The expenditure hadn't dipped, but had edged upward slightly. But the income via the offertory had also... precisely matching the expenditure.

She called Dean Mellors. "How far back did you look?" she asked.

"The last three years. Has it being going on for a lot longer? Those are the only figures I had here. Just part of the summary the accountants send us."

"I don't think it is what you think it is," said Joy. "I'll scan and send the documents through to you."

"What are you seeing?" he asked.

"I'll send it to you, because I'm not sure I am right. But, well, I think that... the treasurer – or someone, has been putting extra in, not taking money out. The endowment is a fixed sum every year, the savings and interest are negligible, the income via fund-raising is generally given to various charitable causes rather than kept for the local church, and looking at the figures, for six, five and four years ago the offertory has garnered less every year. And then it changed direction, to exactly match the expenses"

"I did notice that the parish has been slowly shrinking. Most of the country districts have the same problem with the offertory... except that theirs don't change direction. So you mean someone has just stuck their hand in their pocket and made up the difference," said the Dean.

"That's exactly what I think has happened. And I don't see that as theft, per se," said Joy. "Or a reason to kill anyone," she paused, a horrible thought dawning on her. "Unless, well, unless someone was forcing them to do it."

"Goodness me. It can't have been that much money. I mean, by the sounds of it, surely not worth doing something as terrible as that."

"I absolutely hope that I am wrong. But people do do things for what seem small reason to those who aren't involved."

"I hope so too," said the Dean. "You'd better get to the bottom of it, Joy, without killing your golden goose. It's not like the church can't use that kind of help. We don't want to abuse it though."

"It might be dead already."

"I hadn't thought of that! Well, I will look at those scanned documents, and call off my meeting with the accountants. Perhaps you might have a quiet word with the accountant that signed it all off. Do you know him?"

"Arthur? Yes. He's an unhappy man. I wondered if this could be why, but I don't see how it could be."

"I suppose talking to unhappy people is a very important part of our work," said the Dean, "If not always the easiest. Let me know what you find out."

So a little later, steeled with a cup of tea, Joy went through her list of numbers and called Arthur. The business and home number, for both him and his parents, were the same, she noticed.

"Oh. If you'd called a few minutes earlier," said the slightly nasal voice of Penelope Ambleside-Smith. "He's just left to go up to the city. A University friend's wedding or something. And the Major wanted him to do some pruning this weekend. He has no consideration at all. I'll get him to call you when he gets back."

Joy found it bizarre that Penelope referred to her husband as 'the Major'. "Well, weddings are infectious you know. He might come back down with a bride to be." It seemed vastly unlikely, but Joy had concluded after years of observing people it wasn't always the people who you thought likely, or who would make a good spouse, who ended up married.

"Oh no! Arthur's not like that at all," said Penelope, sounding horrified by the idea.

When she'd put the phone down, Joy wondered what she should do next.

The best answer seemed to be to wander into her living room, and look at the cross on the wall. And then to 'phone Lindsey McCassil.

"Is this something to do with the call I had from Mary, last night?" said the Postmistress, rather guardedly. "I'd like to know quite what that was all about, but I'm not sure that I like it. Is this your doing, Reverend Joy?"

"No, or well, not specifically. We can talk about it if you wish, but what I called about was your role as treasurer for the parish."

"There really is no spare cash for it, Reverend Joy, no matter what it is or how good an idea it would be," said Lindsey firmly.

"I wasn't calling to suggest spending any money. Actually, I was hoping for some help with the parish accounts. I've just been in to the parish office, looking through them. I got a call from the Dean about them this morning."

"Oh." There was a pause and bit of a sigh. "I'll come in after work this evening."

"If that is convenient for you, that would be very kind," said Joy.

"Oh any evening is convenient. I don't really have much of a social calendar. I'll be there about quarter past five. Mr Wiley makes closing up very efficient."

Joy had the kettle boiled and the tea things ready when Lindsey arrived there. "I drink coffee," she said to the offer. "Plain old instant is fine." Joy made it, and offered milk and sugar.

"Drat," said Lindsey. "I forgot to buy milk again. I only use it in coffee and even the long-life stuff goes off eventually. I suppose this is about... what I did with the accounts."

"Well, yes." At least she didn't seem too troubled about it, thought Joy.

"It was my own fault I suppose. I didn't want to admit I had made a complete fool of myself."

This was not the direction Joy had foreseen. "Er. You did?"

"Yes, well Lorna doesn't come across as the most efficient person on earth, does she? I thought she was just making a mess of it. Nothing a bit of good management and housekeeping couldn't fix. No need for Mary's last minute fundraisers. This is the woman who can't remember to buy her milk, thinking that I could do a lot better."

Joy got it then. "You run the post office very efficiently," she said, soothingly.

Lindsey shrugged. "I don't have to find money for PO when there isn't any there. And well..." she trickled off. "And once I had started, well, I didn't know how to stop. Anyone taking over the accounts would see it. I don't like to look a fool."

"You've been very generous of your own money to stop yourself from looking like that." Joy bit her lip. The church needed funds, but it needed to follow the teaching of Christ far far more. "I think I understand why you did what you did. The point is, even if no one ever found out, God knew. We're all fools by that standard, and he still loves us."

Lindsey gave her a crooked smile. "You're very saintly, Reverend Joy. I'm not even sure I believe all of that. It's a lesson that has cost me a few thousand dollars. I think I have learned it."

"It didn't have to."

"Medicine has to taste bad before it works, my mother always said."

"Ah but then it makes us better. My mother used to say that too. I'm not very saintly, Lindsey. I was scared of coming here, I was terrified of 'phoning you about this. I was scared I'd say the wrong thing, just now, too. But that was always my answer, in the end. This is why I am here, doing my best. I'm not good at it but I have help. And that is why I say to you: the church needed the money, but it always needs people more. We need you."

Lindsey looked hard at her. "Nobody really needs me, Reverend Joy. I'm an aging spinster who tried to make herself more important than she really was. I was... trying to prove something."

"I think you did. Just not quite what you set out to prove. And you're wrong. I had Mary in tears here a few days ago. She says you used to be her best friend, once."

"We did a lot of stump embroidery together. I wondered what that 'phone call was about. Your doing, Reverend Joy?"

"Only peripherally. She overheard something you said, and was very upset by it. She wanted to leave the church rather than have to see you or speak to you. I talked to her about it and got her to realize that the issue wasn't you at all, or what you'd said, but her. She'd like to build bridges again, I think. She misses the friendship."

Lindsey sighed. "I'll take her up on the supper invitation then. Although she will cook fancy things I don't like. It still beats cooking for myself."

"Well," said Joy, calmly. "What do you like to eat? I'm doing a mac cheese for myself tonight, if that's not too fancy. You could join me."

"I couldn't impose. It's fine. I've got a freezer full of quick meals and pizza."

"It's not going to take me any longer for two than for one. And frankly after the last few days, I could use a little company. It's scary out here in the country."

"Scary? Here? In Felixtown?"

"Well…besides the brick, there have been a few other incidents." And to keep her talking, Joy told her about them. And about her recognizing the skull and crossbones. It served. Lindsey had been plainly about to take her leave, but now sat and let Joy talk as she prepared the Macaroni cheese. She beat the eggs for her, without realizing she was involved, Joy noted, with satisfaction.

"I don't like him much, myself. But Commander Tom is right. You can hear that car of his a half a mile away."

Talk moved to other subjects. Like her, Lindsey had moved here, taken a job for a few months, and stayed. "I really don't know why I did. I suppose… I was younger then. I joined this church to, um, meet people. I hadn't really been going to church for a few years."

Joy drew her out. The woman was plainly not very socially adroit, but had tried. By her comments she'd hoped to find Mr. Right here in the country, which she liked. "By the time I realized he wasn't coming looking for me, I'd left it a bit too late to go out looking for him. I joined a few local societies. Other than patchwork, I didn't enjoy most of them, and, well it's mostly other women, mostly with children, or grandchildren. And the few men are either old lechers or looking for younger models. So it was the church, or not much else. And I got drawn in to the parish council and well, Lorna was complaining about expenses and, I er, stepped in. Me and my big mouth."

They ate, talking about Felixtown, the people, the place. Joy soon gathered that it was the place, rather than the people, that had kept Lindsey here. "I do quite a lot of walking in summer. I wish we had a ramblers group or something like that. I'm not much on sleeping in tents on the ground but, well, compared to where I grew up, it's just… well it gets to me."

"I love a bit of a walk myself. But I think they'd regard me as far too prissy here. I'm not that fond of getting dirty. Mud has no appeal."

"And at this time of year, you can hardly avoid it! I thought I might try cycling until I saw Donald's son Cameron come in to town, from their farm along the river track, on his bike. The wheels were just a solid layer of mud and he had a black streak of it up his back, and a coating up to his knees."

"He has a son?"

"Yes. He got custody after a long, expensive battle. He's a nice enough boy. Polite, not like some of them."

"I find the local children amazingly polite, after the city kids. Now you were saying you did stump embroidery."

"Yes, but nothing like as well as Mary. I quite liked it, but it's, well, decorative, but pointless. And like patchwork, once you've done just so much of it, what do you do with it? I mean Lorna makes doona covers for endless children. Grandchildren, nephews and nieces, and various relations, but I'm a lonely-only. I suppose the one plus side of having given quite a lot of my spare income to um, balance the books, was that I didn't spend more of it on craft. I only have just so much space."

"You haven't ever tried your hand at tying flies, you know, fishing flies?" asked Joy.

"Goodness no. Why?"

"Peter Hallam was trying to, as a way to get to mingle with the local men. There is all the gear he bought for it, sitting in a box in the spare-room. Apparently it is expensive to buy and hard to resell, we've got it, so I thought I might try to learn to use it. I wondered if you knew anything about it that was all. I know Tom Truman ties flies, but I gather it would cause something of a local scandal if I got him to teach me."

That got a smile out of Lindsey. "I wish someone would cause a scandal with Commander Tom. It was just terrible what that woman did to him."

"Well, I stick to judge not lest ye be judged," said Joy, diplomatically. "But anyway, I am going to try. There's an instruction book."

"It can't be too hard if men do it," said Lindsey.

They ended up looking at the instruction book, setting up the little vice, and finding it was actually both easier and a lot more complicated than they'd guessed.

"YouTube," said Lindsey firmly. "I will not be beaten by this," she said, looking at the odd-shaped creation in the vice.

"Well, we have produced something. But I think it is already coming apart."

"And it doesn't look much like the picture, but it was quite fascinating, getting there. Well, thank you Reverend Joy... it's been the best evening I've had for a while. Shows how exciting my life is."

She took her leave, and that left Joy to wonder if she'd actually achieved anything, except to establish that the church funds were not the reason for Peter Hallam's death. That in itself was of some value, even if the hole in the budget next year was what came of it.

She found out the next day that Mary Truman was not the only effectual individual on her parish council, and that Lindsey was just as good if not better at taking decisions and acting on them, if less loudly. There was to be a parish council meeting at three o'clock.

Lindsey made no excuses and cut no corners. She told them exactly what she'd done, and why. "So: I'd like to apologize to Lorna and I'd like to resign as treasurer."

There was a silence. Then Lorna Smithson stopped her knitting and laughed, a warm, bubbling chuckle, which, by the look on Lindsey's face, was not the reaction she'd expected. "Lindsey, dear, I wasn't born yesterday and my name isn't blind Freddy. I'm just a housewife, but I can keep household, and balance a budget. I knew what was coming in, and what the expenses were like. Of course I knew what you were doing from the moment you presented the accounts that first year. But I was glad to be out of trying to do it, and if you wanted to pretend I was bad at it and you were good it, by putting in your own money, eh, well, you have more money than I do. It was good for the church, and saved me time, and all of us a lot of trouble. Good on you, I thought."

"Er."

"I've got four children, and a half a dozen grand-children," continued Lorna calmly. "They've all done the same thing, somewhere down the line. Not all of them have been as good as you at doing it, or at admitting it. And you're much better at keeping the lid on expenses than I ever was. So I vote you go on being the treasurer."

"But I can't go on..."

"Of course you can," said Mary firmly. "We've all done things like that. We'll just have to raise a bit more money, that's all. We can do it."

"I'll add my vote to the 'please stay on'," said Tom. "But that's only because you said I could have money for a new gutter, and I don't have another two and half hours to spend getting that okayed again." The smile said that it was said in jest.

And by unanimous vote, the treasurer found her resignation turned down, and she was asked to stay on. Joy was good at judging expressions. She'd guess the local church had gained itself a scrupulous treasurer for some years, and the show of support had surprised the woman, and made her a great deal happier than her original showing off had done.

"Good," said Tom. "Now can we declare this meeting at an end and make it the shortest parish council meeting on record? All in favor raise your hands and I'll reward you with extra eggs that I want to give away. That's called bribery and corruption, Reverend Joy. Just in case you want the secretary to record it."

The laughter that greeted his comments showed that at least among the parish council there was a degree of healing and fellowship. "I'll second the motion, without any corruption, or bribery – I have lots of eggs still, but I want a word with you, and Lindsey, afterwards. About a separate matter," said Joy.

"So much for my getting away in a hurry," he said cheerfully. But he waited until the rest of the available parish council had left. Joy noticed Lorna giving Lindsey a hug. That was all good.

When the last had gone, Tom said: "And now? What are we in trouble about? Or do you want to spend money on repairs and get the treasurer at a weak moment?"

"Neither," said Joy. "How did the YouTube go, Lindsey?"

The reason for this dawned on Lindsey McCassil. "Not too well. They start by knowing things I don't." She looked at Tom. "We were looking at fly-tying."

"Likewise. I looked at two displays last night. And I thought we should ask an expert, just to start us off." Joy turned to Tom Truman. "We were trying to tie a fly with Peter Hallam's kit last night. We... I thought we might ask a bit of beginner advice."

"Or just vice," said Tom. "Tch tch. Fancy that! Lindsey, what do you think my sister would say about our new priest asking me to help with her vice. I'm shocked. Shocked."

Lindsey was not impervious to his banter. "You're impossible, Commander Tom," she said with a smile. "Please would you show us your vice skills."

"No, just improbable," said Joy. "So would you? Choose a time, and we will be glad to learn. It's a chance," she said to Lindsey, "to reach out into the community. And I really would appreciate not having to do it alone.

He shook his head. "I'm not much of an expert instructor. I just tie a couple of basic patterns fast, and use them to catch a few fish. But we have one of the best in the country as part of our informal little group. I'll ask him to come along and give you some basic lessons. If you get the hang of it, if you like I'll invite you to join the rest of us on the last Wednesday of every month. We set up our vices, eat pizza, and drink whiskey and swap fishing lies. I would love to see the shock on their faces if you two women turn up," he said, with decidedly unholy amusement. "I don't think they'll have ever met a female fly-tyer, let alone two. I'll talk to him and let you know."

Lindsey looked at her watch. "Heavens! I must fly. I asked Mr Wiley to cover for me for an hour," she said guiltily. "Thank you!" And she scurried out.

Tom watched her go. "And the trick will be not telling Jeff Wiley that it's his boss he's showing his skills to. When I heard Lindsey asking about fly-tying I said to myself: 'Indeed there is a God and he is both just, good and has a sense of humor'. But then I thought I saw your hand in this Reverend Duck. Am I right?"

Joy shrugged. "God uses all of us as his tools. It did occur to me that you'd said something about it, but I assumed she'd know. Obviously she does not. Seriously, I saw it as a way to do what a good Christian ought – to mix with the community outside our own comfortable circle of fellow Christians, and, if by nothing but fellowship, show who we are and what we are. I don't think I could do the shooting and fishing, but I could do the fly tying."

He laughed. "I think you should look up 'cul de canard', Reverend Duck. If I'd thought it through, and guessed you'd try fly-tying, I might have chosen a different name."

"That sounds like a base canard, sir."

"I won't take that up. It would just lead to trouble," he said waving a farewell.

CHAPTER 9

Joy was glad of a relatively uneventful run up to her Sunday, barring calling the Dean to let him know that her treasurer had indeed been quietly supplementing church funds, and would not be doing so in future. He seemed to find that a matter for regret. Joy didn't think it would be. "In the short term, definitely not. It's made us stronger as a parish."

"They're getting to you, Joy. They're yours now."

"Yes. I suppose they are. Isn't that my job?"

He laughed. "No sign of the will yet? I do suppose you have checked his bible?"

"Er. I hadn't thought of looking through all the books. I brought my own bible, of course. I'll look for his. I'm sure I saw it on the shelf in the lounge."

There was one there, but it wasn't particularly used looking, like hers was – and that was even though she used her Kindle for convenience most of the time.

She stopped herself from going through all of the many books in the house, by a force of will, and concentrated on preparing her message instead. It struck her, not for the first time, that those who advocated Sunday as a day of rest worked on Sundays. But the cross on the wall seemed to have an answer for that too. It wasn't so much working as untying the donkey or the ox from the stall and leading it to the water. The real question was: was she the donkey or the ox? Eventually she settled for the donkey. It was small and grey, a humble beast of burden, and extremely stubborn at times. An ox would be strong, slow but enduring, patient, and capable of pulling steadfastly at the command of the drover. She was, she concluded, not a good ox, in physiology or nature.

After the service, during tea, Tom Truman sought her out – while she was in conversation with Lindsey and Isabella, to say: "I spoke to our fly-tying guru, and told him that the new priest and one of the ladies from the church wanted a bit of basic instruction in fly-tying. He's agreed, very nervously, so long as I come along, because he doesn't deal with women easily, for Tuesday about six-ish? Here, rather than in the rectory, if you don't mind. He likes a lot of bench space. He's trying to talk old Mac into coming too, to hold his hand."

"We don't bite," said Lindsey.

"Well," said Tom, with a straight face. "You'll have to be tactful. He's scared of women, and it took real missionary zeal about his hobby to get him to come along at all. Now, I must get another tomato sandwich before they're all gone."

"Is a joke," said Isabella, knowingly. "You can tell with Tom. He do this all the time. His mouth doesn't laugh, but his eyes they do it."

Lindsey nodded in agreement. "Well, whichever Lothario it is, at least Commander Tom will be there to keep him in bounds. It's probably old Seitz. He never manages to come into the Post Office without making some stupid comment. Mr. Wiley has become very good at making sure he deals with him. I was quite surprised at how he read him the riot act the other day."

Joy said nothing, but wondered if Tom Truman's latest jest would backfire on all of them. But she didn't quite have the heart to spoil it. The normal talk that would follow any service, anywhere was still too punctuated by awkward silences – at least one caused by an accidental mention of Reverend Hallam.

That afternoon, she took a long walk and read a book, instead of looking through all the books in the place. The walk, chosen to face into the wind on the way out, and blow her home on the way back, was a little further than she should have taken her ankle, and the stinging wind-driven sand on the track next to the beach made it less pleasant than it could have been.

None-the-less it took her out toward the cape that sheltered Felixtown, and up onto a spit of rock that gave her a view back over the little town and its valley. She could see how the road she'd come in on took a long curve away from town to join the coast road, avoiding the water-meadows. The wind drove wave-patterns across their green, a sea of grass surging up to the road-margin trees. It was still a great deal quieter than the actual sea, today. That was white-flecked all the way out to the horizon – a horizon that visibly wasn't flat. No day to be at sea today. She turned back to the land, to the neat farms taking their shelter from the geology that led to the cape she had been walking towards. She attempted to work out just where she'd come off the road. About five miles from the town... but because the road curved so, following the higher ground, that wasn't actually that far from the town. She could see neat patchwork-paddocks with tiny black and white cows, and a huge shed, the corrugated roof glinting in the weak sun, with a house and a smoking chimney next to it, and coming closer some less neatly paddocked land with black cows. Then a mix of bush and the water-meadows to the slight rise of the town.

It was, she realized, even in this weather, a picturesque area, and the road out towards the cape from the town showed a series of houses set there to take advantage of the shelter and the view of the valley and coastline. Someday she must go up there. But not today, not on foot, her ankle said. So she made her way back to the town, and to her fire and a thoroughly unsatisfactory murder-mystery of Reverend Hallam's where, as Lorna had put it a few days earlier, Blind Freddy could see who-dunnit. Her meditation was a far more satisfying read.

The next morning she started going through all the books in the house. It wasn't in the murder-mystery, which she had decided could go to the book-sale at the church fair.

The 'phone rang, as it will, just when a pile of books had to fall over if she let go of it. Ah, well. It would mean starting that row again.

It was Arthur. "Mother said you called," he said, sounding as cheerful as a wet weekend at the beach. "Something about the church accounts?"

Joy had forgotten that Penelope had promised to get him to call her. "Ah. I am sorry to waste your time. It's all cleared itself up."

There was a pause. Then in a low hesitant voice he said: "Oh. Oh, well, I want..."

"Is that you in there, Arthur?" asked another voice, loudly. The nasal high-pitched tones of his mother, by the sounds of it.

"Yes Mother, I'm on the 'phone," said the slightly muffled voice of Arthur.

"But why in there, dear?" demanded his mother. "The Major is looking for you!"

"I'm sorry Reverend Joy. I'd better go. I'm glad it has been cleared up," said Arthur, loudly and clearly. "Lovely talking to you."

Joy was left wondering quite what he had actually wanted to talk to her about. It plainly had not been something he wanted his mother aware of. Really. The man must be thirty, and still living at home.

She'd just got back to her collapsed book-pile, when the 'phone rang again. This time it was Tom Truman. "Thought you ought to know for your pastoral visits, that Little Willie is away."

That left her floundering a little. "I looked it up, and watched the band sing it on YouTube. Those clothes! But, besides the fact I won't see the star shoe shimmy shuffle down, why is that important?"

"I think I was assuming you knew a little more than you do," said Tom. "Let me explain. Little Willie had words with Reverend Hallam... as in Little Willie lifted him two feet off the ground and told him never to set foot on his property again or he'd... well, not treat him to cream tea. It didn't help that Peter Hallam turned out to be right, and it was his daughter."

"Er. Was his daughter what?" asked Joy.

"Oh she was one of a bunch of kids that ran a bit wild, eh, about five, six months ago," explained Tom. "They painted graffiti on a few places, including the fence of the rectory. They nicked the clapper out of the church bell, set the toilet to indicate vacant when it wasn't and occupied when no-one was in. Of course Grogan caught up with them eventually, and sure enough Izzy was one of the bunch. But by then Reverend Peter had tried to apologize, Mary went down with him, and she got into a yelling match with Willie. It was a mess that didn't get better. Little Willie won't have anything to do with the church anyway, but then his mother leaned on him when Izzy got caught, to go and say sorry, and he got Peter on a day, or a moment, when he was antsy, and, well, it made the whole situation worse. He wouldn't even come out of his house to speak to him. Apparently threatened to call the cops if Willie didn't leave immediately... Jeanie – that's his wife -- stopped coming to church which I reckon she'd only been doing to keep sweet with her mother-in-law – she wasn't exactly regular, but you'd see her there on occasions. Christmas, Easter, sometimes when Willie was away."

"So... do you think this is the moment to make the peace? I mean, I suspect that she, and probably her husband if he got to hear of it, would think I nipped in the minute he was gone to try and take advantage of that. It doesn't seem the ideal moment to me."

"I'd say you were right, except I called old Mac last night to lean on him about the fly-tying. I practically had to twist both of Jeff Wiley's arms off to get him to agree to come, and that was on condition he had backup. And in the middle of all the talking to him, Mac comes out and says he hears you did a home visit to Fred Danyard's place the other day, and were you thinking of going to see his daughter, Jeanie, soon, as Willie was away? And if you knew old Mac like I do, you'd understand that's practically begging."

"Then I'd better go. But I had better 'phone first," said Joy feeling the chill in her stomach that potentially nasty scenes always brought to her.

"Hang on. I'll give you the number. I've got it here from when Willie was working for me. Just tell Jeanie you're meeting all your parishioners."

"Can I tell you how to milk cows, Mr. Truman?"

He laughed. "My sister is rubbing off on me."

"The thought never crossed my lips, Tom Truman. Anyway I think the number is actually on the list your efficient sister Mary gave me. I have it here next to the 'phone." She read it out to him.

"Yes. That's it. Good thing you hadn't got that far. Well, I'll see you tomorrow. Cheerio."

He hung up, and Joy closed her eyes and did her best to compose herself. The procrastination demon was strong, tempting her toward tea at least first. But last time she had put a call off for a cup of tea she had missed Arthur, so she took a deep breath and dialed. It was never easy.

The woman on the other end of the line sounded both wary, and indecisive. "I don't know. I really ought not but..."

"I'm trying to link the families together," said Joy. "You're Marcus McGregor's daughter, aren't you? He's a gem. I met him through Tom Truman."

"I heard about that! You loaded pig-food!" exclaimed Jeanie. "Dad said you were different to any priest he ever met. Um. Look..."

"I'm walking down to the IGA in a few minutes. I'd just like to stop for a minute and say hello. From the address on the parish list I think it is on my way. I'm trying to visit everyone. It's a bit hard for people to get used to a woman priest. I'm trying to work through them alphabetically, but say if some other time would be better."

There was a pause. "Come now. Please," said Jeanie.

"Righty-o. I'll be there in a tick," said Joy, realizing that she had to strike while the iron was hot. She didn't waste time about it, had a quick look at the address and took her coat from the rack and set out.

Jeanie Jenkins was one of those people with an enormously expressive face, one that could never hide anything well. Poker would never have been her game. Right now, had she been playing the game with you, you'd have guessed the entire hand had nothing, and she'd just put the family fortune on the table. She could never have been a pretty woman, she had a broad face overpopulated with freckles and too big a mouth, but now she seemed to be wearing the world's troubles as well. Still, she did her best to make small talk. Naturally the subject of loading Tom's pig-food outside the co-op was the starting point. "I couldn't leave him to load them on his own," explained Joy. "Not after he rescued me from a ditch."

"He's good at rescue," said the woman, slightly tremulously. "We owe him too. Um. Not money, but he gave Willie a job, and, um, helped him."

It was plainly awkward ground. Joy did her best to ease around it. "I heard your husband has a new FIFO job." One of the things a priest got used to doing was reading the small signs. The house was neat and cared for... but that made the signs that cash had obviously been tight slightly more obvious, if anything.

"Yes. It's been a relief but, we've never been apart. Not ever since we got married. I mean the money is wonderful, and especially now with jobs hard to get. But..." she sighed. "I wish. Oh well, as dad says if wishes were horses we'd be knee-deep in horse-ah...manure. Oh, um pardon the expression."

"It's a beauty. Only I bet he didn't say manure. I've been into the shop when he was doing 'surgery' on some piece of machinery. He was talking to the screw that wouldn't budge. I don't think he even knew he was saying it."

That finally drew a smile which quite transformed Jeanie's face. "Dad." She shook her head. "It's not that he means bad by it. It is just what he is. I struggled so with William's family, 'cause... well every time I opened my mouth I was in trouble."

"Well, relax with me. I've heard worse. And plenty of nastiness hidden in prissy speeches too. Give me a rough tongue and good heart any day over hypocritical sweet talk. And that's your father, I'd guess."

"Oh yes. That's dad's trouble, in a way. He'd give you the shirt off his back. He always feels sorry for people and never charges half of them. And he said the new bible-th... priest was better than that... um well." She blushed. "Anyway. I don't know if you know. Willie had a disagreement with your um... predecessor. Which was why I was kind of surprised to hear from you."

"I'm not Reverend Hallam the second," said Joy, with a smile. "I don't even look like him. I'm Joy Norton. We just work for the same boss, and that boss is better at forgiving than his employees ever are. He even forgives Peter Hallam, and me as well, when I mess up, which I do. He's better at understanding too. But I do my best, without too much bible-thumping."

"That's what dad said, he said 'she's a tiny wee thing and could barely lift a bag, but she was doing her best'." She bit her lip. "Look. I said you could come around because I need some advice and I didn't quite know who else to ask. I can't ask dad, and I just can't even think about telling Willie. He'd go spare. And talk to any of my friends... because, because it would get around like wildfire. And she's my daughter and I love her."

"You can talk to me. And it won't get anywhere without your permission. I've been told all sort of things over the years. It's part of the job too."

113

Jeanie looked at Joy doubtfully. "You promise?" She obviously read the expression on Joy's face. "It's not a crime or anything. It's just... they'll call her a slut. And around here that sticks and hurts. See, on Saturday, when I was helping Willie pack up, I... I went into her room. The swags and tent and stuff... they're all in the high bit of the built-in cupboard in her room and I couldn't find the travelling wash-bag."

She stopped.

"And what did you find there?" prompted Joy gently.

"A condom." She stood up and dug in a somewhat worn shoulder-sling bag hanging on the chair, and pulled out a still-sealed little package, garishly bright purple, and proudly pronouncing its extra ribbing and various other properties.

Joy had begun to realize that context was everything out here, and plainly to this mother that was beyond horrific. "I hate to ask, but how old is she?"

"Fifteen. I couldn't say anything to her. Or Willie, not with Willie just about to leave. But... in the car on the way home... I did. And she lied to me. She said it wasn't true. And then when I said I had the bloody thing, she said how dared I search her cupboard and, and she wasn't sleeping with anyone and... well, we both shouted ourselves hoarse. She told me to stop the car and let her out and of course I didn't. I didn't know what was going to happen when we got home... but Dad was waiting. He'd come and cooked tea for us. And... and we both had to pretend things were normal. She's his pet. He spoils her, but, well it's just a little bit."

"I'd be surprised if he hasn't taught her some very good expressions that have got her into all sorts of trouble," said Joy.

"And taught her to weld. He never taught me!"

"I think you should have complained to child welfare," said Joy, "but it is a bit late for that now. Look... how old is the boyfriend?"

"She hasn't got one. Or she's never told me about one. She's, she's popular. I mean not like that. She's just lively, and if there is anything going on, she's involved in it, but... well, she looks like me. This morning before she went to school, I asked her again who it was. She just went all sulky on me. Like when we had that whole graffiti thing. I don't know what to do. If Willie finds out... He'd track this boy down and kill him. He got... so angry again last week when we had Grogan around here, again. Just following up he said. Where was Izzy last Monday? Well, Willie told him to take his 'just following up' to the City and his Cousin Ed's place, because that's where we were. And then he could shove it up his..." She sighed. "It was just lucky it was Joe Grogan. Joe's been a bit on Willie's case, but, well I think he was trying to get Willie to straighten out. Anyway he didn't do anything about it or Willie could have been in trouble again. And we need this job."

"Look, every child is different, and teenagers can be very, um, trying. I was one, and I remember it all too well. I think the first and most important thing you're going to have to do is to tell your daughter you love her. Build bridges if you can rather than blow them up. I expect you and your husband have both done your best to protect her from the tough times. That's good, but it doesn't help her to understand, and as a teenager you really want to be treated as an adult, and part of that is being told what is going on, and being relied on. So: if you haven't told her... tell her it is very hard for you and her father to be apart and that you need her help."

That got a nod. "We just didn't want it all to affect her too badly. But, well, I see your point. And then?"

"And then you're going to have to be patient, trusting and loving. I'd say you could try a prayer too. And you know, there is a small possibility that she wasn't lying to you."

"I don't really see how."

"I once had a parishioner swearing to the police that it was her own drug paraphernalia to protect her son. Maybe

115

Izzy has a friend who can't keep his or her parents out of their cupboards. I know it isn't likely, but there is an outside chance."

"I've never done that before. I have always trusted her. Why is life so complicated?"

"The best answer I've ever heard to that is because death is simple and nasty, and at least complicated can be good sometimes," Joy looked at her watch. "Now, I'm dying for a cup of tea. How about if we walked down to La Zenobia's... uh, I probably should call it the Chamomile whatever."

"Oh no. I, I can't," she said looking embarrassed. "We, we cut back on that kind of thing."

"It's my treat. And you'd be doing me a huge favor and I'd appreciate it a lot," said Joy.

"What? I mean why?" asked Jeanie.

"The town knows Peter Hallam and your husband fought," explained Joy. "Seeing us together will tell them that that's being sorted. That's valuable for me in this sort of community. And besides, this being Felixtown, everyone probably knows you've been having a hard time."

Jeanie sighed, nodded. "We had too big a mortgage, and the ends just kept getting further apart. I thought we were going to lose the house. And well. Um. Willie was drinking a lot. That's... that's why I was so grateful to Commander Tom. He sort of got Willie's pride up again, got him to stop pi... uh drinking it all. And he was one of Willie's referees for this job. But we still have to watch the money."

"Nothing will tell the town better that you're on the way up, with your husband having landed a good job, than being seen having some tea. And cake. And it is entirely my shout. When things do fix themselves up, you can do the same for me. Come on," said Joy, smiling encouragingly.

"Well... I'll have to put some smarts on. I can't go like this. I can't even think how I saw you like this."

"I'm just Joy. You can see me anyway you like. Two of my parishioners even saw me in my pajamas."

That got a real smile. "No wonder my mother-in-law says the church is full."

"I'd overslept," admitted Joy. "I don't take services like that. Mind you, I did have someone fall asleep during the sermon yesterday. Maybe if I suggest he wears his PJ's, he'll stay awake!"

"Um. I'm not sure about coming to church. Willie..."

"I'm not angling to get you there. I'm just doing the job I was given. I don't make the decisions or any judgments about church-going. But I have faith it'll all work out as it should," said Joy, calmly. And that seemed to work, as reassurance.

They walked down to the shore-front, and Joy worked at drawing the woman out. She worked most days, cleaning in various places. "Willie hates me doing it. But, well there was nothing much coming in. I'll have lost a few of the better places going off on his job-hunting trip with Cousin Ed. But some of the jobs, no one else wants. It's been part of the issue with Izzy. I mean I used to be home all of the time. And then I wasn't."

The shop was once again under the control of Zenobia's daughter. She actually gave Joy a tentative smile, and started to say something, before Jeanie came in and said that it was nice to see that she wasn't quite as skinny as she had been. Maybe it wasn't the most tactful remark, by the flush it brought to Madeleine, but it was well meant.

Joy and Jeanie talked easily enough, and got through a pot of tea, and two large slices of lemon meringue, and drew a few startled looks in the process. Jeanie gradually relaxed, stopped minding her tongue, and opened up like a peony in the sunshine. Joy got quite a lot of extra information about 'little' Willie, and a great deal more about their daughter, and also the names of the kids who'd gone on the tagging spree. It was first names, of course, but that, she felt would be enough

117

to track back through her information service of parishioners. The pot was long cold, and a couple of people had started drifting in for lunch when Jeanie looked at her watch, startled. "I've kept you for hours. I'd better get going. But… thank you. I haven't done this for a long time. I used to. A lot. Before…"

"It wasn't a hardship, I promise," said Joy. "Just… keep the door open with your daughter. Any time you want to talk, even if it's about nothing in particular, I can come around or you can come up to the rectory. I'm still learning about all the people here, so it helps me too."

She got a nod and a broad smile. "I'm also going to stop in with Dad on the way back and ask him if he'll come and have tea with us again tonight."

"Good idea," said Joy, hoping it was. She was less sanguine about the goodness and wonderfulness of Jeanie's daughter, who was, however you viewed it, underage and had been in trouble before. She knew, in the reality of a modern world, that a lot of fifteen year old girls thought that they were very adult already. She just hoped and prayed she'd given good advice, as well as good fellowship.

She walked back, stopping at the post-office – which was busy, but not too busy to give her a smile and a friendly greeting – and then on to do some shopping, and get a cheerful 'What can I do for you, Reverend Duck?' in the butcher's shop, showing the spread of that name. It was not one that fighting would do any good, so she just smiled and placed her order.

CHAPTER 10

That afternoon Joy got down to going through the bookshelves. Peter Hallam – and, by the age of some of the books, his predecessors – had been keen readers. He had not been particularly systematic about shelving them, although they were in broad categories. Joy also did that with her books, but she also liked them in alphabetical order. She opened each book, and fanned the pages twice, before putting them in her piles to be alphabetically arranged. There were a lot of books on theology. That was to be expected. She really must get a bible-study group going. There was a broad spattering of novels, largely of the thriller type with a few gory whodunits – not her sort of book at all. And then she came to a collection of books on art and drawing. At first glance she'd taken them for, like his collection of fly-tying materials, an attempt to fit in with the art crowd here. But the books were old, and well-used. And they had his name in the inside cover. One was awarded as a school art prize to Peter John Hallam.

It would seem – despite Amabelle Tilton's opinion – that he hadn't been new to art. The next books on the shelf were several years' worth of collections of cartoons – political cartoons, from a national newspaper chain. They were not recent, dating from twenty years ago, by a cartoonist who signed himself 'Halley'. The signature looked familiar. And the books were in mint condition. It didn't take Joy a great leap of intuition to go and find the parish register and compare the signatures. She was no expert, but it was certainly very much the same in style, and the way the letters were formed. Well. There was nothing to stop a priest being a

119

cartoonist. She turned to the internet and was rewarded for her effort by the discovery that 'Halley' had been the pen-name of the cartoonist Peter John Hallam. He'd risen to national fame, won several awards, and then given it all up suddenly, after what the article described as the tragic death of his wife, Edith. They were very flattering about his ability to caricature, so Joy went to have a look at the cartoons.

It was an accurate comment. This was a man who could, with the sparsest use of lines, convey the whole of his subject's face, expression, attitude – and could change the view of those with a twitch of the pencil. Joy had never been that kind of artist: her skill was in a precise rendition of what she saw. She knew she had been quite good at it, but Peter Hallam had not been quite good: he'd been a master-craftsman. And yet he'd walked away from it all to enter the ministry, and to quietly rot away here in this rural town. Having made that choice herself, she could understand that it brought a different reward.

But it still made her wonder.

Some hours later, having thoroughly filled her sinuses with dust, she was sure that Peter Hallam's will was not in any of the books in the living room. That left quite a lot in the room that was still full of boxes, which he had used as a study, but she had had enough dust for the moment, even if she was now rewarded with alphabetical shelves, and a small window into the life of the dead man.

The rest of the books would have to wait. In the meanwhile she did a little 'fishing'. She had a list of names, and she had Mary. Mary, it turned out, still helped with netball coaching, having been a junior state player, once, long ago. Mary rapidly worked out who they were, and that they were the children involved in the graffiti incident. "I put it down to that Kyra Tompkins myself, and she and her family left town again. They'd only arrived six months before. Her mother was working in the pub, and he was a block-man at the butcher's. She was a piece of work, that child. She wore black nail-polish to school. And she got caught shop-lifting." Joy built up a picture, quite rapidly, from her intelligencer. It was the kids who were in the social B team at the school. A new girl had arrived and they'd all had a bit of rebellion together, by the sounds of it. That was not surprising, really. "Around here, it's really all about sport," explained Mary. "Or horses, if you're a girl. I couldn't stand them myself, but I was good at hockey and netball, so that was all right for me."

"Horses always rather intimidated me. Not that my parents had that kind of money."

"Well, when I was growing up, it wasn't that big a deal out here. A couple of old folk from out Pellah way still came into town in carts and there were lots of ponies around and grazing was cheap. But it has got much more expensive since. Anyway, the others aren't outright bad. They're just the misfits, I suppose."

"Tell me about them. No one is God's misfit."

So Mary did. It was, Joy appreciated, the point of view of a spinster, who had little to do with teenagers, but still lived in a small place where you could hardly avoid knowing something about them and their families. She learned about how fat Jarred Webb would probably take after his father and go and cook in the pub, and how he refused to take part in the footy. About Megan Stott and her glasses and odd parents. About Donald's son Cameron: "He's a nice boy, but he's a bit small. And, well, not very masculine. He's older than the others, I was surprised he was in with them."

"And the other one? Isobel Jenkins?" asked Joy, casually.

"Yes it is a bit odd she's in with them. She's a star netball player. Been first team since grade 8. She's taller than her mother, but looks just like she did when she was younger, except she has her father's hair. That Jeanie was a tomboy and a half. She was always in trouble. Always looked like she cut her own hair."

Joy suspected the family finances, and possibly the situation at home, especially if her father had been drinking too much, might have pushed the daughter into the 'outies'. And it seemed true that parents who were wild often were a lot more conservative when raising their own children. But she filed it into her mind for further thought.

She was lucky the next day to run into Sergeant Grogan outside the IGA. Perhaps doing so with her shopping trolley was not so lucky, but that was how it happened. "I should book you for dangerous driving, Reverend." he said cheerfully.

"Well, I wasn't texting while driving. I was trying to read my shopping list. That's not against the law is it?"

"It should be," he said. "But I'll let you off this time. No more nasty incidents, Reverend... Norton, was it?"

"Yes, Norton." She decided not to answer the question, on the certainty that he'd ask why he hadn't been called. "You haven't caught my brick thrower yet, Sergeant?"

"At the moment I'm at a bit of dead end there, Reverend Norton. My principal suspect was a bit too far from the scene to make it possible, the next lives too far out of town, and the third had a good alibi, like having a leg in plaster, and fourth one would need to be Houdini, her mother locks the place up so. Not that I'm counting it out, but she's often late for school, and I believe it'd take a crowbar to get her out of bed early enough to get up to mischief. Midnight would be a different matter. But this is Felixtown. It'll come out. And I'd better get back to my busy schedule," he said, laughing at himself. "Now you drive that thing carefully. No more reading and driving."

Joy had actually come in to get a few ingredients to make something to feed the fly-tying mélange that evening. She was worried the prickly Lindsey McCassil... or the nervous Jeff Wiley, might take exception to Tom Truman's little joke. Pizza seemed likely to be safe, and would hopefully not involve too much washing up. It would be simple, but at least she'd make the pizza bases. She collected her ingredients and went home.

Joy opened the rectory door to the sound of a ringing telephone.

It was Jeanie Jenkins. "I just wanted to 'phone to say... we, Izzy and I had a good talk yesterday when she came in. She left it 'til late too, got me in a real state, but she'd gone to dad's workshop. She told me that she was going to cadge some money from him and run away. Only, dad, bless his heart, no sooner saw her but he made her work holding stuff for him and then doing some welding, and told her he was coming to tea this evening. He dropped her round, on his way home. When she came in... I'd been so worried I just hugged her. Anyway, I said I was sorry. And I told her a whole lot that I hadn't said about, well, about nearly losing the house and about how I was battling without her dad, and how I needed some help and support from her. We ended up having a good cry together. And I didn't say anything about, you know." She laughed, tremulously. "I suppose it is better that she knows what they are than, well, the alternative."

"That is true," agreed Joy.

Jeanie sighed. "So long as her father doesn't find out. I mean, he treats her like she's five. She's his little girl. Well. Anyway, things are a bit better. And I hear you've been waving your magic wand over dad too. Um. I suppose priests aren't supposed to wave magic wands."

"No, but they do wave incense in some high-church services. It makes me want to sneeze. Jeanie I'm more worried about people not talking to me at all, than I am about the way you say things. I know what you mean... I think."

"Well, Dad says he is coming to tie flies there tonight. I nearly fell on my back. You really are very brave. He had said the only time I'd see him in church would be in a coffin, and he'd be cremated to fool them. Oh, I am only opening my mouth to change feet..."

Joy laughed. "Well, you should be safe. He's only coming into the hall we serve tea in. And only because Tom Truman leaned on him. I just hope it doesn't all come apart. Tom is playing one of his jokes. I'm about to make pizza as a social lubricant."

There was a moment's silence. "Well," said the woman on the other end of the line. "How many people will you have there?"

"Just five, including me. You don't tie flies do you?"

"Good grief, no. I quite liked fishing, but only in the sea. We used to have a boat... anyway. I'm going to make my sticky-date pudding and I'll send Izzy over with it. That way you'll get to meet my girl. I mean, if I tried to bring her to church she probably wouldn't come, but for her grandfather, she will. And then you can try waving your magic wand there too."

"I've only got a cross, but it works miracles," said Joy. "And you really don't have to do that."

"I want to, and I will. It sounds like you think you're going to need it."

That actually did not help Joy to relax about it all. It was at times like this that she really wanted the support of older clergy. But here, there was only her. And God, for which she was very grateful.

She kneaded dough, which was a good occupation for meditation. She prepared the toppings. And then, as she still had spare time, she went into the room with the boxes, and started going through the book-shelves there, resolutely not thinking about mice. This didn't work too well, but there were no mice, despite her nervousness. There was also no will, even though these books were ideal for such a thing. The shelves were larger and deeper here, and he plainly used this to store any books that were too big for the shelf in the other room. It was near the bottom of the book-case, on the last shelf, that she came across the sketch book.

It was 300gsm paper. It was well used, with only a few empty pages at the end.

Most of it was cartoons. Only these were not the cartoons of the other collections. Instead these were everything from Mickey Mouse to Asterix, as well as some Anime style work, and some she could not place. The next pictures were still life compositions – a vase, a set of cups, and repeats of the same, improving, getting the perspective better. And then there was a picture of a girl – all in pencil shades. Young, curly hair, with a very broad-mouthed smile, a gap between her front teeth. That was probably an exaggeration, but the artist had captured the leggy stance, the slight awkwardness in poise that spoke of the uncertainty of being a teenager as loudly as any words ever could. She wasn't beautiful, but the artist had caught the spark and youth in her eyes perfectly. It was the kind of picture that would win competitions, thought Joy, looking at it and shaking her head, mildly incredulously. She should turn the light on and look it better, as it was definitely too dim in here to appreciate that picture. She looked at her watch and realized that time had galloped on, and it was actually that the day was fading. She took the sketch pad upstairs with her, turning the oven on as she went past.

She was back down putting the second pair of pizzas in the oven when someone knocked. It was early for the six o-clock schedule, but not ridiculously so, thought Joy, resignedly, going to the door.

It was Lindsey. "I'm sorry I'm early," she said. "I just wanted to set things up and put the heater on in there, if I could just get the keys. And there was a parcel for Reverend Hallam again. I took the liberty of bringing it round to you."

"We'd better open it I suppose," said Joy, briskly. "And a good idea about the heater. I'm not used to the chill of country evenings, yet." She opened the padded post-bag. It contained art paper, and several cases of Blick studio drawing pencils.

"I thought he had dropped out of the art classes?" commented Lindsey, obviously surprised.

"He needed them about as much as a cat needs lessons on how to chase mice," said Joy. "He was actually a brilliant artist. He had won several awards."

"He did? Really? It goes to show how little we really know of people. He never even mentioned it. I'd better go and get that heater on. We've got that nasty cold rain falling again."

She took the key and went off to do that. A minute or so later, having set a timer on her watch, Joy went across to the hall. She found Marcus MacGregor arriving at the same time. "Tom will be here in a few minutes, I reckon. He's just got to finish his evening milking. He said it was a bloody awkward time to choose if you don't mind me telling you for future reference... Reverend Joy. He's too polite to tell you these things."

"Well, I'm glad you're not. Now I know, I won't let it happen again. And thank you for coming."

"Least I could do," he said gruffly. "It seems like you gave my girl a bit of a hand up. They've been doing it tough, and she's my only kid. My only grandchild too."

"You just keep standing by her. She needs you too."

They walked into the hall, where Lindsey was gingerly patting the urn. "It's not a dog, girl," said Mac.

"I think it bit me, though. And it's not getting hot."

"The light on the heater is not on either," said Joy.

"Unplug it," said Mac, putting a modest plastic case on the table. "You've probably tripped a fuse."

They trooped out to have a look at the fuse box, which was in the vestibule at the front entrance – in the first half of a sensible double door arrangement to keep the chilly winter wind out – and this was indeed the case. "We can manage with a jug tonight, but for Sunday..." said Joy.

"I'll take it away with me," said Mac unworriedly. "Ah here's the man! G'day Jeff," he said to the laden figure who had just struggled to push through the outer door.

Three things saved Tom Truman's idea of a joke from disintegrating right there. The first was that Jeff Wiley, who had just pushed open the door with his elbow, with four large cases in his hands, had literally had no room to turn and run when faced with his boss. The second was that Lindsey was just as surprised to see him. And the third was Tom himself saying "Move, Jeff, I need to get in and take these boots off."

So Jeff Wiley, his escape blocked, edged forward as little as possible, put down his cases just inside the door, and smiled very nervously. "Er. Tom asked me to come and give a quick lesson to a couple of church ladies. Uh." He literally stuck his finger into his collar, which, as he was wearing an open-necked shirt was funny enough to make Joy smile, if in sympathy. "I, um, had no idea you'd be one of them, Ms. McCassil."

Lindsey had plainly been as surprised as he was, but had had a few more seconds to get hold of her mind and tongue. "And I had no idea you tied flies, Mr Wiley. I was just saying to Reverend Joy how little we know of people."

"Well, I wish all of you would move along," said Tom. "I'll be inside in a moment. I came straight from the dairy, and like an idiot I managed to leave my shoes behind, so I need to leave my muddy gumboots out here and join you in my socks."

So they all went through into the hall, and Joy's timer went off, so she had to rush off and take the pizza out of the oven. She thought she might as well just bring it across hot, so she did. She returned, bearing a couple of trays, and struggled to find a place to put them down despite the large table. Jeff Wiley had begun to take over the table-top. He probably had no desire to conquer the world, but merely to take over all available flat surfaces, and fill them with fly-tying paraphernalia... And the other two men were competing too. "I should have brought Peter Hallam's stuff out," said Joy. "I'll go and get it."

"Oh I wouldn't worry," said Marcus. "Young Jeff's got spare vices and enough gear to stock a couple of shops. And I wouldn't have bothered with tea if I'd known you were doing this." He helped himself to a piece of pizza.

Joy had worried that poor Jeff Wiley would feel badly intimidated. She needn't have. This was his field of expertise. He was good at it, and completely comfortable and absorbed in creating flies, once he started. And once Mac had told her not to, because she wasn't in the bloody Post Office now, Lindsey even stopped calling him Mr. Wiley, and managed "Jeff." Lindsey was also far better at her attempts to tie what Jeff called 'a simple pattern' than Joy was herself. After a few flies, they stopped and Jeff Wiley took out boxes of flies he'd made – some of which, Joy judged, would fool an entomologist, if not a fish. It was, Joy judged, a quiet success of an evening. Far better than sitting going through books in search of a will, or brooding on how and why her predecessor might have been killed.

There was a knock on the door just as Jeff had been talked into giving a bit of a master-class in tying something particularly fiendishly difficult.

And in came the girl from the sketchbook. The artist hadn't got the mouth wrong. Or failed to capture the expression on Izzy Jenkins's face, as she carried in the steaming oven-dish of sticky date pudding, while her mother followed behind with a jug of butterscotch sauce. "Hello dad. It was raining so I drove Izzy over with a little present for you. Your favorite."

It was obvious that he wasn't the only person who felt that way. "If you ever want lessons again, Reverend Joy," said Jeff Wiley. "You know how to bribe me!"

"Makes up for the tea they've been threatening me with, to drink," said Mac. "How's my favorite granddaughter?"

"I'm your only grand-daughter, gramps."

"That's why you're my favorite. Now come and meet Reverend Duck. She loads pig food better than any forklift."

"At least when the forklift is broken down," said Joy, praying inwardly for calm.

She was treated to an innocent fairly neutral gaze, as one might give to a friend of your mother or Grandfather. A wave. "Hi."

It wasn't much of a speech to assess anyone on. The girl was looking at the open boxes of flies – not the entomologist's delights in the tiniest of sizes, but the big, garish sea-flies. "Oh cool. Mum, these would make such magic ear-rings."

"And the barb would make sure you never lost them," said Tom cheerfully. "Talk to Jeff Wiley. He can make you some that'll make you the envy of every punk-girl in the school. Maybe even on barbless hooks. "

"Punk is so like, yesterday."

"We'll need some bowls and spoons. Can't let this pudding get cold," said Mac. "Reverend..."

"Oh I'll get them, gramps. Is the door open?" Izzy asked Joy.

"No, but here is the key," said Joy, taking the bunch out of her pocket.

She took it. "Be back in a jiffy," she said and ran off, like a leggy colt.

"She's a good kid when she's not being a bloody teenager," said Mac. "I can tell you're from the big smoke, 'cause you lock your door. The only other person who does that is that crazy Stott woman. She locked herself out and the baby in about two months ago. Had to get me and the SES and the Jaws of Life to get back in. And then, so help me, she had it fixed and made tougher, because we did manage to get in."

Barely a minute and half later, Izzy returned, with bowls and spoons from the rectory cupboard.

How had Izzy known where to find them? The bowls weren't in a logical place, it had taken her ages to find them herself, behind the baking dishes thought Joy, hoping her face did not betray her. She found it easiest to cope by just eating the pudding, and letting the others talk. There was nothing awkward about that, and listening to the easy chatter of various fly-tying materials, the superiority of fishing for steelhead trout and how several of them liked desserts traditional and simple and not foreign muck– and how Tom said yes, he had to agree with that, there was nothing like a good old-fashioned tiramisu. Several people agreed with him. Tom Truman, in the fashion of jokers who are used to being a little brighter and sharper than their audience, managed to retrain his quirking lips. He noticed her shaking her head at him, and laughed, but no-one noticed or asked why.

The group broke up shortly after that, and, as the little hall had a tiny kitchen area, a combined effort saw the dishes washed, and people leaving in various directions soon after.

Joy was left to return to the rectory, with a tray full of plates, and her mind still wrestling with the new information. She tried to slip into her normal evening routine, but sleep avoided her, as she played over again with what she now knew of Jeanie's daughter, her age, and fact that she knew how and where to find crockery and cutlery in the rectory. The worst of all possible conclusions had to occur to her, again and again. It just... didn't fit, although it seemed unpleasantly obvious. Finally Joy settled on reading her bible, the King James Version for the beauty of the language in it. It was nice having a choice on her Kindle. She fell asleep, appropriately, on 'Ask and it shall be given unto you, seek and ye shall find.'

CHAPTER 11

The next morning, just as she'd finished breakfast, did bring the knocking. So she opened the door. Whether Tom Truman was the answer, was less than clear. But perhaps just talking it through would help.

He held out a key on a green tag to her. "I was last out, putting on my boots last night. And by the time I got out, and locked up, I, um, was thinking about something else, and put the hall key in my pocket and drove home. Sorry. So I brought the key in, now, because I've got a pump that needed fixing in a hurry. I've just dropped it off with old Mac."

"I do need to talk to someone about... well about some things I have discovered about Peter Hallam. Will you come in?"

He shook his head. "We have enough rumors in this town. We don't need a newspaper, we have a hairdresser. Come and walk around the front garden with me instead. I have a reason to be there, it needs work."

"Isabella? I've been meaning to go and see her," she said, stepping out.

"Oh, not Bella. But there are always at least three customers there, blowing more hot air than her dryers," he said smiling. "Now, this bed needs weeding, which is more than I know about murder. I'm sadly no expert on crime. All I know about it is learned from the very imaginative pens of fiction writers."

"I think they mostly use keyboards these days, but I am hardly better informed. I know less about it than about gardening, and as I have never looked after more than a window-box, and grew up in a flat, I am afraid I haven't paid the garden much attention."

"Well, you should," said Tom with a smile. "It's at least a third of rural conversation. That and livestock. Chooks will do at a pinch. It's not very exciting out here, which suits me fine."

Joy bit her lip. "I am afraid this is more serious than that... if my worst suspicions are confirmed it will be very bad for our church community, and they'll have little else to talk about. And yet, I see dealing with it as unavoidable. It's a cancer that needs cutting out."

He went back to his murder mystery theme: "Pen, keyboard, whatever. What all of those books have in common is that they almost always eliminate suspects by their alibis. They take the time of death, cause of death, and proof the suspect wasn't there. And the murderer is always the one with best alibi, because that keeps the reader guessing. So what I suggest is, instead of jumping from random suspect to suspect, you need to think about those things, instead of behaving like a wallaby chased by a Jack Russell."

"We don't know how he was killed," said Joy.

"We know how he wasn't killed. No wounds, no blood, no signs of an obvious assault. So, assuming our good Doctor Hammond spotted something he wasn't expecting – it would have to be fairly dramatic. So I decided he either had to find signs of strangulation or some kind of impressive poison. Strangling? Peter Hallam wasn't that small or that weak that a smaller or weaker person – such as most of the older parishioners, and probably a lot of women in general, and most likely more than half of the men are just not strong enough. Poison –they'd have to know enough. Most of us don't. It also means quite a narrow window of time – if you assume, and it seems likely, that whoever killed him then also tried to call the ambos. To me that makes them either horrified by their success, or most likely not planning to do it in the first place, which does away with poison, really. So then you just need people with strong hands or some expertise in secretive killing. I'd say you should start eliminating the males. By alibi, not killing us off. And as I have a pretty good alibi, I'm probably guilty."

"I do wish you'd be serious about this, Mr. Truman," said Joy.

"Oddly enough, I am being. This way I stay dispassionate," he said with a wry smile. "Something has upset you enough to stop you thinking clearly. Best if both of us aren't. And as it happens that particular day, less than an hour before, I was in the Big Smoke, with the Dean of my daughter's university, along with my ex-wife. My daughter is adult, even if she hadn't behaved that way, and I don't see what we were supposed to do about it. It wasn't a particularly pleasant interview. It would take a speed freak to get from the city to here in less than 90 minutes. And as it happens, our Sergeant Grogan had chosen that particular day to set up with a fellow officer who had come down here for that reason, a speed radar trap just this side of where the Hardacre road meets the road from Menham Bridge. So I didn't come through there like a bat out of hell. Arthur, who had to be one of your other suspects, did. In fact he was there when Grogan got the call about Reverend Peter. I know because Grogan told me so. So that's two of your suspects out of contention. Your favorite suspect, Donald..."

"I don't think I was right there."

"Well I was about to say, he's not a large, strong man. I doubt if he'd have the physical strength, he's not an active fellow. He's also a calculating sort of bloke, so, he would have planned it – and does know poisons. To have murdered Peter he would have had to have left the pharmacy untended, and because he's like he is, do so without it being noticed, which is too unlikely and too risky for him. And why he would phone the Ambos is another question. For your next male suspect: The Major, contrary to the impression he may give, was in logistical supply and not a Commando or special services…"

She interrupted again. "The person I was most worried about was Willie Jenkins."

"That was during his stint with his cousin. That's the other side of the city."

"He could have driven. I think he had motive," she said quietly.

"What? An argument about graffiti? Oh please, Reverend Joy," said Tom, dismissively.

"No. I think you will have to come inside and look at this."

Perhaps her tone convinced him not to dispute doing so. He followed her in. She went upstairs and fetched down the sketch book, and showed him the picture.

"It's really very good," he said, obviously not grasping why it was relevant.

Joy found herself struggling to explain. "It's brilliant, but that's not the point."

"I didn't know you could draw that well. But I don't see…"

"I didn't draw it. It was here in the house. It was drawn here, in the house – look at the background, that's the study. Peter Hallam was actually a very good artist. He was a professional cartoonist before he became a priest. But the problem is not how good he is, the problem is Izzy came over to the rectory last night, a place that she ought not to know at all. Yet she came back with crockery and cutlery very fast. And she was very confident about finding her way around a place she had no reason to have ever been into. It took me twenty minutes to find where the bowls were kept, the first time. She did it all in less than two minutes."

Tom took a deep breath. Tugged his beard. "One can jump to certain obvious conclusions, but, well I think you need something more to go on. There could be some innocent explanation. But... well one thing doesn't fit. You'd have to check alibis, but that's just not Willie."

"You mean he's not violent... but his wife said she couldn't tell him about, um..."

"Oh he's got a temper on him, and he's a big guy. But, Willie? Plan something, sneak in, sneak away? You'd have had to tie him down, if he even **thought** something was happening to his daughter. Hell's teeth, Reverend Joy, you'd have had to tie me down too. But the idea of Little Willie being devious? It's just not the way he's ever behaved. Spur of moment, he might. He's big enough, strong enough, but I've seen him in tears over a dying calf," said Tom.

"Perhaps he brooded on it because he couldn't believe it. Look, it seems really horrid, but she went to the rectory as if it meant nothing to her... not the way you might think, um, if, er..." She didn't want to continue, feeling a little sick. "Well, perhaps he came here secretively to confront Peter Hallam. I have to call the Bishop, and the police."

Tom shook his head. "Look. Whatever went on, it has to come out. But Hallam is dead, and jumping too fast won't make him alive to answer questions again. Give me a day or so to try and establish where Willie Jenkins was that day, without making anyone suspicious. I know a few people. I'll go through to town, and see that cousin of his on some pretext. He does irrigation as far as I know, as well as some building. I'll see my daughter as well."

"Um. While you are there, do you think you could go and look at some... newspaper archives?"

"I suppose so. If you tell me where to go. What do you want to know? I don't think that, other than an Obit, there was anything in the paper?"

"I want to know about his life, not his death," said Joy. "It may hold some clue as to why he died. Some motive for killing him. The Wikipedia article says he gave up his cartoonist career, just after his wife's death. I want to know what she died of, or if there is anything there that adds to this."

"He was a cartoonist? He didn't even have much of a sense of humor," said Tom, doubtfully. "You get my jokes. He mostly didn't."

"A political cartoonist. He used the pseudonym of 'Halley'."

Tom looked rather startled. "I remember the name. He was in the papers! You mean that he was our local priest?"

"So it seems. He'd given up drawing cartoons by then."

"I'd better look this up myself." He sighed. "Anyway, look, I'd better go. I can't get into town until tomorrow morning – I really need to fit that pump."

She nodded. "I have work to do, but I think I need to get out. Just to do something else. I think I'll take a walk."

He nodded, sympathetically. "There's a nice trail along the beach."

"I went that way a few days ago. I was thinking of walking down to the river. I think I need peace rather than the tumult of the sea."

"That's more difficult at this time of year. There's a track along the town bank, goes through crown land, Donald's place and then mine, but it's pretty muddy. The fellow who owns the other bank doesn't allow access. Then at old Pevensie's place, the next farm along, you can go down along the bank, all the way to past my place. At O' Halloran's you have to stop, because you run into the Major's bottom boundary. He doesn't allow fishermen on, so there is no real path."

"Well, I do have gumboots."

He managed a smile, "You'll need them. It's wet and muddy at this time of year. It's a nicer walk in summer."

"Everywhere is muddy after the rain we've had, I should think."

"Well, it varies. The coast is mostly old beach-sand and dries out fast. Along the river you've literally got the historical

Egyptian situation – it floods into the river flats and makes them very fertile, and very glutinous. I even keep my cows off it until it dries out a bit, or they get stuck. And a bit of mud in dairying is normal, but black mud to the belly tends to mean you get a tail-full in the face too often.

"That does sound a little deep for me."

"Well, you don't weigh as much as a cow," he said, keeping a straight face.

Sheer obstinacy, she admitted a little later, as her boot came free of a particularly gluey ditch, had made her go that way anyway. It was probably a good track for fishermen, bird-watchers, and by the tire tracks, crazy cyclists, but not for priests needing a brisk walk. After twenty minutes, she turned around, and found her way back to the outskirts of Felixtown, in her now muddy floral-patterned gumboots. The mud had not got to belly height, but it had reached her knees and one hand, when she'd stumbled. Inevitably Mary Truman was walking away from the rectory as she arrived. "Have you been moving cows, Reverend Joy?"

"No, I was proving I wasn't as heavy as one," said Joy. "What can I do for you, Mary?"

"Nothing," said Mary. "I was going to the post office, and so I stopped to drop the updated parish list in the parish office. Oh and to tell you old Mac says you can collect the urn. I offered to get it, but he said he couldn't trust me with such a delicate task. That man!"

"Oh, well I'll take the list in for you if you're in a hurry."

"I've dropped it in already. Um, you do know that Lindsey and I have keys to the glass sliding door into the parish office? That's why that interior door has a lock, so it can be shut off from the rectory."

"I hadn't realized that," said Joy.

"Now I feel that we have invaded your privacy. But, well, Reverend Johnstone set it up like that, and Reverend Hallam thought it was a good idea. It meant he didn't have to be home for us to come and go. You can lock it from the inside with a bolt too."

"I'll have to think about it," said Joy.

And she did. It was an obvious entry to the house, now she had established that it wasn't just a large window. It led out into the back garden. This was much less visible from the road. There was an old shed, and an unused chicken yard there. Perhaps she should keep chooks. It would give her something to talk to her parishioners about – half of them seemed to have chickens, to judge by Sunday conversations, and the gifts of eggs she'd been given. The chook pen, however, was more due for demolition than chicken-renewal. But there was a gap down between the shed and the chook pen that took her attention. The grass outside the pen and shed was neatly mowed. The gap, however, had had a population of tall weeds, some of which were broken – there was a little path through them.

She was wearing jeans and muddy gumboots anyway... so she followed it. There was a rusty little gate in the hedge, and that opened into a very narrow lane along behind the houses. She knew exactly what it was – a Victorian relic. Access for the poor fellow who would have fetched the nightsoil buckets, before waterborne sewage. Well, the little town was old, and the church one of the older buildings...

The cobbled lane was really too narrow for modern traffic, but it was plainly used. There was even an oil-stain on the stones.

It was logical, natural for it to be there – but still not pleasant to find that there was a secretive way into the rectory – and one which was at least occasionally used.

She went back inside, washed her hands and her boots, and changed out of the muddy jeans – and could not settle. So she locked the door from the parish office into the house. The key was in that lock, but she had just not noticed it before. Then she set off to collect the urn. Considering... well everything, it would only be more unpleasant if her worst suspicions proved right, and she had to do so later. It was still a difficult task.

She decided she'd walked enough for one day, and besides, carrying the urn would be awkward.

'Junk and Mechanical Repairs' was open. It was also empty of any living person. The church urn stood on the counter, but it wasn't telling where old Marcus might possibly be. Neither did a polite 'Hello? Anyone home?' yield any result. Joy wandered around the shelves for a minute or two, and then heard a metallic scream. She followed the sound to a door – which was partially ajar, and walked out into the yard behind the shop. The scrapyard behind the shop might have been a more accurate description. On one side was a large lean-to, in which Marcus MacGregor was wielding an angle-grinder in a shower of sparks.

He stopped when he saw her there. "Just finish this," he said and resumed the metal shriek. It didn't last long. "Sorry, I hate stopping a cut half way," he said, pushing back the safety glasses, pulling off the ear-muffs, and wiping his hands on a bit of rag. "Your urn is ready, and won't be biting anyone again. The wire had just chafed through. I've put a rubber insulation layer that'll outlast the element, and certainly outlast me, and probably you. If you women would just put the thing where it is going to be and not move it around like a yo-yo it wouldn't have happened in the first place. Lindsey is lucky she didn't get a proper belt from it."

"A good thing we have decent earth leakage!"

"Yer right, one of the better bits of not living in the good ol' days." He made his way towards her. "Wanted to say thank you for talking to my girl. Those two are all I got," he said gruffly. "I been worried about her, and Izzy too. That kid has been givin' me grey hairs."

It was far too late for grey, but Joy didn't mention it. Instead, she said: "What's been wrong?"

He shrugged. "Teenage rubbish I reckon. Combined with things being tough at home. She hasn't been herself. I see a lot of the kid. She and her mates used to come in here all the time, junior school, a whole mob of them chattering and lively as box of budgies. Lately it's just been that Megan and little Cam. He comes to hide out in the back instead of doing his homework. Noise I can handle. The sulky quiet makes me want to clip the lot of them. But I'll say she seems to be doing better with her mum since you had a word. She said that her mother told her for the first time just what financial strife they were in. I mean she knew it wasn't roses, but I don't think the kid had any idea it was that dire. I didn't either."

"Tell me about your son-in-law."

"William," Marcus sighed. "He was a bit of a good-time boy. I didn't have anything against him, mind you. Not while things were good. He got to being number two at the brickworks, got a bit fat from driving a desk, and then the company got bought out, and they decided it was cheaper to truck the bricks and tiles in than make them here. He got made redundant, had a huge fight with the company over his severance, and didn't work while it was going through all the motions... and battled to find any work when he lost. They did him over all right, but Willie's too bloody inclined to do first and think later. He scruffed the company lawyer at the arbitration meeting, and basically that was that. Most of his mates from when he was doing well suddenly weren't his mates now he wasn't shouting the drinks. He was trying for other jobs... but shooting for the moon, wanting to get back into management. By the time he started to get the idea that wasn't gonna work, they'd had to sell his car, and the boat, and the bank was hassling them. Jeanie finally had enough and started working at cleaning jobs, but Willie, well, he got in with Joe Denton. And the two of them were gunna make a fortune fishing. Only they'd just get stoned first... lucky Zenobia got the hell in with Willie, and put a stop to it. Then he gets a DUI ban on his licence... so he can't take any job that needs driving for a year. And then, well, just when I was saying to my girl she'd have to leave now, along comes Tom, sees him half-cut one morning sitting in the street. He hauls him out to the farm, gives him a bloody good ear-bashing, and makes him work off a half ton of lard. And gets him to give up the grog and the weed, and start getting himself back together again. The lot with his cousin didn't work out as well as he hoped, mostly because he couldn't drive anywhere, but he did start applying for jobs he had a chance of getting."

"Tom Truman does Christianity the way it should be done."

"Well, I'd just say he was a top bloke myself," said Marcus. "Not that I'd tell him that of course," he said with a smile. "But it does mean that when he says he needs me to help with Reverend Duck and fly tying I'll go as far as the church to help him out. I'll even try and weld the aluminum on his blasted pump for him."

The mention of welding aluminum brought an errant memory back to Joy. "MIG welding?"

"Don't tell me you do that as well as load pig-food and tie flies? And cook too!" said Marcus McGregor grinning. "I was wondering what your bishops and those fellers thought sending a wee girl here, but now I think they're so sharp it's a wonder they don't cut themselves. You were born for this place."

"Um. I don't do any of those things, or at least not well," admitted Joy. "I like to make bread, but that's all, really. No, I just wanted to know where someone would get a piece of aluminum MIG wire from?"

"Me. How much do want? It's a bit soft for most things, but I can give you a bit. Izzy tried it for some bracelets, but it bent out of shape too easy."

"Er. I don't want to buy any, just to clear up a little mystery. So, is it common around here?"

"Around here? Like hen's teeth are common. I've got some, as I weld aluminum. There's a MIG on the Major's place but I don't think he knows how to use it. They had a farm manager before who did. And there's another bloke with one about twenty miles towards Hardacre. I know of that one, because I fixed it. There might be others of course, but those are the only ones that have come my way."

They'd been walking while they talked, and had arrived at the urn on the counter. "Well, there she is, Reverend Joy, good as new and twice as natural – I used a protective rubber sleeve from a trashed welder for it. It's never going to do that again."

"Thank you. I'm not supposed to shock my parishioners. How much do we owe for that?"

"Nothing. I used junk I had on hand and it wasn't a hard job. Besides I owe you for looking in on Jeanie."

This was awkward. "She needs your help. Probably will quite a lot in the next while, Marcus."

He nodded. "Me and Izzy are conspiring on 'how to help mumma'. It's good for the kid, I reckon. Keep her mind off boys. And we'd take it kindly... well, she said you were easy to talk to."

"I'll do my best. And, well, no matter what happens, I'm...available to help." It seemed an awkward and inadequate thing to say.

She took the urn back to the hall, and then went back into the rectory. She had decided that, unpleasant though the idea might be, she'd better finish going through the last shelf.

It proved a fairly innocuous task. Yes it did include a book on figure drawing, which had a section on nudes, but the book was thirty years old and was a text-book. The only other thing that the shelf contained was a daily diary. The book was put in upside down –as if someone had just shoved it in the gap.

The diary proved, however, only that Reverend Peter Hallam was no diarist. He had used the book to record things he had to deal with. He did so in a shorthand of initials, which made it even more confusing. She was mystified at first. 'Par Co 3.30 re St Fr. Day at Sanctuary. App. L. AJ to lead? M to do hymn-sheet

Then a flash of inspiration hit her, and she went into the Parish office, and got the minutes of the last Parish council meeting – which began at 3.30 PM, on the day in the diary, had apologies from Lorna Smithson, at which they discussed among other matters, the outdoor service at the local wildlife sanctuary, that Mrs. Jenkins was asked to lead.

It could take a month of Sundays to figure it all out. They all seemed to be time related appointments, though.

Joy bit her lip, and looked up the Wednesday he had died. There was only one entry, in the same slightly shaky handwriting. '10.30 AM'

And that was that.

He'd been dead by 10.45 AM that day.

CHAPTER 12

Joy had taken some time in meditation and prayer after that. The knocking on the door was both welcome and worrying. It proved innocuous though. "Wednesday afternoon. Is my afternoon off, I come to clean the church," said Isabella, smiling up at her from the step. "I just want the bucket. The bucket from the vestry we brought here, when we clean the kitchen after Reverend Peter died."

"I'll come and give you a hand," said Joy.

Isabella looked faintly shocked. "Is no need," she said. "Is my gift to the Church. It is what I do to keep up God's house." There was a calm devoutness in that, which was very powerful in itself.

"Please can I still come along? Perhaps some other day I'll have something I have to do, but today I would like to come and help, and learn what must be done. And talk a little."

Isabella smiled. "You are a very nice priest. Like Reverend Peter."

They went together and Joy learned that normally two of the parishioners did the job, but Lorna was nursing a grandchild with pink-eye. It was always two of them, but one of those two was always Isabella, every Wednesday, even on the day Reverend Peter Hallam died. "Someone has to cook, clean, even when people die," said Isabella with a shrug. That, reflected Joy, was very true. Joy learned a fair bit more about Isabella, fifteen years out of her native country, she was comfortably settled here. She seemed a happy, generous and kindly soul, who struggled to say anything even vaguely nasty about anyone, and to whom hard work was second nature. The worst you could say about Isabella is she believed things had to be put away, and not necessarily where they belonged. Just away. As Mary had told them that Martine the organist was very, very precise about her music, and how it was ordered, Joy had to be glad she had decided to come along. She learned a great deal about her parishioners' hair, the niceness of their children and spouses, the habits of people leaving the strangest things in the church, and not much else. Isabella did not betray confidences, or not on purpose anyway.

It was a long haul into the next day, and through the morning, waiting to hear from Tom Truman. Joy filled the time as best she could, while mentally going through the possible next steps she would have to take.

Tom 'phoned at about 11.30 that morning. "I thought you'd be sitting on eggs, so I decided I'd call," he said. "You can effectively write Willie off your list of suspects. He's too big to wear his underpants outside his trousers, and that's the only way he could have got to Felixtown. I'd forgotten he'd had his license suspended, and they only have one car – well, he was on a building job half an hour the other side of the airport – two hours from here, having gone there with his cousin. The bloke remembers it pretty well because it was the day Willie decided it wasn't working out, and then got a call from the Fly-in Fly-out crowd. The license issue was basically why the building and irrigation contracting didn't work out, besides the fact that living with relations is all very well for a week, and short of selling up they just didn't have the money for anything else. Anyway, so he didn't have a car, couldn't have vanished for four hours and was far more interested in the possibility of a good job, and how he was going to break the news to his missus and his daughter."

"Well. Thank you. At least Marcus's daughter should be relieved from having that issue too."

"Yes, and I found I could access your old newspapers online. I'll send you the URL. It's a grim story, I'm afraid."

"Um, what happened? It never occurred to me to look online."

"To summarize: Peter Hallam left his heavily pregnant wife at home, flew to the Adelaide Arts Festival to get an award... and she was hit by a hit-and-run driver, and died before he could get home. He lost his wife and unborn child. There was a very moving tribute to her by him, and he said he was giving it all away. Makes me feel as if I didn't know the bloke."

"I wonder how much of anyone any of us know," said Joy. "Thank you."

"Yes. Anyway, I'm going to have lunch with my daughter. I'll see you on Sunday if not before, Reverend Joy. You can ask God to forgive the lies I told Willie's cousin and that those irrigation fittings I've bought as my pretext are worth having."

"I can't make any promises about irrigation fittings, but in my experience," said Joy, "God is far more understanding than we humans are. Besides, we have a good advocate to plead our case. And thank you again."

"It needed doing," he said.

Joy sat for a while. It didn't really answer the questions that were posed by the circumstances, but it did at least add another layer of knowledge, and more alibis to the situation. And no matter what else came of it all she was glad that Jeanie's husband was not the killer. Whatever old Mac thought of his son-in-law, his daughter still obviously loved the man and missed him, badly. Of course it didn't rule her out, or even the old fix-it man himself. He was more than strong enough, and more than capable of being calculating. And he was a repository of all sorts of knowledge, she'd realized at the fly tying evening. He hadn't had much schooling, but he read voraciously, apparently. He'd have known what goji berries were.

The wire had probably come from his workshop. But that certainly hadn't been him running away, and Joy was fairly sure that it hadn't been Izzy either.

She dealt with the mundane aspects of the parish for the week: A discussion on hymns for Sunday with the organist, deciding on someone else to ask to read, as Lorna would not be in church in case she gave everyone pink-eye. Small problems, and solvable, because they required small solutions and small steps.

In that quiet it came to her that perhaps she had been taking far too big a steps with her enquiries. Jumping to conclusions. What it needed was a systematic lay-out of possible people and possible motives, and of course, possible alibis – but she barely knew half the people, and it seemed the more she delved the more human they all turned out to be. Humans were flawed, but they were, after all, made on the pattern of God, and were his children, no matter how flawed.

The answer had to lie in those flaws. She began writing a list of the people known to have had conflicts with Peter Hallam, and wrote down what she knew about them. When she came to the graffiti and the children, it occurred to her that she knew very little about any of them. And a fifteen or sixteen year old could be strong and very angry. She'd learned that herself, the hard way.

But of course there were other tasks to do, and one of them was to write the message. So she left her lists and went to work on that. Over the next day she added a little to it, and to her sermon too, and then went and visited old Mr. Porter. The old man was fading away to a place where he wouldn't need hearing aids any more.

The next morning brought an unexpected garden party, or at least a party of gardeners, headed by Tom, carefully reversing a small ride-on lawnmower off the back of a ute, driven by Arthur, and three ladies: Isabella, Martine-the-organist, and Mary, all with gardening gloves and implements of destruction. "There'll be a few more along later. And this is all Arthur's fault," said Tom generously heaping the blame on him. "If he hadn't called to offer to do my mowing duty as I was away, which I wasn't, then this would not have happened. You have him to thank, and me I suppose for betraying your ignorance about gardens to the force that cannot be resisted," he said, pointing at his sister.

"I got the wrong end of the stick," said Arthur, looking faintly gloomy, but resigned.

"We'll see to feeding you at least," said Martine-the-organist. She was also a treasure, Joy had decided, even if she wanted to talk about music in general and not just next week's hymns. Joy wasn't sure how to break it to her that music was not one of the areas her new parish priest had been blessed with talents in.

Joy had had a few other plans for her Saturday, but she was also quite practiced at reading into the thoughts and actions of people – and what she got here cheered her. They'd come to say, in their own way, that they cherished her, as well as their Church. She couldn't ignore that, so she found a hat, was given a pair of gloves and found herself in for a morning of garden instruction. They stopped for tea in the shade at about half past ten, Joy being glad of the repaired urn, but wondering what she could feed this steadily growing army – there were a few that she'd never seen in church, spouses roped in for the labor. But they provided their own loaves and fishes too, or at least fruitcake and sausage rolls. All she had to do was sit down, and rest her already sore feet and back.

Arthur came over to her, "Um. Reverend Norton..."

"Some more cake?" asked Mary brightly, waving a piled plate at them.

"Uh. No thanks," said Arthur.

Joy wondered if he was sickening for something. It was the first time she'd ever seen him turn down food, and took a piece herself, although she really didn't need it. Arthur started again. "Um. I..."

Tom arrived with a sausage roll on a plate and handed it to him. "Nabbled the last one for you. How's the gardening going Reverend Joy?" he asked as he sat down on the grass next to them. It was, for a winter day, a fine one, already showing the first tiny promise of spring.

"Arthur was trying to talk to me," said Joy, hoping he would get the hint.

"Oh. Didn't mean to interrupt," said Tom, starting to get up.

"It... it's nothing important. I just wanted to ask about, um, the daffs."

"No use asking her then," said Tom, obliviously, settling down again. "She wouldn't recognize one if it bit her, would you Reverend?"

"No, but I would recognize one in flower. I think," admitted Joy. "If you mean daffodils. I am better on wild flowers. I know most of those. But I will learn. This being in the country is a steep learning curve for me. So is a new parish. Who is the lady in the magnolia hat?"

"Janet Webb. Came out of curiosity I think. I suppose it's easy for us, we know each other, and just had to learn who you were."

"Would she be any relation to Jarred Webb?" she asked. Despite having refused cake, Arthur was eating the sausage roll.

"Mother. Her father cooks in the pub. He's a good pub-level cook. You're getting to know the links, Reverend Joy."

"Oh. He was one of the tagging children. The graffiti artists. I was trying to work out who they all were. So far I've only met, um, Isobel Jenkins."

"Oh Jarred would have gone along just to be part of something," said Arthur. "Or so I was told. I've uh, got a friend who knows the younger kids better than I do. It was that Kyra who got it started. She's left now, but apparently Donald's son Cam took to it like it was the best ever. He got my friend to buy him cans of paint, away."

149

"I haven't met him or... Hayley or Megan," said Joy, dredging deep, wondering just who Arthur was friends with, and what sort of friend was buying kids cans of paint.

"Cameron probably thought it would make him look tough. Poor kid," said Arthur.

"Why?"

Tom and Arthur exchanged looks. "Because he's pretty," said Arthur finally.

"Small and pretty," added Tom. "Verging on what you could call beautiful, according to older women, who used to come and demand that he show them his eyelashes." He took in Joy's look and explained. "Donald's quite fine-boned, as we say around here, but Cameron's mother was a model. She won a few beauty competitions, and had a few acting jobs. She was quite a looker, but very petite. She didn't last long in what she considered the howling wilderness, but she left the boy with her looks and size. Which is hell on a boy. The kid's actually quite robust, but he doesn't look it. He's always trying to prove himself, and we've had a couple of search and rescue incidents because of the little menace." It was said with good humor. You could tell with Tom that he approved rather than otherwise.

"So um, isn't he a possible brick thrower?" asked Joy

"Except that he lives at the end of a long loop out of town. Their place is next to mine – except they can't get to the Hardacre road like I can – my place is the right side of the bridge, but to get to Donald's place takes a fair bit longer, because he has to come out of this side of town, and then take the loop back along the ridge."

"And the other two?"

"Oh, well, Megan. You know her mother is the town paranoid. Fort Knox ought to subcontract her to keep their gold. The girl was trying to shake free of some cotton wool, if you ask me," said Tom. "She'll get out of home eventually and go completely wild, I suspect. She's why they got caught, as far as I know."

Arthur nodded. "The mother is really strange. Single mum, goes through fads. She claimed to be a Muslim for a while, about five-six years ago. And then it was Scientology..."

"And I think the other girl, Hayley, was just looking for a camp, any camp, to follow. She's one of those kids that manages to be out no matter how hard she tries. And the harder they try, the more excluded they are. They're the kids who are different and get ostracized for that."

"Come on. Work to be done, lazy-bones," yelled Mary, and they all headed back to various tasks. Fortunately, many hands made it go very fast. They were just finishing up with loading garden waste onto one ute, and the little ride-on onto another – the Ambleside-Smiths kept it for cleaning up their rental properties as well their own gardens, when they had a noisy display of how to ride your motorcycle on one wheel come burning past... and do a donut and do it again. And a third time.

"It's a good thing the Major isn't here. He'd have called the cops by now," said Tom. "He absolutely hates that girl, even more than her mother. Always trying to get her into trouble. Not that she doesn't help," he said with a wry smile.

"It doesn't always take two to quarrel, but it does help," admitted Joy.

Back in the rectory, Joy took a deep breath, and washed her hands thoroughly and went upstairs, to re-examine the sketch book. She wasn't just leafing through it now, but looking at each page. The start of the book, oddly, was mostly copies of other cartoons. They could actually all have been copies, but she wasn't that up in contemporary cartoon art. The skill in copying the ones she did recognize was excellent.

About half way through the book she finally came across a 'Halley' cartoon, and shortly thereafter the artist seemed to get bored with cartoons, and start on more typical art subjects. Joy wondered if that had been when Peter Hallam had joined the local watercolor classes – except the artist had kept to pencil, although moving from just HB, to a range of softer leads. It was obviously a practice book. There were little corrections, little side-sketches in places. The work varied from landscapes to a scene out of the office window, to various still-life pictures, to what was obviously the artist's strength – portraiture. He had been a good cartoonist, but there were a few flaws in the more conventional artworks. They were still a long way from amateur, and far better than some of those for sale in the shop on the foreshore. Joy could just imagine how frustrating he must have found the 'Art group'. Then she came to an obviously unfinished head and shoulders portrait – Joy had never actually seen a picture of Peter Hallam, but it seemed likely to be a self-portrait as the man wore a clerical collar, and the recognizable rectory study window. It showed a man with somewhat sunken eyes with deep shadowing under them, whose cheeks were pronounced and flushed. He had a small, clipped moustache, a slight smile, and a firm chin. The left side of the head needed finishing – it was just sketched, but the rest was finished, down to the detail on the throat. That, oddly had a bite-like mark on it.

Then there was the picture of Izzy Jenkins, and that was the last thing drawn in the book. There were only about four pages left, which could account for the newly ordered ones. Joy hadn't found the pencils anywhere, but they had probably been packed away.

She reached her decision. Asking might not be easy, but it would have to be done, and there was no time like the present to do the things she didn't want to do. She had a fairly large cloth shopping bag, so she put the sketch-book carefully into that, and went down and called Jeanie Jenkins. She got a cheerful welcome on the 'phone. "Is your daughter also home?" asked Joy.

"No, she's nicked off to Hayley Miller's with a couple of girls from school. They say they're doing a project." This was said without too much worry, or, by the sounds of it, too much belief. "Megan and Hayley and Linda. Megan's mother was having fits about it, as per normal. There's a limit to what four girls can do in Felixtown in daylight, I said to her, although I got up to a few tricks in my time. Anyway we had a long proper talk to Willie not an hour ago. He's doing all right, he says. He says there's not much to do except drink, watch TV or work, and as he's given up the grog, he's putting in a lot of overtime."

"He's given up drinking?" That was always a problem in lonely professions.

"Yes. Not that I think he was an alcoholic or anything, but he went through enough of our money on it. Tom gave him hell about it, and kind of, well got him to prove he could stop. He said he bet Willie couldn't stand up to peer pressure. That he was too bloody soft to do it... heh. He psyched Willie perfectly, and Willie even knows it, but he won't let it beat him now."

"Look, I know I'm asking a lot, but I really want to talk your daughter alone. Can you trust me?"

"Of course I can. I asked you to find out," said her mother.

"Yes. Well sort of. Anyway, please understand I would keep her secrets as well as yours. I am just trying to build bridges."

"Well you helped me build something of one with her. I won't say she's different, because she's still a teenager, but, well we've been a bit closer. And she's actually offered to help with some of the chores! I mean I thought the world was going to end. Now, look, we're going to the pub with Dad for a Parmy for tea this evening. His treat, he reckons he won't have to cook. Big treat for me! So... probably tomorrow. How about, um just after lunch? Two o' Clock? I'll shoot down to the supermarket to get some stuff before it closes, and ask her to mind some baking for me, and also that you're bringing um..."

"A book," said Joy.

"That'll work. I read too much now that Willie's away."

"I'll find something suitable. I have a feeble murder mystery."

"I like romances more!"

So Joy, having hardened her resolve, had to put it on hold until after church. That of course was followed by tea, and of course, people wishing to talk. That was also her work here: to listen.

Also, of course, to ask relevant questions. Of Mary she asked: "And how are you at cryptic puzzles?"

"Not brilliant. Why?"

"I found Reverend Peter's personal diary," Joy explained. "It is just scheduling by the looks of it, but he only used initials and rather scrawled writing. I was hoping you could help me interpret it – it goes some months into the future, although of course, most of it is in the past. I puzzled some of it out, because it referred to a parish council meeting and a special date."

"Well, I'll have a go. It shouldn't be too hard."

"I'll get it for you later," promised Joy.

Lindsey was looking remarkably cheerful. "Sorry to miss the gardening. Guess what I was doing yesterday?"

"Headstands," offered Tom, from the sideline.

"I did fall down a bank and nearly land on my head, but no," said Lindsey with an assumption of dignity, which failed to mask the cheerful touch of excitement which lent life and happiness to her face. "I went fishing, of all things."

"Trespassing," said Tom, cheerfully. "Jeff asked my permission but I said no. I said to him 'we can't have women doing this. Next thing they'll want flush toilets along the banks.' Those were my very words."

"Have another piece of cake, Tom," said Joy, smoothly. "And pay no attention, Lindsey. You're casting pearls before swine. He wanted to go fishing himself."

"And I caught my first sea-run trout! On one of my own flies. It was just... such fun. One of the best days I've had in the last five years," said Lindsey, ignoring Tom's heckling. "You must come next time, Reverend Joy."

Joy shook her head hastily. "I don't think I'm ready for fishing yet. I, er… Well, fish um, wriggle so. I don't think I could."

"And they're slimy," said Tom. "You really should avoid it." His shaking shoulders betrayed his words.

Lindsey shook her head, and lifted her eyes to heaven, and was buttonholed by another person, wanting to ask, on Sunday, about postal schedules. Tom beamed as they walked off. "That has worked well, so far."

"I gather that's not your first bit of social engineering," said Joy.

He shrugged. "Why should women have all the fun? What else am I supposed to have done?"

"A lot of good for Willie Jenkins."

"I treated him like a new seaman," said Tom. "Bawled him out, challenged him a bit. He knew I was pulling the reins, but, Reverend Joy, he was willing… in fact, desperate to have them hauled on. I think, from experience with that sort of man, that he'll stick to the rails like glue now."

"You did what was needed, when it was needed. As you did with your… trip to town. You're a good man, Tom Truman."

"You'll have me blushing any minute. And actually, it did me some good with my daughter. I hope you don't mind… she was very angry, in fact downright nasty about me coming to check on her, so, um, I told her why I had come. Took her mind in an entirely different direction and by the time we'd dissected it, we parted on the best of terms. Of course, she's convinced that Peter was, er, molesting the girl in some way. She's… she's pretty anti-church, and a priest as a villain suits the narrative they're indoctrinating her with. It's one of the few things I agree with Donald about. If you're going to go to Uni, do a STEM course, not Arts."

"I didn't do a STEM course," said Joy, calmly, "My indoctrination was obviously not successful. And I held down a respectable job after that, before I felt I was called to the Ministry, a job that did not involve 'Do you want chips with that?'"

"You're an exception."

"So are most of us in some way. And I think you underrate your daughter. She's your daughter in the end, and that suggests to me she will have an independent mind and a fair amount of intelligence."

He sighed. "Sometimes. Anyway, at least she was talking to me. And I told her about Peter being a successful cartoonist and losing his wife. That gave her a bit of a pause."

"It does explain his... bachelor life... ah, yes I would love to try a piece of the cake Mrs. Smithson."

Confidences were at an end and Joy was swept into other conversations. But rather like a vast jigsaw puzzle, more pieces were fitting into the picture that was this small rural town.

It was a lot more complex and interlocking than she'd realized.

They were busy collecting the last cups for washing up when Lindsey added a further piece to her puzzle. "By the way, Jeff, er, Mr. Wiley said Reverend Peter left money to some of the town's children in his will. He said it was all the post office's fault for teaching him to read upside down, and Tom's fault for signing everything so slowly. It's a bit odd, isn't it? We don't really have any children in the church at the moment."

It occupied Joy's mind so much that she forgot all about giving the diary to Mary and took herself for a quick walk down to the sea, trying to gather her thoughts and pray for strength and guidance.

CHAPTER 13

At two minutes to two, Joy got into the Micra and set out. She decided it would be easier to drive – she'd walked too far and too fast, earlier. She was armed with her cloth shopping bag, containing the sketch book and a Maeve Binchy novel she'd brought with her from her little flat. She really had to think about what she was going to do about that flat, in the fullness of time. When all of this was over, when she knew quite what she would be doing for the next few years

She opened Jeanie's gate and walked to the door, hoping her timing was right. The garden had seen work, since she was last here, and it helped the house to look less neglected. She knocked, and got a call of 'Coming'. A few moments later the door was opened by a smiling Izzy. "Hi, mum said you might bring her book. She said to give you a cup of tea, she just forgot stuff she needs and had go to the supermarket quickly before it closes."

"Oh. Do you mind if I come in for a moment?"

"Sure. If I know mum and the shops she'll be ages. I offered to go because at least I can get in and out quick, but she said no, and she promised she wouldn't be long. She's had all morning," said Izzy, almost certainly imitating her grandfather in tone, and probably using his words too, "And she thinks of it now."

"Um. Not really. I asked her if I could talk to you alone."

Izzy promptly got angry. "She said she wasn't going to ask about that thing anymore. So, like, she gets you to do it. Well you can both f..."

"I'm not going to ask you about condoms," interrupted Joy. "You can sort that out with your mother, or not."

"She doesn't believe me," said Izzy, defensive, sulky.

"I know," said Joy, keeping her voice as level and as even as possible. "But I came to talk to you about a different matter."

This was met with suspicion rather than the outright anger. "Like, so... have you come to talk religion at me? Go away. I'm not listening."

"Neither at you, nor with you," said Joy reaching into her bag.

"I'll just throw your stupid books in the fire... oh," she halted mid-track at the sight of the sketch-book.

Joy said nothing, just waited.

Izzy bit her lip. Stood equally silent for a moment. Then to Joy's amazement, she began to giggle. "I really got that wrong, didn't I? I'll give it back to him. Like, was that all you came for?" Her tone had totally changed and Joy didn't quite know what to make of it. And who was she giving it back to?

Joy nodded. "Well, I wanted to ask about the picture of you."

Izzy blushed slightly. "I told him not to draw me. But he did anyway. Like, he doesn't listen."

"It's a great picture," said Joy.

That drew a smile, slightly embarrassed, but entirely natural. "My mouth's too big. But the old guy thought it was really good too," said Izzy.

"Trust me. I trained as an artist, I wish I was in that league."

"You too? Is it, like, something all priests do? Hey, can I show you some of my pictures? He said he was terrible at color, and I only like doing things in color."

"I'd love to see them," said Joy, "I did colored illustrations of birds and flowers, so I do know a little. I'd be happy to help you if I can."

"Oh this is way cool! So, like can we come on Wednesday and Friday again? Megan can't do the Tuesdays, and I've Netball on Monday and..."

"So, um, Reverend Hallam was teaching you art?" asked Joy, feeling a weight lifting from her shoulders.

She nodded. "Yeah. It's pretty funny really after the trouble we got into about tagging the church. My dad just didn't get that he didn't want to give us stick about it, the old guy just wanted to know which one of us was doing the cartoon figures. Dad got all defensive and started shouting saying he'd deal with disciplining me. And the more the old priest guy tried to explain, the angrier dad got, and then, well, yeah, anyway. Maddy told us, like about three days later just why he wanted to know who it was, because he really thought they were good, and he knew something about drawing."

"But... but why in secret?" asked Joy.

Izzy rolled her eyes. "Like, if you think my dad is bad, you've just got no idea. Megan's mother was convinced the priest was gonna brainwash her into becoming a nun or something." She pointed at the sketch-book, "His dad would go absolutely spare. He already threatened to send him to boarding school when we got bust. He'd go completely off the freaking wall..."

The mobile phone in Joy's purse began to play 'Morning has broken.' It was not the ideal ringtone, but Joy liked it. She took the 'phone out of her purse, wondering why anyone had to call just right now. It was Mary, and she didn't waste time on 'hello' or niceties. "Are you far away from the rectory? I've caught your burglar."

"Do you need me to call the police?" asked Joy, hastily. "I can be there in a minute... or two at most."

"No. I'm not too sure what to do with the brat, but I think we should leave Grogan out of it, for now. But if you can come fairly quickly, it would be good. Ow! Stop that!"

The last part wasn't addressed at Joy. "I have to go, Izzy. I'll come another time," she said, hastily pushing the book back into the bag.

"Sure. The book?"

"Wednesday!" said Joy, over her shoulder.

It was only half way back to the rectory that it occurred to her that Izzy might possibly have also meant the book Joy had promised her mother. It wasn't likely, but given the history of misunderstandings... A little Nissan Micra was not a racing vehicle of the classic car chase, but Joy did her best. She arrived home to find Mary's station-wagon in her driveway, and stopped – barely -- behind it, and got out at a run, calling, "Mary, Mary are you all right?"

"Fine," came a voice from the back – so Joy ran that way. One of the windows of her office was open, swinging gently. Joy peered in, and then decided she'd just climb in that way. Mary, who was not a small woman, was sitting on someone, on the floor. All Joy could see was some kicking feet.

On getting herself into the room, which was not a great challenge, she could see the person Mary was sitting astride of. He was not large, and despite his fury, yes, Joy could see how his face could be described as beautiful. "He's a strong little beggar," said Mary.

"Cameron, Donald-the-Pharmacist's son, I assume," said Joy. "I want to talk to you, young man. There are certain things I need to know..."

"I've got nothing to say to you!" he said terse and angry. "And I'm not a thief. I only wanted..."

"Your own property back. And I wanted to know if Wednesdays and Fridays would still be suitable." The look on the boy's face was proof, thought Joy, that God's wisdom and justice were really too much for human understanding. And also something of a reward for the worry the boy's actions had caused her. "I think you can let him up now, Mary. Your sketch-book isn't in the house anyway, Cameron."

Mary shifted her weight. "You knew about this, Reverend Joy?"

"I had just arrived at that last piece in the jigsaw, or at least this section of the jigsaw. Do let him up, Mary. I remember being pinned like that at school, and it wasn't very pleasant."

"I haven't done it since then," said Mary. "Will you behave yourself, Cameron?"

"All right," he said sulkily. "Just get off. You weigh a ton."

"Tch," said Joy trying not to laugh, and failing, partly at the situation, and partly with relief. "You should never say that kind of thing to a lady, young man. Or at least not until you have a running start."

"It's not funny," he said, as they both stood up.

"Well, it is, actually," said Joy, cheerfully. "But it helps to know the context. I only know part of the story. I do need to know the rest. And," she said looking around at the tipped out boxes, "I think you owe me, and Peter Hallam, an explanation. You frightened me very badly, you know. You could just have come and asked."

"I couldn't," he said. "I mean, for sure you'd have said something. Told my father about it."

"Not if you had asked me not to. But I don't suppose you know much about me, or about the responsibilities and duties of a priest. But surely it wouldn't have mattered that much. I don't understand and I think I need to. I know your father's feelings about religion, but he was at least civil enough when I took Reverend Peter's medications in to him, to dispose of," said Joy, inspecting the boy.

"Donald's not that bad. He's got a sharp tongue, but then so have you, brat,' said Mary, still sounding more than a little angry. "You're being remarkably silly and you're just lucky you haven't ended up in worse trouble. And you could still. Look what you've done to this place." Boxes were tumbled and spilled, and plainly scrabbled in.

161

"It can be fixed," said Joy. "Mary, dear, why don't you go and put on the kettle. I think Cameron and I need to talk in confidence and alone."

"I've got nothing that secret to say," said Cameron, still more than a little surly.

"None-the-less, I have," said Joy, firmly. "And I really need that tea, and I think Mary does too."

"You can certainly give orders," said Mary, but with a smile, now.

"I am following them myself," said Joy. "Now, please close the door behind you, Mary."

Cameron faced her in silence, his eyes slightly narrowed, assessing. Tom and Arthur had been quite right, thought Joy. With a wig, he would have been a very pretty girl. He had long eyelashes, deep blue eyes under a delicate brow, a retroussé nose, good cheek bones and a complexion of peaches and cream, set off by his dark, slightly wavy hair. A bit of a scowl, right now, actually did nothing to lessen the impression.

Joy waited. So did he.

As he seemed in no hurry to speak, she did. "Izzy is in all manner of trouble about that condom," said Joy, fishing, in truth. "Her mother found it."

She saw by the flush that she'd been quite correct. "It's not what you think. I mean, she's not..."

"She said so. And I believe her. But you've still made things very hard for her."

He swallowed. "Well, I'll go and fix it up."

"How?" asked Joy.

He looked at her, frowning. "I dunno. I suppose, I um, I could tell her mother I was gay. And I just asked Iz to keep it for me."

Joy had a keen ear for tone. "And you think she'd believe you? I don't."

"Everyone else does," he said bitterly. "Even my father."

"What everyone thinks is less important than the truth," said Joy. "It may take you a while to get around that fact, but it is so, in the end."

He shrugged. "You can get used to anything."

Joy tried a different tack. "I can't see why you were so worried about it. I mean, it would be sad to lose all your work, but was it worth frightening me, and breaking into the house? Let's say it hadn't been Mary, but someone who called the police, and they'd caught you here."

He shrugged again. "I had to do it. Like, eventually you had to find the book and then you'd have given it to my father. And then he'd have gone completely ape. I mean if I was lucky it would be boarding school, or he could do something crazy and get himself arrested."

"Why would I have given the book to your father? How would I have known it was yours?" asked Joy, puzzled.

"Duh." He shook his head. "My name is on the back cover, of course."

"Um. You wouldn't believe it, but none of us noticed. Why on the back?" she probed gently.

He shrugged. "It was mostly white, and I thought it would be cool to fill it up. The other side has a picture on it."

"Well, I have more sketch pads and more pencils that Peter Hallam obviously ordered for you and your Wednesday and Friday sessions."

"You mean it then, about... going on?" he sounded both amazed and doubtful.

"In the short term, yes," said Joy. "I agreed. I really, to be honest with you, dislike keeping this a secret. As you know, people jump to conclusions about secrets. And they can be abused to hide things. Let me think about it, pray about it. See if I can find a way to make it work without hurting more than I fix, and to heal the past. Peter Hallam's memory deserves that these rumors go to rest. I think he's been misjudged, and that says more about us, than it said about him. I promise that I will do my best to heal, and not harm. Peter deserves that."

That, she could see, made an impression on Cameron. "I do owe him," he said with a simple, deep sincerity which was hard to doubt.

"Then you could tell me how it came to this situation, where you were that scared of your father knowing that you'd break in here. That you'd do things which are not in your nature. I need to know, Cameron. At the moment it doesn't make a lot of sense, and I think that's because I don't understand enough. If I am going to protect you, and keep your secrets, I need to know what lines to avoid. What happened to cause this?"

He sighed. "My father was going on about... you know, like he does about religion and stuff. That priests only joined the Catholic Church so they could beat little boys, and they were a bunch of con men, and they were all homophobes because they were hiding being like that themselves. He was... you don't know my father, he can be really horrible. And, and I was stupid, I said that Peter wasn't like that. That he was kind and gentle and he understood. And then he said, "I'll kill him. God, I'll kill him." And, and he went to the gun cupboard and, and I had a big fight with him. I said... if he hurt him I'd never speak to him again. I'd hate him forever. I tried to explain it was about art, over and over, but he wasn't listening. He just doesn't. He'd made up his mind and, and I snatched the safe keys from his hand, and ran. I took the keys from the car and I ran down the swamp-track. I dropped the gun-safe keys into the river," he swallowed. "I nearly threw the jag keys in after them, but, but I put them in a tree. A hidey spot I use when I go fishing. I could hear him calling. He... he can't run. His hip, he had a car accident. It even hurts him to stand too long."

The boy was actually panting himself, remembering, telling. The pain of it was still sharp. Joy resisted hugging him, but nodded, understandingly.

He found the words. "I knew I could run faster than he can so I, I went back a bit. I didn't answer him or anything. Just went back to where I could hear him. And I sort of realized there was something odd." Cam swallowed. "He couldn't walk anymore. He was dragging himself along the ground. Still calling for me. And he sounded really afraid, and sort of desperate." Cameron paused. "He can be really nasty, I mean, not hitting me or anything but I almost wish he would instead. But just with what he says. But, well, he's my father. And..."

"And you love him," said Joy.

"I guess. I had to go and help him. He's an idiot," said the boy crossly. "He was in trouble, struggling to breathe properly, and really, really sore. I, I thought he might die on me or something. Anyway, he kept saying he loved me anyway, and it didn't matter, and gay people were normal. And, and he promised he wouldn't do anything to Peter. I tried to tell him he was wrong. He just wouldn't listen, and kept getting himself more upset. And so I said... I'd never see Peter alone again. Like, I hadn't ever, it was always Izzy, and Meggle and me, but it was the best I could think of at the time, but he would have to swear to leave him alone too. And he did promise."

Joy could read that terrible niggle of doubt in the boy's voice, but decided this was not the time to follow that up.

"But, like, it was after that he kept... giving me these condoms and, and saying I could make my own choices, but I had to be careful. I just hated, hated, hated it! I tried telling him he was wrong, and just to leave it. But... you can't talk to him. When he's made up his mind like that he doesn't **listen**. And so there are a whole lot in my room. Um, and then when Grogan hassled Izzy's dad about their car rego again, well, uh, we were going to go and... well, you know he sort of does like a 'I'm watching you' slow cruise around town every morning, first thing? I thought... well if we made a small hole in one, and put it on his exhaust it would stay blown up behind him.

165

Only the first one just exploded. And I brought that really garish one with me to show Izzy and Meggle when we were at the rectory. I showed them while Peter was out taking a 'phone call. We were killing ourselves laughing when he came back, and Izzy had it just then and hid it quickly. He came in and said someone had told him they went into the pharmacy and my Father was packing up early, as he wasn't feeling well. So I lit out of there like a rocket, to get back to school so I could pretend I was at footy practice when he came to pick me up. Ha, ha, as if I'd play footy! And then next thing Izzy went off to stay with her cousins, 'cause her dad was working there. It was just an accident. I... wouldn't drop her in it, not for anything." A flush betrayed him again. He would make a poor lawyer, thought Joy. "She didn't tell me her mother found it! I'll... I'll have to explain."

"I did say to her mother that other reasons could exist," said Joy. "And I think you should be glad you have such a loyal friend. I'll see what I can do, if you like."

There was a timid knock at the window, and peering in was Izzy Jenkins. "I brought your bike in from the lane and put it in the shed. If you leave it there they'll nick it or kick the spokes in again," said Izzy.

"Hello," said Joy. "You can either climb in the window, like everyone else, or come in through a door."

"Iz! What are you doing here?" demanded Cameron.

She shrugged and climbed in through the window. "I kind of figured that you might be here, in trouble. I sort of couldn't help overhearing the 'phone-call and did a bit of thinking about what was said, so I nutted it out. So I told mum I was coming up to talk to her new friend, and had a look in the lane. When I saw the bike I knew I was right."

"What 'phone call?" asked the boy.

"I was off talking to Isobel when you broke into the rectory," said Joy. "And no one is in trouble. Actually I'm feeling very happy and relieved." She noticed, quietly, that the two kids had squeezed hands, in coming together.

There was another knock – this time on the office door. "If the tea gets any stronger it'll break the door down," said Mary. She took in Isobel's presence. "I'll get another cup."

"And I think we need to have some cake with that tea. I was given some fruit-cake by someone," said Joy with a wink, knowing full well that Mary had baked it.

"It's barely edible," said Mary.

"We'll put it to the jury," said Joy getting it down from the shelf. "If you can bear to help us out with this?"

Cam nodded. "I'm starved. I, uh was hiding in the dunny-lane watching for you to leave right through lunch-time."

"Then you'd better have something a bit more substantial than cake," said Mary firmly, mothering instincts coming to the fore.

"My kitchen is all yours, Mary," said Joy. "There is bread, cheese, tomatoes, lettuce, salami... and a few other things. I am just going to sit and drink tea and be thankful."

"You know she's an artist too, Cam?" said Izzy, taking a seat, as if she was at home in this kitchen – which she probably was. Cameron sat too, but with less ease.

"An illustrator, merely," said Joy. "I did museum illustrations. Not like Peter Hallam's work. Nothing like as good either. I can't teach you what he could."

Cam nodded. And then Joy realized tears were running down his cheeks. He tried to hastily blot them away with his sleeve, to turn away from them. And then he put his head forward onto his hands, on the table and wept, the loud anguish of a young man who had kept his sorrow, fear and loss bottled up for too long.

CHAPTER 14

Cameron was, naturally, as embarrassed as a sixteen year old boy could be at having broken down. "Sorry," he said, drying his eyes, and blowing his nose on the proffered tissues. "Just... he was, brilliant. I mean, he could change the expression, the whole feel of a face, by just changing the angle of a line. His hands were like, shaky, but he could still just... do it. I get it right by accident sometimes, but he could do it on purpose, every time."

He took a gulp of his tea. "He showed me so much. I never got a chance to tell him how much it meant to me. And it did. It was like... well a whole new world or something."

Joy patted his shoulder. "He knew then, and he knows now. And listen: a friend of mine once told me, you can't fix the past, but you can change the future. Or to put it another way – there are things you can't pay back, but there are always things you can pay forward. Reverend Peter obviously thought you had talent and he tried to nurture that. The best thing you can do to reward him for that, is to be the best artist you can be."

He nodded. "I'm going to be. But, well. One day." He pulled a bit of a face. "After Uni. Now can we see some of your pictures?"

It was said with a deliberate intent to lead the conversation away, and Joy allowed it to happen, and went and fetched out the guide books. "It's not what people think of when they talk of fine arts degrees. It's very precise, and not at all imaginative. Rather like me, I am afraid."

They admired the pictures of flowers and birds. Joy had steeled herself to the fact that they might well find it boring, or that young Cameron would find her old work very inadequate compared to Peter Hallam's. That, in her mind, was fair, because he had had a level of genius she did not. But the boy was fascinated by the detail, and the accuracy of the pictures of the birds and animals he recognized. He actually appreciated just how hard that was to achieve.

"I'm better at drawing something I have seen. Some people can do the imaginary stuff, but I like to draw what I see," he said, explaining.

He also was fascinated by the idea that artists could work at something besides drawing cartoons or painting portraits. "Well, it's competitive, and not as fashionable, but yes, artists end up working on everything from movie sets to painting book covers. You don't get rich and famous at it but there are jobs you can make a living at," explained Joy.

Cameron pulled a face. "According to my father, they all involve asking people if they want chips with that?"

"It's not an easy way into a sure job," conceded Joy. "But life is about taking your talents and doing the best you can with them."

"Yeah?" said Izzy, challenging. "All I'm really good at is welding!"

It was interesting to see how the boy came to her defense. "You're good at lots of things. Like, I mean netball, pictures, um, running. Uh, practical jokes," he grinned, trying for a laugh.

"Well, what's wrong with welding?" asked Joy. "I knew an engineer at my last church who said no one should ever qualify in his field unless they had some idea how to use every tool in a machine shop."

"Whatever your far future holds," said Mary, "Right now, Cameron van den Vaestermark, it holds you clearing up the mess you've made. I have to go and do some work on my garden this afternoon, and I'm not leaving until you clean it up. Or, I know you, you'd leave Reverend Joy to do it."

He nodded, and stood up. And then looked somewhat shame-faced. "Uh. I can put everything back in the boxes. But the window... I broke a pane. Um... I... I'll pay for it. But I haven't got any money right now."

"Well," said Joy. "I'm not going to go and demand it from your father. I am sure we can reach some kind of arrangement." He'd broken it. He should pay for it, she decided, in the fullness of time.

"I will," he nodded, "It's just like my pocket money got stopped because I'd used it to pay for the paint. So, um, it may take me a while."

"Weeding and grass-cutting," said Mary. "I could use some, and I'll pay you for that."

"Well," said Joy. "I have another idea. Maybe an additional one. If you would finish that picture of Reverend Peter, I would like to buy it for the church. We don't have a single picture of him, and I'd like one. I think he deserves to be remembered."

Cameron's eyes filled with tears. "Yes. But that should be... must be my gift. And I'll make a copy. I'm not wanting to forget him. Ever." He sniffed. And Joy handed a tissue.

More to distract him than anything else, Joy said, because it had struck her earlier. "That mark you drew on his neck..."

"He said it was his cross to bear, but it wasn't killing him yet," said Cam.

"He used to cover it up as much as possible," said Mary. "He didn't like people seeing it. Come on let's get to this clean up. I have to get on.

"Well," said Cam "I'll need a brush and dustpan, please."

"To deal with the broken glass? Good thinking," said Mary. "Under the sink."

"Er. A little. The glass is mostly stuck to the paper. With honey. To stop it making a noise."

Joy shook her head. "You are a young man of some resource, even if it's a waste of honey. Where do you get all this expertise in burglary from?" It was said in jest, but the two youngsters looked at each other and both giggled. She raised her eyebrows, and tilted her head questioningly at the reaction.

"Oh, like, they won't split," said Izzy. "You know, like Megan's mum is um kind of always locking everything?"

"I... have been told," admitted Joy.

"So Meggle spends all her time working out these escape plans and practicing with lock picks, and reading up on how to break windows and saw through bars."

"Only, she's a bit of a wuss. She never, like, does any of it," said Izzy, in a tone that said she would. "She's big into all the martial arts... in talk. So, like I made her some nunchaku. And she hit herself on the head. But she's always talking about sneak attacks and stuff."

"She told me about the brick through the window distraction thing," admitted Cam.

"You chucked that brick through the window?" Izzy looked mildly aghast.

"It was open," said Cam. "You were supposed to come running out," he said to Joy, "and then I'd nick inside as soon as you opened the door. Only, um, you didn't."

"You frightened me quite badly," admitted Joy.

"I'm sorry," he said, sounding genuinely contrite. "I didn't know you then. I wouldn't do anything like that now."

"Now you know just to ask," said Joy. "Let's go clean up."

He nodded. "Then I better get back. The track's a boggy mess right now, and I said I'd be home by 3.30."

With four of them, putting everything back took relatively little time. Joy listened a great deal, and learned a little.

She got a solemn handshake and a formal apology from Cameron, before he left. "I feel really bad about all of it now. Um I didn't mean to frighten you. And, and I'm sorry I blubbed all over everyone."

"I respect you a lot more for it," said Joy. "You loved him, I think. Not in the way your father... assumed. People are too inclined to confuse sex with love, I suppose. Now, you haven't taken your book."

"Uh. Can you keep it, if, if you really mean we could come in on Wednesday afternoon? I don't want to get it muddy. I, um was going to go and hide it in Izzy's granddad's yard. I didn't want to ride home with it."

"I think Wednesday will work," said Joy, solemnly. "As a temporary measure anyway."

"Like, I'd better get home too," said Izzy. She'd been hanging in the background while Cameron took his leave and made his apology.

"Do you mind if I walk down with you?" asked Joy. "I really have got a book for your mother. And she's likely to be a bit concerned by now."

"Yeah. Like she's suddenly gone all protective."

"Well, I'll be offski too," said Mary. "I'll get hold of Tom and ask him if he can come and fix that window. You can always lock the door, if it worries you. Cameron should have been burgling my place – the door is never locked, and the window in the 'loo won't close. I'll give you a call later."

This left Joy walking with Izzy. After a few yards she said, awkwardly, "So like, what story do you think I should tell my mom?"

"It's always terribly hard to keep stories straight," said Joy. "And I think by now, to be honest with you, that your mother has worried herself so much about you... we all do about people we love, that she'll be glad to be told about Cam. The things we imagine, well, they can be pretty dreadful. I think the truth is likely to be a lot milder than what she's been readying herself for." She took in the questioning look. "Really. Trust me on this. Look at what Cam's father imagined. How much of that did you overhear?"

The girl colored. "Not a lot. Just my name, but he sounded miserable. I mean he did promise not to tell anyone we were like going out. I'm not allowed to date."

That wasn't all of it, Joy could tell, but she responded to it anyway. "And he didn't break his promise. In fact he was ready to tell your mother he was gay to distract attention from you."

The girl stopped dead. "But like, that makes him as mad as a cut snake."

"I saw that," said Joy. "But he values you and your reputation above himself. So, I think telling your mother as much as possible would be a good thing."

"You don't think she'd freak out?"

"In a word, no," said Joy hoping that she was right. "Look, most mothers would be glad if their daughter's boyfriends were as nice a boy as that. He's intelligent, good looking, and cares a lot about people. You are very much among those he cares about. I should think you'd be the envy of half the girls in the world."

"They tease him all the time. They're worse than the boys at school."

"Oh, not silly school-girls. They tease him because he doesn't notice them, and they feel he ought to, and that's their way of getting noticed," said Joy, carefully putting as much genteel disdain in her voice as possible. God would forgive her, she hoped. "They're very like sheep. All do the same thing, and play at spite and pecking order, if I remember right. Boyfriends and fashion and money, mostly."

"Yeah. And I haven't got any of them," said Izzy, in a way that told Joy that that aspect of high school girls remained the same.

"You've got the boyfriend, and I promise you this, by the time that boy goes to Art College or Uni, he's going to BE the fashion. If you're still an item you'll probably have to stand guard on him. And he comes from money, I think."

"Cam says his mother cleaned them out," said Izzy with a comforting lack of concern. "And his dad is dead set on him getting in to do medicine or something. I think that was why Cam liked the old priest so much. Because he said that somehow Cam needed be an artist."

"I think he has a lot of talent," said Joy. "I'm surprised they didn't pick that up at school."

"Oh, like art's a joke at school. Ms. Johnstone can't draw a stick figure. And she can't stand Cam. He cheeks her a lot. Funny, he was always really polite to the old priest."

"Maybe because he could draw stick figures?" said Joy, and then did her best to recover. "Maybe because he knew something about how to draw, and wanted to share that knowledge? That would appeal to Cam I think. Or did Peter do that? I want to know as I'm going to be expected to fill the same role, and I'm not anything like as good! Did you enjoy it too?"

"Well, he was always nice about our pictures, and gave us, like, pointers and stuff. And it was kind of fun, because everyone thought we were in trouble with him. But Cam, well it was different. I mean I quite enjoy painting, but it's, like, not what I want to do with my life or anything. But for Cam, it is his life. He always draws on everything. And he just couldn't wait to show the old guy what he'd done since last time. Megs and I only, like, drew anything at the rectory. Cam had always done, like, half a ton of stuff. He's really intense about it all. Sometimes I think he didn't know if I, um, either of us, were there with him."

They had arrived at the house by this time, and by the speed the door was opened before they quite got to it, Izzy's mother had been peering out of the windows.

"Hi mum," said the girl. "Uh, like, what is wrong?"

"Nothing honey," said her mother. It would not have fooled anyone, let alone her daughter.

"You've been crying," said Izzy, putting her arm around her mother... and being enveloped in a hug.

"I should imagine worrying, and doing her best not to 'phone or come looking for you," said Joy. "We should have called. I am sorry. We were talking and time got away from us."

"I had you dead in the river, or, or... Oh I was just being stupid."

The look Izzy gave Joy spoke volumes. "I'll leave you to talk about it," said Joy, smiling. "I did bring a book for you."

"Stay a little bit," said Izzy. "Please. Um. Mum. I've... got a boyfriend. I know you and dad said... but like, everybody..."

She was falling over her own tongue, and Joy had to restrain herself. But no harm in righting the ship a little. She gave a calm smile. "I'd panic much less if I were you, Jeanie. The condom was for a practical joke. I believe it was to be attached to Sergeant Grogan's police vehicle. It and the word 'boyfriend' are only slightly related subjects." She winked at the woman, hoping the daughter, now with her face downcast, didn't see it. She would have to explain later.

She got a slight nod in reply. Jeanie managed a very credible, even, loving voice. "I figured about the boyfriend. And thank you for telling me. I didn't tell my parents about my love life, and I was involved with several boys, uh, not sleeping with them, but, well involved when I younger. You're our little girl, but you're not so little anymore. We forget. Am I allowed to know who it is?"

"Like, uh, Cam."

There was a perceptible blink. "Oh. Cameron!" That was a definite lightening of tone. "Well... I suppose I should have guessed. He's a good boy at least, Izzy."

"I think," said Joy, "That I really should leave you two to discuss Cameron's merits. Do tell your mother about Reverend Peter, and what the three of you have been doing in the study at the rectory for the last while, please. Then I won't accidentally give away any secrets. You can call me, if there are any further misunderstandings. But I think you have a wonderful daughter, Jeanie. You should be proud of her, not worried about her."

Joy succeeded in disengaging herself, amused at the play of expression on Izzy's mother's face, slightly tempted to stay and hear it all, but she had a few more things to do. And it was best that they talked to each other, not through her. This was not her success, it was theirs.

Still, she would be very surprised if she didn't get a call later from Jeanie.

And she was not disappointed. "Izzy has gone to take a box of Anzac cookies to her grandfather. I just wanted to thank you..."

"And I just want to explain – now that you know the kids were meeting here in the rectory, three of them..."

"Yes," there was a slight laugh. "What a mess we all managed to make of it. Um. The best I can say is Willie was still drinking a lot then, and he's very defensive about our girl. It's got a funny side too. I nearly bust myself laughing when Izzy was telling me about when Willie came pounding on the door, and they were all eating a pudding someone had given the priest, and that he thought he might be allergic to, in the kitchen. They all thought Willie knew they were there. The kids ran off to hide, Iz said. She had to put her hand over Megan's mouth to stop her screaming. Izzy said it was kind of funny now, but just then they were all frightened out of their wits."

"They would be. But what I am wanting to tell you about, I do, because I trust you not to repeat it, and I only tell you because your daughter is involved with the boy."

She proceeded to explain how Cameron's father had jumped to a wrong conclusion about his son... and exactly why Cameron had condoms. "I have no reason to believe he was lying. He was terribly upset about it all."

Jeanie's comment on Donald was pithy, coarse, and more or less what Joy had been tempted to say, herself. "But by what Izzy said... sort of, reading between the lines a bit, but I was that age myself once, he'd be quite keen to put them to other uses. I told her to tell him I'd break his neck if I found out he was, but otherwise he's welcome here. And at some time I'll talk to her dad, but she's got my support. She told me she's not that dumb...which, er, I guess means she won't get pregnant, at least. It's a bit odd... I know, they're at school together, and got into hanging around together, but you know, he's old money, dad's a pharmacist, and none of us ever even went past year ten."

"It is early days for both of them. But I think it shows that they have both got good taste."

That brought a laugh. "Yes, a taste for trouble. But thank you for... what you did. And thank you for, um, filling in the background."

"So you're happy with Izzy coming here on Wednesdays and Fridays then? I want to move this whole performance to something more open."

"With you? More than fine."

"I'm going to try and recruit some extra help."

"So long as it's not old Stilton. The school asked her and she decided that she'd have them drawing a nude model... there was a fuss about that."

"Oh my. Not in my Rectory and not on my watch!" said Joy. "Ah. I have another call coming in. Good bye. We'll talk again."

The other call turned out to be Mary. "Three things quickly, I'm going out to the farm for tea. Tom's daughter came home while he was at church, and I'm going to try and keep the peace, or at least provide a distraction. Tom will be in to fix your window tomorrow. He says it'll cost you coffee at Zenobia's. Secondly, I am making pretty fast headway with the diary. It's not code or anything. He just used initials instead of names. But I'm not sure who the AM was he was seeing.

"10.30 AM – in the morning."

"No," said Mary. "He never wrote times like that – just the numbers, next to the part of the day. There are hours down the side of the page. And besides there were earlier AM entries. Two of them, both in the afternoons."

"Oh, how strange. Well. I'll have to go through the parish list."

"I have. I have even been through the 'phone book... no real candidates. Anyway, the third thing I have to say is when you decide to go and deal with Donald, take me along. We go back a long way, and I can deal with him," said Mary grimly. "He deserves a good slap around the chops, but I promise I won't."

"You were listening in, weren't you?" asked Joy, mildly irritated but not really surprised.

"Yes. Glass against the door. I thought you might need help. And, um, I have a big soft spot for that boy, even if he said I weighed a ton."

"I'll think about it," said Joy.

"Talk to Tom about it. Anyway, must rush. Bye!"

Thinking about it all, Joy suddenly realized just how right the Bishop had been. She had coped. Done what had to be done. In her old parish she would have turned to others for help, instead of to the help she had within her all the time. Now she just had to decide what to do next, and find the courage and strength to do it. She knew that she was rather too timid to find it easy, but she was still upset by the hurt that had been done... It needed meditation and prayer.

That evening Joy had made herself lasagna, with the intention that it would feed her for a few nights. Before she went to bed she wanted to put it into the fridge, which given the overcrowded state her fridge always evolved towards, needed a smaller container. She went looking, and found a fair number of plastic containers in something of a jumble in a low cupboard. Naturally there were no lids... except on one container, a lunchbox of startling pink and transparent violet. Well, lasagna was probably not color conscious, thought Joy, fishing it out, looking at it curiously. It had a girl guitarist picture on the lid. Perhaps one of the young artists might have left it here, she thought, turning it over. On the bottom was a name, written in glitter-ink – surprisingly un-obvious, because it was written in the same violet on the pink plastic. 'K. Truman'.

Joy hunted out another box, and covered it in cling-film, and left the lunchbox on the counter meaning to give it to the owner's father in the morning. Presumably it had been left in the church hall or something.

The next morning, Tom came along with a tape measure, but left again before Joy even emerged from the house, to return his property.

He came back just after lunch, with a pane of glass, and a hammer. "I thought I'd break it first and save time later," he said when she asked him why the hammer. "Actually, it is because it's one of those small panes held in by little wooden strips and not putty, which would be too easy. So I have borrowed a hammer and this little punch gadget from Mac, so hopefully I don't have to break the glass, putting it in.

He succeeded, against the odds, as he put it. "Now I need to drop these with Mac, and then we'll have a coffee at Zenobia's. My second visit today. I had morning tea there with my daughter which is why I had to rush off. She likes to go and catch up, but it was so busy they barely had time today. Can I give you a lift down?"

"No, thank you," said Joy. "I will need to shop on my way home." He left, and it was only after he'd gone that she remembered the lunch-box. She put in her car, on the passenger seat so that she wouldn't forget. Of course, that meant that she was distracted by a cheery greeting as she getting out, and did forget. Small town dynamics meant it took her a good five minutes to get from her car to the table where Tom was sitting.

"Getting to know everyone, I see," he said.

"It is rather different from the impersonal crowd in a city shopping mall. Drat. I have something of yours in the car. I forgot."

"Coffee first. It'll help your memory," he said. "And I'll remember."

They sat and talked – while just drinking coffee, Tom had had his weekly lemon meringue fix earlier, and Joy decided to forgo the temptations of the steak, kidney and oyster pie. It was good timing as most of the other customers were leaving when they got there, and they could sit in solitude. "My gossipy sister told Katie about what she overheard while I was out milking. When I heard about it I did the big brother thing and put my foot down and told her it stopped right there. It was not easy because I'm younger than she is. Hopefully with Katie back at Uni, she won't be repeating it, either. I asked her not to, but I'm only her dad."

Joy sighed. "I am not delighted at the news."

"I didn't think you would be, but better that you know. And yes, when you go and talk to that little squirt of a pharmacist of ours, take Mary. She's about the only one who ever could get him to shut up and listen."

"She won't get into a fight with him and make matters worse?"

He picked up the reference. "Willie was drunk. That's not exactly typical of Mary, in her defense. Seriously, for some people, no she wouldn't be my choice. But for Donald, yes. She'll actually make him listen. We had what could have been a major blow up with the fishing access, and he was on one of his crusades about the litter from fishermen and cruelty to fish... and I got Mary to come with me to chat to him. Ten minutes and we'd gone from absolute NO, to um, well now you put it like that..."

"Then that's what I'll do. I prayed about it last night. Normally, well, I need help with putting off doing hard things. Now... I believe I was told to let myself cool down. To wait."

"I don't see what harm waiting will do. And I'm rather pleased to have my worst thoughts about Reverend Peter turn into illusions. We want to be careful, but..."

"The balance is a hard one. To be fair to Peter I think he saw that too. He made sure they only came to him as a group. Cameron told me he'd asked if he could come in in the afternoon, the day he died. And he said no, only in threes."

Joy, after a very brief argument with Tom, paid a rather pallid-looking Madeleine, who barely spoke to her, and was about to bid Tom adieu when he held up a hand, and said: "My property."

"Your daughter's, actually," she said. "It's in the car."

She handed him the box when they got there, pointing to the name underneath.

"Ah," he said. "Katie's old school lunch box. Yes, I've brought cheese for the Sunday teas in it. I make a cottage cheese every now and again. I must have left it behind in the hall."

"It had found its way into the rectory, seeking others of its kind."

"They do that. Well, cheerio."

Joy drove the few hundred yards to the supermarket, feeling vaguely guilty about doing so. Of course everyone did, here. There was parking everywhere. She'd shopped – it took a lot longer than it had at first, because traversing an aisle meant three conversations. Still, there was a warmth about it. People should know and care, and if that came with a level of curiosity and gossip, that went with the territory.

By the time she got herself out of there, school was also out, a couple of kids on scooters were hooliganing down the pavement. She'd just got into her car, when she saw Izzy positively bounding along the pavement, still in school uniform but with a carrier bag in her hand. Joy waved, and got a huge grin as the girl came running up to her. "Would you like a lift?" asked Joy.

"Like, I'd love one. Mum asked me to get some fish, and I think Maddy put rocks in the bag. Well, ice-bricks."

"Hop in," said Joy, moving things off the seat into the back. Izzy got in, and they drove out. "So, like, what did you say to mum?" asked Izzy. "You know what she said to me this morning. She said I should go and get busted kissing Cam at school! And she was, like, serious!"

"I'd guess she was telling you that she approved, and that would tell certain people he was interested in girls."

"Okay..." said Izzy. It was a very considering 'okay'. A quick glance showed Izzy biting her lower lip. And smiling very widely. "I, like, talked to Maddy about it. Like, about what girls would think about Cam, like, at Uni and so on. She said I'd have to lock him away. Huh. And she said I had caught a beauty. And you were right about mum, yesterday. You're pretty smart sometimes, Mrs. Priest."

"Um. No. But I have help from someone who is."

"Who?"

"I'm a Christian priest, Izzy. Who do you think?" asked Joy as she negotiated the corner, waved to a pedestrian, and pulled up at the gate.

"Oh. Yeah. Um so, like what you said yesterday..."

"I said quite a lot. Which bit in particular?" asked Joy rather warily. But she was still unprepared for the direction the reply took.

"About welding. And engineering. Like, everything any of the other girls ever talk about doing is like... I'm not interested. I like well, doing real stuff."

"Why not? It's real enough, even if very few women seem to do it. But it's quite a lot more than just welding. You have to do well at math, computing and I think the sciences just to get in."

"Um. Actually, I can do that stuff pretty well. I just don't want to look like a nerd."

"Similar to having a boyfriend," said Joy, smiling, "Sometimes you have to decide whether what people think of you is important, or the thing itself. I had to take that decision when I entered the ministry. A lot of people thought I was crazy, but it was important to me. There are a few people I really do care about what they might think of me, but really, what the world thinks is not that important."

There was a pause. "Yeah. It was funny. I, um, decided I'd tell Gramps about Cam and me. Like, Mum said I should. And you know what? He said if I wanted to keep the fact I was kissing Cam secret from him, then I should remember that shiny metal makes a great mirror. And he said I could do worse, but couldn't I find a mechanic or an engineer instead? Like, he was teasing me. He likes Cam."

"I'll arrange for you to meet my engineering friend sometime," said Joy. "If you're really interested, I know they take some year 11 students to do a bit of work-experience. And he's got two sons about your age, so he's quite used to talking to them. He says they know everything about engineering. Now that he's fifty he knows he knows nothing."

Izzy got out of the car. "Thanks for the lift," she said, and went on her way, so Joy did too, knowing that sometimes seed fell on good ground.

CHAPTER 15

There was no escaping the fact old Mr. Porter's health had gone downhill in the last few weeks. He'd been at her first two services, but not this last Sunday. Mary had noticed of course, and had followed up through her own local channels. She let Joy know, late in the afternoon, that it might be a good idea to visit that evening. Joy took her little travelling communion case, her bible, and drove over to his house. There was another vehicle parked outside, and as she drew up Doctor Hammond came out.

He looked at her. "You're quick off the mark," he said. "I was actually considering 'phoning you, simply because you might have some influence on the old boy." His tone said he did not think priests were a first resort. "Look, he needs to go into care. He's refusing to leave."

"I'll try to talk to him," said Joy. "What's wrong with him? And if you tell me its patient confidentiality then I shall ask him. And he will tell me, and get it wrong, because his hearing is awful. And that won't help either of us."

"Emphysema. He smoked all his life and his lungs have had it."

"I wondered about his struggle to talk. Look, I will do my best. I know you probably won't tell me, but if it was those marks on Father Peter's neck that worried you..."

"No," said the Doctor, tersely. "I knew all about the lupus, of course. I was treating him. It was the oleander branch in his mouth that I didn't expect to see!"

"Oh," said Joy, somewhat nonplussed. "Well, let me see what I can do for old Mr. Porter."

As he had just been nebulized, the old man was breathing easier, and he was sitting up against his pillows. He still did not look well, but gave her a weak smile. "Where... where's my... ear? Took it out... so that sawbones... couldn't lecture me."

Both Joy and his wife had to do a bit of searching until the device was excavated from under a book, inserted, and with a high-pitched squeal switched on and settled in. "Really, Sam. Why didn't you just switch it off like you always do," said his wife, Sarah, crossly.

"Heh... he's got wise... to that one. Made me... switch it on."

Joy gave him communion, and prayed with him. She told them both about what Dr. Hammond had said. He shook his head. "That's in... Hardacre. Sarah can't drive... anymore."

"But can you look after him?" Joy asked of Sarah.

She nodded. "Mostly. And our daughter Sandy is coming home at the end of the month. She's taken the nursing job in the surgery."

"It's... winter. Always hard.... on chest. Spring... is getting here."

Joy heard more about the excellence of the daughter, and how she'd be able to manage the nebulizing so much better. And going into care would mean either selling their home or it would cost an arm and a leg. That Dr. Hammond didn't like being called out, and was always trying to get the older patients to go to Hardacre, where he wouldn't have to be. At length Sarah trotted off to the kitchen, still quite spritely for her late seventies, and the old man, when he heard the clatter there, said: "Wanted to tell you... while Sarah was out... everyone thinks... I'm deaf. Always switch... the hearing-aid off. So they forget... I can hear... with it on. Was sitting... down on the bench, next to the rectory... Day before the vicar was killed. Was doing better...I went for a walk... got tired. Vicar came out... and he got a call on his mobile. Didn't... hear a lot. But he said... 'If I don't die first... your marriage will kill me.' Woman was... talking to him.

Couldn't hear ... what she said. But... he said 'Well... I think it'll be the... death of me, too."

At this point, Sarah returned, saying that his tea would be ready in a few minutes, and Joy took the hint and left.

As soon as she got home, Joy promptly looked up Oleander. She'd had it pointed out to her as a poisonous flower before. And it was... but it was not that poisonous. Not strong enough to kill someone with a branch still in their mouth. They'd have to eat the stuff, and a fair amount of it, and then they'd be sick and in most cases, live.

Shaking her head she looked up lupus. She'd heard of the auto-immune disease, but knew little about it. On reading the symptoms, many of the little mysteries about Peter Hallam cleared up – his sensitivity to sunlight, his reputed flares of temper, his allergies, his medications...even possibly the goji berries. The mention of heart conditions... perhaps that tied into the Oleander, which, did after all cause cardiac reactions.

Well, she was somewhat better informed, but not, it seemed to her, much wiser.

Joy had been rather nervous about Wednesday art classes, and had wondered who, if anyone, she could ask to help her. She'd eventually decided that at least for the first session, she'd just do it herself. She had a long hard look through the sketchbook to try and pick on areas that needed work. Inevitably perspective was an issue – a minor one, but at least it gave her something to look up, to refresh her own memory about. She found she had not forgotten, so much as just not thought about it, which helped her confidence at least.

In the event, she need not have worried. She did a little fishing when they arrived, and established that Peter's 'method' for what it was worth, was to pick on a different type of drawing, each time. He let them have a go, and helped as they went along, if they wanted it. Joy did a bit of explaining about geometric perspective, and how it worked and the math thereof. She suggested that as structures with parallel lines were easiest to learn to do it in, and their view of architecture from here was limited, maybe the shed and the ruined chookyard would have to do. Yes, of course, if Megan wanted to draw gnomes and bikers in it that was fine. So long as the further away gnomes were not bigger than the closer bikers.

After a while she went out to get some tea, and heard a clattering sound in the direction of church. So she looked out, to see that Isabella had obviously dropped a metal bucket, in her attempt to carry too many things up the stair to the little door to the sacristy. So Joy went across to help. The artists could do without her for a minute or two.

Of course, by the time she got there, Isabella had retrieved her bucket, and Mary had emerged to help.

"I thought you were at work?" said Joy with a smile to Mary, having greeted them both.

"I do a couple of hours on the Saturday morning, at month end. They let me take time in lieu to come and do my turn. I set the roster up, I need to do my bit!" explained Mary.

"Oh, well, you don't need me. I'd better get back. Um, I'm attending to something," said Joy.

"Ah," said Mary. "Yes. Well, quickly come and look at this. Isabella and I were talking about shifting furniture around back here. It's just impossible to get through that door if you're in a hurry without banging into that little cabinet. I wanted to move it over there to that corner," she pointed, "but Isabella thinks it'll be better over next to the hanging rack."

"Is closer to the basin. We use for flowers," said Isabella.

"Yes, but you'll have to walk around the robe hangers."

"Talking of flowers," said Joy. "Oleanders..."

"They're finished now. We had the very last from Lorna's garden, just the week before poor Reverend Peter died."

"Someone tip them out next to the altar," said Isabella, showing the first sign of anger Joy had ever seen on her tranquil face. "No respect! Like they sick in the toilet and don't flush."

"Oh. When?"

"I see it when I clean the day Reverend Peter died."

"Yes. Well, about this cabinet," said Mary, obviously keen to move the subject on.

"What's actually in it?' asked Joy. "I must admit I found dodging around it to get out of the door awkward. But do we need it in here at all?"

In answer, Isabella opened it. "Is cleaning stuff on the bottom. Brasso, mothballs, window cleaner, some polishing cloths, some small vases. Here," she pointed to the second shelf, and then leaned forward and pulled things out. "We keep the candles, matches, the little watering-can for the flowers, clothes for the small hall-stand..." The next item was a well-worn, rather ordinary bible. "Is Reverend Peter's. I find on one of the pews, the day he died," she said sadly. "I do not want to leave it there."

Joy took a deep breath. She could see various bits of paper protruding from it. "I think I will take it back to the rectory," she said, priding herself on keeping her voice even. "I'll think about the cabinet. I must get back." And she took the bible from Isabella, and ran.

Back inside, she looked in on the three budding artists before she could start to look at the bible or its contents. There seemed to be cause – there were gales of laughter coming out of the room. Joy found that Megan had drawn a biker kissing a gnome in her dilapidated shed. She wasn't a bad artist either, really. Joy cheerfully pointed out the problems in her perspective, while admiring the biker. Of the three young artists, Megan had by far the most imagination, Izzy the most methodical approach, and Cameron had natural talent in abundance. She disciplined herself to spend the fifteen minutes with them, until they took their leave.

This secrecy had to end, and soon she decided, but it was good to see them comfortable and easy with her.

When they'd left she opened the bible. And, yes, one of pieces of paper in the back of it read 'Last Will and Testament of Peter John Hallam'.

Joy decided she was going to look at it. It wasn't sealed, and was germane to her work here. Then she would call Dean Mellors.

It was both simple and startling enough. As Tom had said, his personal possessions were to be used by the parish or sold if they were of no use to them, with the proceeds donated to St Andrews Children's home. There were a series of small bequests, including one to Lindsey McCassil – 'as a small thanks for her services as the Parish treasurer where her kindly work had not gone un-noticed.' Well, well. That would surprise her. Mary got a gift of several books. It was the rest of the will that was startling. It seemed that Reverend Peter Hallam owned a home in a good suburb of Melbourne, and had various investments for his retirement, which were lodged with a respectable firm of solicitors in Melbourne. The house was to be sold, and the proceeds to be held in trust with the investments, and disbursed as deemed necessary by the nominated trustees for the education, board and lodging and such discretionary expenses as they saw fit, at a prestigious Fine Art college, or an equivalent institution, for Cameron van den Vaestermark to study art, fine art or design or a similar course. Should that not prove possible, Cameron van den Vaestermark, (and his age and home address were carefully stated) was to be given the sum of 50 000 dollars when he reached the age of twenty-one in the hope that he would pursue further training in art. The Trustees were named as Dean William Werthe and Mary Truman. There were similar, smaller bequests left to the other two children, but simply for their choice of further education. Any remaining monies were to be equally divided between the Parish of St. James and Bush Church Aid.

It was, considering the value of property these days, not the trivial amount Tom Truman had thought it would be. It was also going to be a hot potato. She turned the will over. It was neatly signed and dated some weeks before his death. In doing this she noticed that the next thing in the bible was a letter, with a stamp on it, addressed to Dean William Werthe, Dean Mellors late predecessor. Attached was a bright puce post it note with a morbid message: 'To be posted in the event of my death.'

Joy picked up the phone, and spent the next twenty minutes explaining to Dean Mellors that she'd found the will, the contents and what complications it was going to create.

"The other trustee, this Mary Truman. What do you know of her?" asked Dean Mellors.

"She's efficient, knows the boy and his father, and is probably the best possible choice for the job. Peter Hallam knew what he was doing, naming her. Now, there is the letter addressed to Dean Werthe..."

"I suspect that Peter Hallam must have been unaware that he had died during the trip he took to his native Germany," said Dean Mellors. "It happened around that time. I think this probably comes under the heading of business correspondence, and thus will be my concern now. Have a look inside and tell me. If it is personal, well, I can forward it on to Dean Werthe's son. If not, you can read it to me and send it on if need be."

The letter was addressed to 'Dear Bill'. Joy rapidly decided she had better read it out aloud.

"Dear Bill, If you are reading this, it will mean that I have predeceased you after all. The disease proceeds at an uneven rate, and I have been in much pain, lately. This, and the circumstance I have found myself in, have motivated me to make my will, and to name you as a trustee in it.

My dear friend, I know I am handing you a problem. I also want to tell you that you were right, all those years ago, after Edith's death. God gave me a talent and I should not have just buried it in the ground. I can see that now, with blinding clarity. At the time, with my beloved wife's death so raw I never wanted to draw again. I eventually tried to move past it here, and try painting instead, as a way of reaching out into the local community. Alas, watercolor was not something which I had any skill at. But God works in mysterious ways, and I saw his hand in some of the most brilliantly executed pictures painted by some young 'vandal' on the town's walls. My fellow townspeople here saw graffiti – I saw purity of line. I followed it up, and found the artist. And he has talents which far eclipse any I ever had. He's also fated to have a parent who will not consider the boy using this talent. I tried on several occasions to reason with him, but he is a somewhat aggressive atheist, who slammed the door of his shop in my face when I tried to go and plead, for the boy's sake, that he see to his training and education. The boy needs help to be able to use this marvelous gift to its full potential. It seems that his father has taken me into a personal vast dislike. I am hoping to enlist some help in speaking to him – the lady I have nominated as your co-trustee has some influence with him. Anyway, this letter is to plead with you, for the sake of an old friendship to undertake this trusteeship (or to appoint someone suitable to act for you), should I have been re-united with my beloved in the mansions of our Father. It was something I have longed for, but you helped me understand that I still had work here to do. Now I know what it was, and, if you are reading this letter, I pray that you will help me to finish it."

There was a long silence down the telephone line. Then Dean Mellors said: "Sometimes I get so caught up in administration that I forget why I entered the church in the first place. Well, I will look into the legalities, but I think that we're bound to honor his wishes. I'll talk to the Bishop. In the meanwhile I think you need to make certified copies of both the will and that letter, and post the originals on to me, so that I can get the process in motion. Now, you spoke quite highly of this Mary Truman? Could you, in confidence, broach this with her? It may be too much for her. She may end up as sole trustee, for all I know."

"She effectively runs the Parish Council and I doubt if it would be too much for her. So, I could show her the will and the letter? She's also the Justice of the Peace so she can certify the copies."

"Yes, I think that would be reasonable."

So: when Mary came around a little later, Joy was ready.

"I waited until Isabella had gone, but I have to know," said Mary. "Was the missing will in his bible? I saw the papers sticking out."

"Yes, and now we'll need some tea, and then I will show them to you, and we will need to talk. Peter, um, entrusted something very difficult to you."

"And I'll need tea first?" said Mary, raising her eyebrows. "Well, I'd better make it then."

"You sit and read these. Did you know about Peter's wife?"

Mary nodded as she sat. "Katie – Tom's daughter -- told me last week, when we were talking about Donald and Cameron and his drawing. So sad. We never knew, here, of course, but it did explain... so many things about him. There was, um a sort of melancholy about him. I... I tried to cheer him up, jolly him along a bit. I felt terrible about that when I was told."

"Don't feel bad about something you could not have guessed. Just read those. I'd start backwards, with the letter. Dean Werthe is dead, unfortunately. I've just talked to his successor, and got his permission to show the will and letter to you."

Joy made tea, and turned back to the table to find Mary sitting with tears trickling down her cheeks. Joy gave her a tissue, and poured the tea. "So," she said, giving Mary the cup. "Are you prepared to be a trustee?"

"Of course," said Mary. "I wouldn't dream of refusing. It's such an honor that he trusted me to see to something he saw as so precious. I wish I was even faintly artistic. You'll have to help in that respect, Joy."

"What help I can give is always yours for the asking. And there is always prayer. God knows everything there is to know, even about art."

Mary managed a watery chuckle. "Try not to say that to Donald."

"Oh, indeed. We have a job to do, not merely a point to make. That would be at best a Pyrrhic victory, and be failing to do what Peter believed was best for the boy. No, we'll have to try and keep the matter as secular as possible in dealing with Donald."

"Well, we'd better go and see him," said Mary. "There is no point in putting it off."

"I think it might actually be better if we went down tomorrow morning. Cameron will be in the pharmacy, right now, and we may both say things I'd rather he didn't overhear. I think the less people involved the better."

Mary nodded in agreement. "Can I talk to my little brother about it?"

"Tom does seem to be a sensible ear," said Joy. "But please ask him to keep it to himself."

"He's good at that," said Mary. "Too good, sometimes."

She took her leave, after they had made copies of the will and the letter. Joy wasted no time, and put both originals into an envelope, and took them down to the post office.

It was still Mr. Wiley and Ms. McCassil while they were working together, Joy noticed to her amusement. But both of them were rather cheerful, and happy to send her envelope off, certified mail. Joy had to smile herself, knowing about the will and the bequest in it.

That evening Tom called her. "I've had my sister talking to me during milking. She never comes near the dairy, usually. I was thinking maybe you should take at least a book of those Halley cartoons with you. I was telling Mary, Donald was in touch with me a few months ago – before all this blew up, about the possibility of selling off at least his river flats. He was just fishing for interest, but plainly money is still tight. He said at the time he had to consider Cam's education, and whether Donald wanted to live out on the farm on his own, when the boy was out of home. But I wouldn't place too much on him wanting to save money. Donald, to be fair to him, puts his idea of what is right for the boy before his own interests. If he'd given up custody, he'd have come off a lot lighter."

"How does Cameron's mother fit into all of this?"

"Completely disinterested, except if she can screw more money out of Donald, to be honest. I know it's not how the world likes to see women, but it is plain and simple, she was only ever interested in herself. A gold-digger who had enough of living in the country quite rapidly. I gather – via my own ex-wife who at least knew her, that her pregnancy was her way of getting an apparently wealthy man to commit to marriage. She doesn't even bother to contact the boy. That much I know, from a conversation I had with Cam a while back. To be honest, he didn't seem too upset about it."

"Well, thank you for telling me, at least."

"A pleasure. I wish you the best of luck in dealing with it. I'd offer to help, but I doubt my presence would be of any benefit. We're neighbors, and on speaking terms, but we don't have much common ground. Oh, by the way, I've sent that pink and purple container... or its twin sister, back to its owner with Mary. I opened my kitchen cupboard to put it away, and it was there already."

"Oh. But it had your daughter's name on it."

"Yes. I've kept that one. The one I had, had MAD on the bottom written in the same violet glitter ink. The girls both went through a phase of using it on everything. Obviously I've had the wrong one for years. I have no idea how Maddy's one got into the rectory. She wouldn't have been a frequent visitor! But I daresay she left it somewhere, and then it got used to bring something to the church. I've put some more eggs in it for you. My hens think it is spring again."

The next morning Mary came to the Rectory at about 9.30. "The office thinks you're a force for ill. This is the second time I've taken time off since you've been here," she said, putting down the pink lunchbox. "Eggs. Tom is relieved to have another person to give them to. His hens lay less in winter, so instead of buying a few eggs, he has extra chooks. And then he spends the rest of the year giving away eggs."

"If it makes him happy, it seems harmless enough. Now how are we going to approach Donald about this?" They discussed it for a while, and then after a brief prayer, went to do battle.

As with most battles, it went according to plan only as far as: "Good morning," and that came rather warily from Donald.

"Sit down," said Mary. "We've come to talk you."

He looked at Joy. "I don't really need to be preached at, or to discuss theology today. I have a business to run and no interest in sky fairies."

"I said sit down because your hip is plainly hurting you," said Mary. "And we haven't come to preach, or to talk about religion."

"We've come to talk about your son," said Joy.

Donald went white, and raised himself up. "He has nothing to do with you, or your damned church. Now go away!"

"I can prove that he does have," snapped Mary. "Now sit down and listen, Donald. I've known you for more than thirty years, and I have known your son all his life. When have I ever tried to do either of you any harm, you fool? I spent half your childhood getting you out of trouble. I am your friend and I always have been."

Donald literally deflated. He sat down. "I really didn't expect it to happen. Look, please, please can we keep Cam out of it? If need be I'll admit to killing the priest. I hated the bastard enough. Cam couldn't possibly have known. I never guessed that Hallam's reaction would be that violent, that he'd go into anaphylactic shock. The boy hasn't been himself since it happened. He's been in tears and silent. It's like having a ghost in the place... and he just seemed to be getting over it the last three days."

They both looked at him, trying to come to terms with what he said. Mary was the first to say: "Just what are you talking about?"

"The latex allergy that killed him. Cam was in tears when I got home. He wouldn't even speak to me. Didn't come out of his room..."

"Latex?' Mary looked puzzled. "Cameron was in school and..."

"He said he was feeling sick that day. I let him stay home. You don't know how often I have torn myself apart about that."

Finally Joy had pieced the references together. One of the Zoologists at the museum had had to wear plastic gloves to work with the animal specimens preserved in formalin, because he was allergic to the rubber of surgical gloves... Isabella and the hair-dressing cloth, and Peter Hallam's reaction to that. "Well, here is something new for you to tear yourself apart about. Your son's girlfriend has been in a great deal of trouble about those stupid condoms."

Donald's mouth opened and closed. "Girlfriend?" he croaked out.

"Yes. And you need to wash your brain out with bleach," said Mary, who had finally worked out what 'latex' meant.

"Are you trying to tell me that I got it wrong? Look I'm sorry, I'd love to believe you. But I know Cam went into that rectory... what an appropriate name for a place. He's my son, and I love him no matter what. But he was devastated when that bloody pervert Hallam died."

"Watch your mouth," said Mary crossly. "You weren't that badly upset when your own father died, but you were in tears when my father died, because your father barely saw you, and mine was kind to you. Cam was in the rectory all right, always along with two girls of his own age. Never alone. Never doing anything he couldn't do in public, if his father wasn't such an idiot."

"He promised you that he would never be alone with Reverend Peter, and it was a promise he had no problem keeping," said Joy.

"How would you know?" demanded Donald.

"Because he told me, and the girl he's seeing confirmed it, independently."

"Who is this girl?" asked Donald.

Joy and Mary looked at each other. Joy nodded, so Mary replied. "Izzy Jenkins. And you'll keep your mouth shut about that for now, because Willie said she's not allowed to date."

"She was in trouble, deep, with her mother about one of your condoms," said Joy. "I think Jeanie Jenkins would tell you. She'd also probably give you a lesson in bad language about it that would make a sailor blush, and box your ears for you."

"Izzy? I mean. They're just friends," said Donald.

"How many girls a year younger than you at high school, were you 'just friends' with, Donald?" asked Mary scathingly.

"And old Mac has been watching them kissing," added Joy. "He's a cunning old man with reflective surfaces, to let him see what is happening behind his back."

Donald took a deep breath. And closed his eyes briefly. And then shook his head. "I'm sorry. Look I'd be a liar if I didn't say I'd be glad if Cam was fooling around with girls... but this doesn't make sense. You're just avoiding a painful truth. Hallam's dead. Let's just move on. I love my son, no matter what."

Joy reached into the shoulder-bag she'd brought along. She pulled out the cartoon book. "Have a look. Have you ever seen any of these before?"

Donald looked at it. Nodded. "Halley? Yes I remember his cartoons in the papers back when I was in Uni."

"Halley was the pen name of Peter Hallam. He gave up being a cartoonist, when his wife was killed. He joined the ministry, and ended up here."

"He was married? I mean, it has to have been a front if it was true."

"Yes, he was married. Nobody here knew. He obviously didn't want to talk about it, but if you check the records, and you can do it online, right here and now, his wife and unborn baby were killed in a tragic hit-and-run accident while he was away getting an art prize. He never drew another cartoon. But he did see, and encourage, your son's genius, which you didn't," said Joy.

"Which you forbade him to waste his time on," said Mary. "Which you gave him hell about when you found him doodling in his text books. He told me all about that a while back."

Donald just looked at them blankly. Then shook his head. "This is too much for me. I need... I need to check on few things."

"Do," said Joy. "In the meantime I see a customer, walking up your steps. We'll wait. And when you're done, 'phone old Mac, or one of us can walk down and ask him to come in. Look up Halley on the net. We found the story of his wife's death in one of the Melbourne newspaper archives."

The customer came and went, having exchanged polite greetings, and, because this was Felixtown, curious glances. The time and the routine had plainly given Donald time to think, to collect himself. "Mary," he said. "You've always been a friend. I can't see why you'd be doing this to hurt me. You must be very sure you're right."

"Absolutely certain," said Mary.

"But... what killed Hallam?" asked Donald.

"Not your son. Peter was supposed to meet someone at 10.30. All we know is that a piece of Oleander was found stuck in his mouth," said Joy with as much confidence as she could muster.

"Oleander?" Said Mary and Donald together.

"But that wouldn't kill him, unless it was through his carotid artery or, or he reacted to it or something," said Donald.

"I only know it was in his mouth. But that is another matter. I think you'll find that your son really was not feeling well, and heard, via the normal means – the telephone, and then was upset at losing a mentor and a friend, a natural and normal thing to be, worsened by the fact that he couldn't talk to you about it, and Izzy was away. I think it is time we showed Donald the letter that Peter wrote to the Dean about Cameron, Mary," said Joy.

She nodded.

So they handed over the copy of the letter.

Donald read it, and got up from the stool he kept behind his dispensing counter, and walked past them.

"Where are you going?" asked Mary.

"Well I should go and shoot myself," he said with a wry smile, with the first trace of humor they'd seen. "For being a fool. But instead I am putting up a closed sign and locking the door. Customers normally start dragging in from surgery about now. And they can wait, today."

CHAPTER 16

"Your one redeeming feature, Donald," said Mary, "Is that when your nose is rubbed in it enough, you can actually admit that you were wrong."

"That is an honorable character trait, and rare too," said Joy. "And for the record, you have a very brave and honorable son. And in spite of the fact that you have made his life a living misery the last while, loves you very much and cares for you greatly. You should be very proud of him."

Donald took a deep breath. "Let's go into the back room, and you can start at the very beginning."

So they did. Joy told him about the sketch-book, Cam's attempts to retrieve it, and how finally they had caught him in the house, filling in the details.

"He's had a rough few weeks. Not only did he lose a friend and mentor who, finally, saw his talent, but he was terrified he'd send you over the edge if I showed up here with his sketch book."

Donald sucked his teeth. "Look. I... jumped to the wrong conclusion. There is a history..."

Joy nodded. "One evil undoes much good. And to be fair, we worried too. People tend to imagine the worst. One has to be careful. And sometimes we create the worst out of nothing."

Donald nodded. "Thank God I didn't kill him, that's all I can say. I thought about it. I even planned it. I could have tainted something with seafood..."

"That's rich, you thanking God," said Mary.

He managed a wry smile. "Just an expression. But if there were a God I should be grateful. I don't believe a God needs winding up on Sundays though."

"If you come to church," said Joy, "I'll preach a sermon on that. As it happens I agree with you."

Donald drew breath, and Mary put her hand in front of his mouth. "No, you two are not going to argue theology today," said Mary. "I'm sorry I said it. Now let's go on talking about Cam. You've also got a business to run, people to help."

Donald nodded. "Well. Look, I'll have to mend fences with my boy. I'll probably feel stupid and guilty about it for years. Thank you for clearing it up, and um..."

"We're not finished yet. Your son – and the other kids, but especially Cam, get a big legacy from Peter Hallam for their education. That was what the trustee part was about in the letter. I didn't show you the will."

Joy could that see they'd hit a wall. "Look, I know the priest thought art was important. And I do see that... well, it has its reason and a place. I like a good picture as much as the next man. I'm a friend of Amabelle's, but there's no future in it. I can't leave the boy a fortune to dribble away, unfortunately. My father had burned away most of his inheritance – as we found out when he died. My ex-wife took most of what I had. And there's not much in the Pharmacy trade now. It is very capital intensive and I just don't have the assets for it. Cam needs a profession, a future. Very few artists make a living."

"Well," said Joy. "There is truth in what you say. Very few footy players make a living out of footy. But those who do... so it comes down to whether you have faith in your son's ability. My own take on this is that you need to get his skills professionally assessed. And while an awful lot of people do do fine arts degrees, and don't use them afterwards, there is work for artists besides painting portraits or pictures for people to hang on their walls. Book covers, advertising...you've got a little guide book on flowers for sale in there. I still make a small percentage from each sale, and I earned a reasonable living as an illustrator."

"You?" he asked, blinking.

"I was a museum illustrator, before I went into the ministry," said Joy. "Donald, it's a very generous legacy, and even if your son never does work as an artist, there is nothing to stop him training as anything else, before or after."

Donald's eyes narrowed slightly. "What does the church get out of all this?" he asked with sudden suspicion.

"Nothing at all. The man that Reverend Peter asked to be the one trustee was a priest, but he is dead. The other trustee is Mary," said Joy. "I don't know how these things work, but my advice to her would be to see if you could also be made a trustee. Look, Peter Hallam was a priest, but his money isn't clerical. He was a man, I gather, in both physical pain from a hereditary disease, and psychological pain from the loss of his wife and child. Your son, well, made his life somewhat more worth living. He believed that Cameron had great talent. Maybe that was a bit of displacement for his own lost child, but, regardless, he tried to do his best for him. That's all. If you close up on this, Cameron gets a lump sum when he turns twenty one, and he can do exactly as he pleases with it, art school or whatever. Although, my guess is: he is an honorable boy, he'll use the money exactly as it was intended."

"And," said Mary grimly, "If you want to drive him away from you, still further than you've managed so far, that would be the best choice, Donald. Don't do it, Donald. You love the boy."

The man sighed. "Look. I'll think about it. Do some research, I suppose. I'm going to have to talk to Cam about this... and I haven't got it right on my own. Mary, can I ask you, as an old friend, to come and sit in on that? I don't want me getting angry or Cam getting angry. Could we get together this afternoon, after work?"

She nodded. "Yes, of course. Come to my house. I'll make tea for you both. That way it's on neutral ground as it were."

He stood up. "Someone's knocking. I'd better go and see to them. Thank you both for this... I think."

"I hope it works out for both of you," said Joy. "Whatever comes out of it, I think you should be very proud of your boy."

Mary nodded. "Yes, you should be. He's more credit to you, than you are, you silly man." But she did allow him a small smile in saying it.

"Probably. Er. You're sure about the girlfriend?"

"Absolutely certain. But don't you dare say a word about her to Cam, or her, or try any of your other tricks," said Mary. "I'll see you just after five."

As they drove back to the rectory, Joy was very grateful Mary had been with her. She said so.

"He was rattled. Otherwise, well he's got a smart mouth and a glib tongue. He's used to being a little cleverer than anyone else," said Mary.

"You did manage him exceptionally. How do you know him that well?"

"I used to babysit him. We lived on the farm next door, and his parents were very much into entertaining and social high-life. Mine weren't. I am only five years older than him – but they thought an eleven year old girl could take care of a six year old boy... even one as capable of trouble as he was."

"Well, you must have succeeded," said Joy, with a laugh. "Let's hope and pray he weighs it all with common sense. Thank you so much for doing a wonderful job, Mary."

"That might be hoping for too much," said Mary, "But I'll do what I can."

"Better out in the open than in, whatever happens."

"My father used to say that when he, um, burped. I'm not sure I agree," said Mary, as they stopped at the rectory. "Now I had better get back to work. Oh, I'd better take that lunchbox. What a pain."

"Oh, I'll drop it in," said Joy. "I still need to get the eggs out and give it a wash. And I'd like to buy some fish."

"That'd save me a trip," said Mary. "If you're sure you don't mind?"

"What's dealing with the town pagan after a meeting with the town atheist?"

Joy soon discovered: a great deal more abusive in this case. Neither Madeleine nor her mother were outside the Chamomile Natural Foods Café and People's Store. So Joy went in. She saw Madeleine carrying a tray of crockery she had just cleared from one of the tables, heading into the kitchen behind the deli and fish counter. "I'm just bringing back some of your property," Joy said, holding out the lunchbox.

Madeleine dropped the entire tray with a clatter of breaking and flying crockery.

And then Zenobia, who Joy had not seen standing between the shelves restocking from a basket, started swearing and throwing things at her. "Get the f... out my f...ing shop, you f..." and considerably more. Joy retreated hastily, to the surprise of the customers having a late coffee under the awning. Zenobia followed. Joy was only saved from certain death, inflicted by viciously flung whole nutmegs, by Zenobia being ambushed by her own doormat and falling flat on her face.

Zenobia scrambled and clattered up, still swearing, and Joy decided that discretion was the better part of valor, and that she couldn't reason with the woman. Zenobia screamed that she'd better never dare f...ing come near here again, and flung a pack of dried shiitake mushrooms at Joy's head as she backed away. Fortunately they didn't weigh much.

Puzzled and unsettled, Joy went home to the rectory. It had to be something to do with the pink lunchbox. But what?

She was going to 'phone Mary, but then decided to 'phone Mary's brother instead. After all it had been Tom's daughter's lunchbox that she'd found here. The 'phone rang and rang. Well, he had a farm to run, and she did not have a mobile number for him. She resolutely tried to put it aside, and addressed herself to her sermon. When that failed, she settled on a novel, a light and fluffy thing with a good ending, that made her feel more at ease, and happier with the world. She finished it as the afternoon was slipping into evening, and she put it back in her shelves grateful to an author she'd never meet, and who would never know how welcome that book had been. She tried Tom again, and this time he answered, even if he too had no answer. "Zenobia doesn't need a lot to set her off," he said. "Look, why don't you ask around among the folk who tend to clean up after tea at the church on Sunday, if anyone has lost that box, or knows how it got to the rectory. So how did your session with Donald go?"

So she told him as much as she could, and after that made a short list of the people – largely the women, who cleaned up in the hall after the Sunday service. She could, of course, wait until Sunday. But that, a quiet voice inside her said, *that might be too long.* So she started 'phoning. At the second call, she struck paydirt. Lindsey said, "Yes. I remember that. I found it in the washing-up rack, when I went in to set the tea things up. It was the Sunday just after Reverend Peter died. I took it across to the parish office, meaning to ask Mary to add it in to her notices. I thought it might be her brother's. We were at such sixes and sevens that it completely slipped my mind. I suppose in the chaos and packing up it ended up in the rectory, and got put away by someone. So... um I'm going to join the fly-tyers for their evening session every fortnight," she said airily. "You wouldn't like to come along as well, would you?"

"Well, maybe one day. I am not sure that it's my thing," said Joy.

"I wouldn't have thought it would be mine, but I'm finding it fascinating. Oh, um, I won't be in church this

Sunday. I'll be away for the weekend. I'm not deserting you or anything, I promise."

"I'm relieved to hear that. I have a small enough congregation already."

"Oh no! I'll be back, next week. I just haven't been away in, forever. I feel like a little girl going on holiday."

"You certainly sound very happy about it. Enjoy it!"

After a few more pleasantries, Joy put down the 'phone, and sat there, thinking. The lunchbox had come from the church hall, four days after Peter Hallam's death. She took a deep breath, and 'phoned Isabella. Her name had been on the list, anyway.

She described the box.

"Yes. I find it in the church," said Isabella. "Someone leave it there, with a little meat pie in it, and a cup-cake with the pink icing and the little heart decorations. So pretty. I ask, but no one says they know. So I throw the pie and cake away and wash the box."

Somehow, that box was tied to Peter Hallam's death... and Madeleine Denton, in the church, of all places, on the day of his death. The question for Joy, now, was whether she immediately told the police, or tried to find out more.

Given the way things worked out here, it seemed important not to jump to conclusions too hastily. But she needed some kind of local input, and for that Tom Truman seemed to be the calmest person, and the most able to give her that information. So she 'phoned him next, and told him what she now knew.

"Hmm. This sounds a bit like Donald, all over again, Reverend Joy. Someone who dislikes Christianity kills the priest. Let's look at motive – yes she, and her mother have had a long record of little pokes at the Church, mainly just to be irritating and prove they can. I recall Zenobia sitting in her car in the street outside the service playing Black Sabbath at ear-shattering volume a few years back. Maddy did the same with her bike. But that's a long step from there to murder in the church. And why bring lunch with you if you are going to do it? But I'll try and ask her on Monday, when her mother is not around. Look I know: 'She's a good girl really, wouldn't hurt a fly' is what most friends and relations say about cold-blooded murderesses, but Madeleine and my daughter are still friends and were right through school. There's a bit of her mother in her, but she's more like her father."

"Er. He seems to have a substance abuse problem."

"Anything to escape reality, especially if that reality includes Zenobia. Joe's all right. He's just weak... I mean willed, rather than physically. Zenobia tells him what to do, and he either gets stoned or does it, even if he doesn't like it. But Maddy, no, I don't think she'd kill anyone, except maybe herself."

"Suicidal?"

"No, that bike of hers. Anyway, I'll ask her on Monday, if I can get her nose out of a book for long enough."

"Well. Thank you," said Joy.

"Not a problem. I shall see you on Sunday. I'm dying of curiosity to see if a certain member of the congregation is there."

"Oh?" said Joy.

"Yes, I was asked for some advice, man-to-man this week," said Tom, the laughter in his voice apparent. "And if there is one thing about Felixtown, if you don't want the entire town talking about your taking an interest, you'd better go away for a weekend. That's what I said, and he's cancelled a fishing trip we were going on together."

Joy hoped it was quite a convincing fit of coughing that she had.

Still when she put down the 'phone. She was left thinking... That meant waiting until Monday.

A still voice in her head said: *Don't wait.* But how could she do otherwise? Then it occurred to her that Izzy seemed to know Madeleine – at least well enough to ask advice about boyfriends. Which, if Joy was any judge was not a subject younger girls would be anything but wary about with older girls they did not know and trust.

So she decided to try Izzy. "Yes," said Jeanie. "She's home and you're welcome to talk to her. Mind you," she said with a laugh. "I don't remember that my having a boyfriend suddenly made me do math homework. If we'd known, we'd have encouraged one earlier."

So Joy got to talk to Izzy, who had obviously promoted her, in the rank of adults, to 'almost human'. Joy knew that was quite flattering. "Yeah, like she used to stop the older kids beating up Cam," she said, when asked about Maddy.

"Do you think you could ask her if she could please come and talk to me? Soon? Without her mother knowing... Zenobia seems to have taken me in dislike."

There was a silence. Then Izzy said: "You know, like, Reverend Duck... uh sorry that's what my Grandad calls you, Mads is... well, she's not like goodie-two-shoes. I mean she was in trouble for...uh, smoking at school. And other stuff... uh."

"That's okay, Izzy. Tell her I've been going through some things in the rectory, and have something of hers, I would like to give back. And, um, if you can, tell her I'm all right to talk to. I like to smooth the waves, not splash people, just to prove that I can."

There was another thoughtful silence. "Like, I guess I can tell her that."

"I do my best," said Joy, hoping Mary, Donald, and Cameron would not prove her a liar.

"I can nick off to there at break. I know she's off just after two."

"I'd be happy to meet her any place she likes. Here, or anywhere she likes."

"Cool. I'll tell her."

And with that Joy had to be content. She half expected a call from Mary, but that didn't happen.

She did get the call from Mary the next day. "I thought that you'd like to know it went all right. We ended up talking until after two in the morning. If I hadn't sent them off home to bed, they'd be talking still," said Mary. "Donald is still putting a few objections up, but we've won, I think."

"No, Mary. You, Cameron, and most of all Peter Hallam, have won. With a little help from God," said Joy, feeling immense relief.

"With a lot of help from his local representative! Anyway, do let me know what you hear from your Dean."

"I will just as soon as I have anything I can tell you. These legal issues take time, you know."

"Oh I know. But do you know what that idiot Donald said to me? He got there just before Cam. He made some crack about Isobel Jenkins not being a bad start, but hoped that Cam would find a dish among these arts students. I bit his head off. Told him his father found a society beauty, he had found a stupid beauty queen, and maybe Cam should learn from his father's bad example, instead of being as dumb as he was."

"You said he had a rough time growing up."

"He was a bit neglected. I mean, plenty of money, just not much attention. He's tried not to do that with Cam, I'll grant. And of course at school, well he was too bright and not too sporty. And sport is pretty important out here."

"He probably wanted a trophy wife to bring home to show off," said Joy. "Anyway. The discussion went all right, other than that?"

"Yes. Of course, Donald is determined Cam should follow the money, but we can work around it. Cameron is just so stunned that he's going to be allowed to do what he actually want to do, that he's happy to go along... for now. I can see this will be like herding cats."

None-the-less, it sounded as if she was pleased with the job of cat-herder, thought Joy. She wondered if Izzy had managed to speak to Madeleine Denton. Well, there was no use thinking endlessly about it, so she turned herself determinedly to other tasks. Of course, trying determinedly not to think about any subject, be it pink elephants or just how the girl could tie into Peter Hallam's death, that was exactly what she thought about all day. Joy thought she heard a motorbike half a dozen times too.

Eventually she picked up the pink and purple lunch-box and walked across to the church, and, unlocking the small back door into the vestry, she walked down between the rows of pews.

CHAPTER 17

Later, Madeleine would say that she had no idea why she actually did it, except maybe that she needed to tell somebody before she went through with her plan for the afternoon. There was a reasonably straight piece of road, she'd be able to get the bike up to at least a hundred and forty before she hit those stupid imposing stone gate-posts. It should be quick enough, surely? Especially if she took her helmet off first and tossed it away. Let her hair blow in the slipstream one last time.

It still took her three attempts to get herself to go back to that church.

Joy knew none of that, when she chose to sit on the pew near the back of the little church, half a dozen steps from the vestibule, with its glass fronted cupboard full of hymn books and prayer-books, and the door to the toilet and hand-basin.

She just saw that the young woman in the black bike leathers, knee-high boots, and crimson hair, had a very white face when she came in through the vestry door. And she knew that the front door of the church was locked behind both of them.

God moved in mysterious ways she thought, reading something in Madeleine's gait as she walked down the three stairs from the chancel around the altar towards her.

That suddenly clarified something in Joy's mind. And like a vision dimly seen, the rest of the picture began to form.

Words, however seemed to be having trouble forming for Madeleine as she looked down at Joy. Her mouth worked several times. Finally she came out with: "Iz said you had something to say to me?" It was almost an accusation.

"Thank you for coming." said Joy.

"You've got a cheek after shopping me to the cop and getting me that fine. I should..." Madeleine raised a hand, and then lowered it.

"I've certainly never shopped you for anything," said Joy. She did not add: 'yet'.

"So who set the cop on me last Saturday?" demanded Madeleine.

"Ah. When you came past us, while we were gardening?" asked Joy.

"Yes. I've got a four hundred dollar fine... Not, not that that matters."

"Of course it matters! Look, it wasn't me or anyone in the gardening group. You could ask anyone who was there... Tom Truman perhaps. Or Arthur Ambleside-Smith. He was trying to talk to me just then." It occurred to her as she said it, that that was a tactless choice. It must have been because the young woman promptly sat down on the floor, and then put her head between her knees. Joy hastily got up. But she got pushed away by a hand.

"I'm fine," said Madeleine in a voice that said she really wasn't. "I'm just feeling lousy and I shouldn't have come and I don't know why I did."

"You could tell me about it," said Joy.

Madeleine looked at her. Plainly didn't like what she saw. Well, Joy knew that she was nothing much to look at. A small, slightly plump woman, with a simple bobbed haircut, a touch of grey starting on the temples, with a clerical collar above her plain blue blouse. A long step from leather with a lot of zippers.

"You wouldn't f...ing understand," she snapped. "You couldn't. Oh hell. I'm going," she started to get up.

"You know," said Joy, thoughtfully, injecting as much calm into her voice as she could. "I probably don't understand. I have been pregnant, alone and in trouble, but it takes more to understand someone than just a bit of shared experience. It helps, of course. But I'm lucky. I have other help, and he understands things I don't. And he says that just because I don't understand doesn't mean I can't try to help. And I will, I promise."

Madeleine stopped half way up on her knees, and sat down again. She gaped. Finally she managed a choked: "You?"

"Well, someone who looked a lot like me, but was, oh, fifteen years younger, and a lot more scared of everything than you are," admitted Joy with a twinkle of a smile. "You know, everyone comes from somewhere. Priests don't just pop into existence any more than bowls of petunias do over Magrathea." The reference to the Douglas Adam's book was in itself a test... to see how that piece of her puzzle fitted. It might be possible to help if she knew a little more.

Maddy might have been stunned, but she obviously knew the reference by her reply: "But what about very surprised sperm whales?"

"They're infinitely improbable, so that means you probably get them nine times out of ten."

"You're... um, not quite what I expected," said Madeleine. Her tone was still wary... but it was just a little less brittle.

"Well, I hope a priest who knows the Hitchhiker's Guide to the Galaxy will be easier to talk to than one who doesn't. I can say 'Don't panic', at least. Maybe that makes me less alarming?"

"You'd have to say 'don't panic' a lot... I'm... not in a great place. I suppose you know that too. And I'm starting to feel like the whale."

"Well, you're not one, so I'll have to see what can be done about catching you. That's a good thing because churches are harder to clean than alien worlds, once splattered with whale meat."

That almost drew a smile, but it did draw the oft-quoted response. "I bet you're thinking 'Oh no, not again'."

Joy drew herself up and did her best pose of a look of affronted dignity, with a smile to show it was in jest. "I hope I don't even look like a bowl of petunias. And I am not about to blame Arthur, even for the first time."

***

The Hitchhiker's Guide to the galaxy had been the right thing to mention, thought Joy, patting the sobbing girl's shoulder. *Even if Arthur hadn't.* "There, there. It'll be all right," she said. *It was a terribly inadequate thing to say, but on the spur of the moment it was always the best she could do.*

The woman in her bike leathers sat up, tossed her flame red and purple dyed fringe out of her eyes defiantly, proving that this time it wasn't. "No, it won't," she said in a voice full of hurt.

"I know. A stupid thing to say, isn't it?" A detached, calm piece of her mind said: *This was the last person to see Peter Hallam alive. Or at least, the one who reported him dead. And if Inspector Morse was right, that meant there was a very good chance that she'd killed him.* But that was on TV. This was real life, and tattoos or no, this was someone who needed her help.

Madeleine sniffed again. Joy gave her a tissue from her pocket. She blew, noisily. Wiped her eyes. Pushed the tissue into her sleeve, and looked at Joy again. "You're about as unlike my mother as any human can be, but you both say the same dumb things," she said, twisting her black-nail-varnish garnished fingers into a nervous knot.

"I think all humans do. It's the best we can manage at the time. Take it as it is meant: we'll try. It's our way of saying we care."

"I thought it was a priest's job to tell me I was a slut and to get out of here."

"If I remember rightly the advice I got on the subject was to let him who was without sin cast the first stone." That earned Joy a blank look. Well, the girl had probably never come across it before. "I mean I'd be a fine one to choose to do that. I've been there."

"My mother will," said the girl gloomily. "Never mind stones. It will be me out of the house. Except I'm not going to..."

"Why? Because you've got pregnant? I thought she believed in free love. That ends up in free babies sometimes. Only they're not so free, I believe," said Joy.

"No. Getting preggers is fine. She's been telling me she wants a grandchild for years... since I was about fourteen, but it's who the father is."

Joy bit her lip, "Ah. True. Well..."

"Yeah. She'd have been on my case, morning, noon and night, because the father must pay maintenance for what he did wrong. You don't know her, but it's like a dripping tap, honestly. So I came here... It was better than leaving the bastard a note. Don't tell anyone else... but tell him I loved him. A lot. Even..." she broke off again, sobbing. Joy held her.

Eventually she took a deep sniff and wiped her nose and eyes. The tissue wasn't really up to the job, but right now, Joy felt that comfort was more important than fetching tissues. "I will, if you want me to. But... look, part of my job is dealing with, and trying to help, unhappy people. Reading their expressions, reading what they leave unsaid. I don't always get it right. I didn't know how you felt, obviously. But I did see Arthur... looking after you, when you rode past. And some of his statements... now that I know a little more, make a great deal more sense. I don't know what has come between you, but I am sure that he is heartbroken and upset about you too."

That produced even more tears. "I... I didn't need to hear that." But it was plain, by the way that she held onto Joy that she did.

"So, I know something of the family difficulties, but those can be overcome or worked around. Can I try to mend it?" ask Joy.

Maddie shook her head. "I'll just go. I... I'm not going to kill myself any more. But, I don't know where to go, or how to manage. Can... can you just tell me where to start? I mean, a place I can go? Like a shelter or something? I haven't really got any money."

"Of course I can," said Joy. "Right up front you can stay in the rectory with me for a day or two if you need to." Joy caught the start of a shake of the head. "If you want to get away from Felixtown, I have a lot of contacts elsewhere. But it'll make it a lot easier for me to help if I know as much as possible. What are you running from?"

Joy caught Maddie's sudden look around at the church. "I... can't tell you. Please. Once you found that lunchbox I knew I had to go. Like either go away or... die. And I didn't want to go away."

This was incredibly hard. Joy searched for the right words. In the end she said: "Was it an accident?"

"It must have been. He wouldn't have done it on purpose! He's... he's not like that!" There was a frantic plea for reassurance in that cry.

The next piece of the puzzle dropped into place. Joy hugged Maddy hard. "I think," she said then, holding Maddy by both shoulders, "that I can tell you something really, really important about traffic fines, that may get you to go and kiss Sergeant Grogan and invite him to your wedding. Fines have a precise time on them and are signed by the issuing officer."

"What?" The poor girl was utterly bewildered now.

"I bet you didn't know that Arthur was clocked speeding... I would guess driving to this church to meet you and Reverend Peter – so that's what the AM in the diary stood for!... Just after 10.30 in the morning. He has the most bomb-proof alibi in the world. He was getting a ticket from

Sergeant Grogan and another policeman when the call came in about Reverend Peter being found dead."

Madeleine looked at Joy, eyes full of a desperate hope. "You swear? You mean... it wasn't Arthur?"

"I will put my hand on a Bible and swear to that, happily. For me that's the most binding oath I can make. It could not possibly have been your Arthur. He is as innocent as it is possible to be, even when caught speeding."

The look on Maddy's face was worth five million speeding fines. "Oh, I've been so unhappy..." she was managing to smile now, through her tears. "Oh, thank you, so, so, so very much. I didn't know how he could have done it. But it **had** to be him... Peter promised us there'd be no-one else here. The front door was locked."

"Suppose you tell me exactly what happened. Actually, suppose we go over to the rectory, because I bet you need some tea. I'm very like Arthur Dent in that way. And I promise we're going to make this right."

"It's going to be pretty hard," said Maddy, but she didn't resist being led out and across to the rectory kitchen. "I... I messed up. I texted him to tell him never to call me again. Never to speak to me, never to show any sign of knowing me. And to throw his mobile in the river so they couldn't trace his calls. I don't know how to tell him..."

"I don't think mobile records work quite like that. But it doesn't matter, and I do think that soonest is best with telling people."

"I don't know how? I... I told him never to speak to me again. And then... and then I tried to talk to him. And it's just so f...ing hard. He never answers the 'phone. It's always his bloody mother or father. I tried a few times. And he's never in town, and I can't go out to their farm. I've been to those big stone posts a dozen times... That's why I did the wheelies... I was trying to tell him."

"I'll sort that out. You make tea. And when did you last eat?"

That got a watery chuckle. "You're starting to sound like you live here. I didn't have breakfast. I tend to throw that up. But now I could eat a horse... maybe it's, it's the relief or something."

Joy clicked her tongue. "I'm all out of horse, and the supermarket doesn't carry it. I think they expect you to catch your own. But I have bread, butter, cheese, vegemite, lettuce, tomatoes and if you want more than that I only have the eggs that came from Tom Truman – they came in your lunch box, as it happens. Did you know the one left in the church actually belonged to his daughter? You had hers, and she had yours. Now – you fix some food, lots. I know you're good at it. I shall summon Arthur, and he always eats a great deal."

That drew a real smile. "Poor guy loves his food, and, um, he says his mother could louse up boiling water. But she controls the menu, because she's got to watch his old man's diet." She swallowed. "That... that's why I brought some pies and, and a little cake I made for him to the church. Only... when the priest was dead, I forgot it. And then there was the lunch box left there. I was scared if they started to ask me questions I'd..."

Joy was dialing, and waved her at the bread-bin, and the 'fridge. Inevitably she got Penelope. "Good... afternoon, I see it is," said Joy looking at the clock on the wall. "I wonder if I could have a word with Arthur about some alterations to the frontage of the new part of the church."

"Oh that would be Mr. Truman you need to speak to," said Penelope. "He does all the repairs and maintenance. He's here right now, discussing leasing some fishing access."

And Joy heard her put down the phone, and call Tom Truman. Well, that would just have to do. "Hello, Reverend Joy. I'll give you a call when I get home," said Tom. "Unless it's urgent, that is?"

"It's urgent, but on the life-and-death urgency I've affected a temporary repair, that I believe will hold for now. Still, it is one of those things best fixed as soon as possible.

And you can't do it, I am afraid. It needs Arthur. And... don't speed into town."

"So can it wait ten or fifteen minutes?" Tom asked. "I've got some tools in the ute. What is it, brickwork or wood?"

"It's the very stuff of the Church, Tom Truman. And could be expensive, so we need our accountant, and we need Arthur to do the job. You can't get into the place that needs working on."

"I'll have him out of his office and at the church with me before you can say Jack Robinson. The very stuff of the church won't wait," he said. And she could hear the amusement in his voice.

"But we'll be waiting, however long it takes."

Joy discovered that Maddy hadn't been paying any attention to the food side, but was watching her intently, obviously listening in. "Tom Truman will bring him in, shortly," she said, comfortingly.

"I don't know what I am going to say," Maddy said, twisting her hands together.

"It'll sort itself out," said Joy, calmly.

"So, um, do you think those lies will fool his mother? Arthur says she always stands and listens to him on the phone."

Joy smiled. "Lies? I'll have you know that I'm a woman of the cloth. The church isn't a building, Maddy. We are the church. The very stuff of the church itself is hearts and souls, flesh and blood. Tom would understand that. And Arthur has altered your frontage."

"Um. I haven't told him," admitted Maddy.

"Oh. I see. Well, let's see if it matters. I don't think it will," said Joy, re-assessing yet again. She'd made an error of judgment, again.

"I didn't want to tell him. In case, um in case he thought I was trying to force him. The getting married bit was his idea. I said we didn't have to, but... he said it meant a lot to him. A public sign of commitment."

"I think he's right," said Joy. She didn't say, *and brave too*, but thought it. Romeo might have had an easier time of it with Juliet. Marriage was at least an accepted norm on both sides of that relationship.

"I did like that way of putting it... once I got used to it. I wasn't sure about the whole church thing..." she looked at Joy, realized who she was talking to, colored slightly and gave a shy smile, which did a great deal for her face. "Um, I am beginning to get it, I think."

"Well, I hope so. I presume you'd have to at least accept it, if you were talking to Reverend Hallam about getting married in the church."

"Uh. We hadn't really decided to do that. I... I wasn't keen. And neither was the priest, really. He wasn't sure we were doing the right thing, I think. But Arthur wanted Peter Hallam to help him in telling his father. Arthur thinks that the Major will have a heart attack if he gets upset."

Joy snorted. "It is possible, but I have certainly seen him very angry and still alive afterwards. It does show that Arthur is considerate."

"Too much so! His bloody mother **uses** it against him. She won't let him do ANYTHING!"

"Ah well," said Joy. "I love doing weddings. I would love to perform the ceremony of marriage for you, if you decided that that was what you'd like. And whatever you decide, I will stand your friend."

"Mother would say you're just trying to catch me, trap me with honeyed words," said Madeleine, not quite suspiciously, but somewhat warily.

Joy laughed. "Well. They say you can catch more flies with honey than with vinegar. And anyway, that is the commandment we of the church were given by Christ himself. That we love one another as he loves us. It's important to me to do that." She left it there for now. There'd be a better time, later. Instead she said: "So, I'll butter the bread, you decide what goes on it, and while you're doing that you can tell me what actually happened that Wednesday."

"Yeah. Well, I got there a little early, like I did the time before, but the priest had obviously remembered and the door was open. So I went in... I was just going to get a book out of my pocket... but I opened the lunch box to check that the icing had made it there in one piece... and the smell of the pie made me feel really sick. Especially in the morning, some things just set me off. So, uh, I went out into that lobby – I used the loo there last time, and went in there to throw up. Like I was hoping Arthur wouldn't think I'd run out on him. I didn't have my mobile with me, so couldn't even send him a message. I mean, the time before had been a bit fraught. We'd, um, had a bit of an argument with the priest. And I did hear some noises... Sort of someone trying to shout, but I had my head in the toilet. I just couldn't stop puking. I came out as quickly as I could. And Peter was just lying there in the middle of aisle. His face was sort of purple. I don't know anything about first aid or stuff like that. I mean, I felt for his pulse, and then I ran out the back... Ran to his 'phone. Called ooo. I guess I was kind of hysterical, but they said they'd send an ambulance. So I came out to go back, and there was Mary Truman's car, pulling up. I panicked. I mean I couldn't explain why I was there. I didn't know what to do. So ran back to my bike in the dunny-lane. I thought... Arthur got... defensive about me, last time. I thought he must have got angry and k...killed Peter, panicked and then run off."

"I think it will turn into just particularly bad timing, and nothing to do with you at all," said Joy, knowing it wasn't much of an alibi. But she had faith something more would show up. "I hope none of this is making you feel nauseous."

"Oh no. It was just the steak and kidney pie smell."

"Yes, I remember smells setting me off too. Even ones I liked."

"So. Um. What happened to your baby? You weren't just... saying that?"

Joy sighed. It was never an easy part of her own life to revisit, even if there had been a reason for everything. "I had a miscarriage. Ended up in hospital," said Joy. "It... wasn't a very happy time in my life. But that memory too has got better with time. I am very blessed, now. It is not something I talk about much. So tell me, how did you and Arthur ever get together?"

"Oh. I went to a sci-fi conference in Hobart. A tiny thing. A bit too literary for me, and not many young fans... but still. It was cool being with other fen. And there was this guy in an Imperial Storm Trooper outfit. I had my Kitsune mask and outfit on, and he barely knew me, anyway, from Felixtown. And his room was next to the one I was sharing with Tom's daughter Katie. It isn't her scene really, but she came along to check it out with me... and um, this guy and I talked books a bit at the masquerade. He had to drink through a straw, and then I'd just gone to bed after the filk-singing – He'd been there too, and it was about two in the morning. He knocked on my door. I, um, told him to get lost. And he said he was so sorry to disturb me, but please could I help him, he couldn't get the helmet off, the catch at the back had broken. So, I went out, and I got his head out of it eventually. It was pretty funny, trying. It took me quite a long time and we were laughing a lot. And then... the helmet came off and there he was."

"I bet you were just a little surprised," said Joy with a snort of laughter.

"Yeah. And how! I mean he was supposed to be a real creep, according to my mother. I'd never actually spoken to him, because they don't ever come into the shop. Anyhow, I was swearing at him and Katie wakes up and comes out, and asks me why I'm chewing out Arthur. See, she knew him a little, he'd been finishing up at Uni when she got there, and had been kind, and had given her a lift home a couple of times, and hadn't had my mother's version of him. Anyway... we ended up talking all night. He reads the same books as I do, and yeah, he was just nice. I mean, I don't think I'd ever had a guy not trying to come on to me." She blushed slightly.

Joy smiled inwardly. She'd bet it had been a challenge of sorts.

There was a knock at the door, and Maddie dropped her knife, and took a step behind Joy. Joy turned a little, and put an arm around her shoulder.

"Repair crew," said Tom, cheerfully from outside.

"Come in," said Joy, and they did.

CHAPTER 18

The one thing Madeleine need not have worried about thought Joy, with some amusement, was what to say. She hadn't managed to get a word out so far. Arthur's "Mad, I love you!" on seeing her, was not exactly a Shakespearean soliloquy, or a beautifully crafted sonnet, but was exactly the right thing to have said.

The two of them would doubtless get around to talking later, when they'd finished kissing. Possibly when Tom Truman stopped laughing. It wasn't going to be simple for these two, but it was worth doing, Joy decided.

But she underestimated Arthur. He still kept hold of his love, but at least he turned to talk to Joy. "I killed him. Not Maddy."

Joy shook her head. "She didn't, and unless you used mind bullets, or some imaginary science fictional device from a mile away, you didn't either," said Joy. "And we'll have to deal with that later. And we will. The point right now, is that Madeleine needs you, and has been desperately trying to protect you, just as you have just lied to protect her. It's very caring, but the truth is better. You can lie to me, but not to my boss."

"She said she'd like to marry us, Arthur," said Madeleine, "And... um."

"The rest of it, Madeleine," said Joy with mock sternness.

"Well, um, I was going to say I'd like that too, but I have to tell you, uh, I'm pregnant. So you don't have to."

Tom no longer able to support himself, clutching his sides fell onto the sofa. "That's," he gasped, "The wrong script."

"No," said Joy. "It's the right one. She's being serious, Tom. Stop laughing. And yes, I would love to perform a marriage ceremony for the two of you."

"You know, Mad," said Arthur still holding on to her, cementing Joy's opinion that he'd make a good partner for her. "It doesn't matter at all to me. And, er, it might be a good thing, for my father."

"Yes, I can see the Major telling you that you have to do the honorable thing now," said Tom, with a twinkle in his eye, and a smile still on his lips.

"It's not a joke to us, Commander Tom," said Maddy. "I thought... you might be on our side."

"And so I am," said Tom. "I'm a pragmatic old seaman, Maddy and Arthur. You're old enough, ugly enough, both of you, to be able to make decisions for yourselves... and of course the future generations. The funny part is, firstly, the fact that I didn't see it, though it was right under my nose, and secondly, that it is going to give Felixtown the excitement it craves. Now, you two need to stop all the dramatics, ideally crack a bottle of champagne if Reverend Duck's got one, and start to work out the practical details. And we should eat the sandwiches I see there, because I haven't had lunch yet."

Joy nodded. "Your two families are complications, but I think Tom is right, subtly and silently really isn't going to work, unless you both leave the area. And I would be sad to see that happen. But if that is what it needs, that is what it needs. There are a few formalities which stand in the way of a celebrant doing the ceremony right here and now, but no matter what your families say or do, as I have said, I'd be delighted to do so for you."

Arthur bit his lip. "Whatever happens I am going to marry Madeleine. But, Reverend Joy, um, leaving here would be hard on the Major."

"I don't think his health is that bad," said Tom. "Your mother just uses it to lean on you, boy."

Arthur looked uncomfortable. "Look, it's not just his heart, and she really believes it is dicky, but, well, I run the finances. They were in terrible shape when I got back from Uni. Things are better now, but honestly, I could leave them to sink, but I don't do that kind of thing."

"And my mother will just throw me out of the house, and the shop, the minute I tell her. I'll be lucky if she doesn't attack me. And er, I don't really have much money. I could sell my bike I suppose. But I still owe quite a lot on it," said Maddy, showing no sign of letting go of Arthur.

"Tch," said Tom. "I think the two of you need to remember Admiral Farragut's advice: 'Damn the torpedoes, full speed ahead.' Maddy, if you need a place to sleep, come out to the farm. My daughter Katie has just announced that she wants to chuck in the course she's been doing at Uni, and this will give me a wonderful opportunity to ask her to come home, to help her poor enfeebled father with her best friend from school. Arthur, you need to man up with the Major. And as soon as possible, move out. The town could use an accountant, and your parents don't need you out there running errands, let alone their business. You can do the finances just as well from a bit further off."

Joy had gone and looked in the fridge, where, as she recalled, someone had failed to throw out an elderly bottle of champagne. She brought it to the table, along with the sandwiches. "Sit down and let's talk about it. You'll have to make do with wine glasses."

The cork had just popped, when there was a knock at the door. They all looked up like guilty school-children, as the door, which was not locked, opened.

Donald van den Vaestermark, took in the scene with his quick, sharp eyes, and turned to Izzy and Cam, next to him, and said in a voice of decidedly unholy amusement for a rectory, "See. I told you so. That's organized religion for you. Debauched. Drinking in the middle of the day."

226

"Come in and shut up," said Tom. "And have a glass of champagne to celebrate our happy couple's engagement."

"You know, I think I will," said Donald. "I was just dropping the kids here in a public show of approval. But the pharmacy can stay closed for a few extra minutes. My son and Izzy have been given detention today," he said cheerfully, "and you can drink to that too."

"So, like, can I be a bridesmaid?" asked Izzy.

"You two don't seem in the least surprised," said Joy. "And where is the third member of your crew?"

"Oh she's coming along the back way. Didn't want her ma to know. Like, this is Felixtown, Reverend Joy. Meggles and I saw them kissing out in the dunny lane. Megs even drew them in her last picture."

"Well, it does seem as if the town had enough people trying and failing to keep secrets," said Joy, laughing.

"Except for who killed Peter Hallam," said Tom.

"Oh I think that answer was in front of us all the time. No-one killed him. It was just a tragic accident which no-one could have anticipated, as I will explain to whoever comes to investigate. They don't think it was murder either, or they'd have been here. And if you think about it, all this has done is to expose us to the fire, to burn away our worse natures, the nasty things we thought, the faith we failed at, so we could see the true metal," said Joy.

Tom looked quizzically at her. "I suppose we'll all know in good time, is what you're saying."

She nodded. "Yes. I need to talk to my superiors, and to the police. But I think, oddly, that Peter Hallam managed to achieve more for Felixtown, and its church, in dying than he could have done in any other way. And in the end, death is such a small thing to a Christian. We know what happens to us then. It's the living we leave behind that find it hard."

***

That afternoon, after they'd all left, two of them to face their families in what was bound to be explosive meetings,

Joy called Dean Mellors. He listened, and then said he thought that Bishop Michael should hear it all too. It took a long time to tell and explain. But the end result was that the bishop said that he, personally, would talk to someone in the police service, as there seemed no reason why this should drag on any longer.

And then, of course, there was nothing but to wait, a wait that was eventually broken by a call from Tom. "I've got your little prodigal lambs here, for tonight. They're mildly mauled, but surprisingly happy about it. Apparently the Major did have himself a towering, bellowing rage, but, according to his admiring fiancée, the young man stayed calm and stood firm, I suspect for the first time in his life, myself. The Major didn't die. And I wish I could have been a fly on the wall because he even lived through hearing his son's future wife telling her mother-in-law to stop bullying Arthur."

Joy couldn't help chuckling. "I suspect that will be the first of many such instances, if those two ever speak to each other again."

"Oh, we'll work on it," said Tom, cheerfully. He didn't specify what they'd work on, or how, and Joy knew better than to ask.

The next morning Joy found that the town was abuzz with the story, and all of them naturally wanted to tell her about it. She had a string of both visitors and calls. The story that seemed to delight people most was that Zenobia had thrown a spectacular temper tantrum with a customer that morning, who had innocently inquired after Madeleine. She was no daughter of hers, and would never set foot in the place again. "And a lot more that's not fit to tell to a priest," said the elderly woman, primly. "That poor girl!" Joy wondered if Zenobia would ever reconcile, or accept her daughter's partner, let alone their marriage. She seemed the sort who would nurture a grudge just as well as the Major could, if not better.

However, about the latter, she was wrong. Donald called a little later in the morning. "Is that the infamous Reverend Duck, the destroyer of families, scourge of the peaceful countryside?" he asked.

"I do my humble best," said Joy.

"Well, you'll be happy to know I've just had the pleasure of continuing your excellent work in our community. Penelope called out Dr. Hammond last night. And apparently he was very rude. But the fellow did make the Major come in for an ECG this morning, which was, to her disappointment, very normal."

"I think Arthur will be relieved to hear that," said Joy.

"Ah yes, but my work did not finish there," said Donald, his voice positively scintillating with delight at his mischief. "I congratulated him heartily when he came into the pharmacy, after his visit to the surgery, on the magnificent coup he had finally achieved in his war with Zenobia. Telling him he must be so proud of his son to completely outwit the woman, and how a church wedding was going to gall Zenobia until she died."

"And his reaction was?" asked Joy.

"Hilarious. He didn't know what to say. It nearly made his moustache wilt. And there were a good four customers, who just happened to be in the pharmacy at the time. Pure chance of course. They would never have come in just because they saw the Land Cruiser draw up at the pharmacy. And all of them congratulated him, and told him they hoped it would it would be a big flashy wedding, to really rub Zenobia's nose in it. Oh, and the woman who told Penelope she must be so delighted to be going to be a grandmother was priceless. News gets around."

"Oh my word," exclaimed Joy.

"Oh, it didn't end there. They wanted to collect some bit of machinery for the farm from old Mac. I don't quite know what he said to them, but the Major came out of there looking like a stunned mullet. He could barely walk straight. And people were stopping their cars to congratulate them."

Curiosity got the better of Joy. She went down to 'Junk and Mechanical Repairs' and asked.

"Well now," said old Mac. "I just told him his son and the girl were driving up to visit old man Denton this morning, to tell him they're getting married. My suggestion to them, as it happens, but I didn't tell him that. He's in the care facility up at Hardacre. Old Denton doesn't see eye to eye with his son about Zenobia. He hadn't had any real contact with the girl as a result. But he actually owns the property the shop is on, as well as the farm, that's leased out to Masterson's. And he has told me a good many times that he doesn't want to see his son p... uh waste away what the old guy put together, and he and Zenobia hate each other's guts. I'd be very surprised if he doesn't leave it to his new great grandchild, what with the girl getting properly married in church to a respectable young bloke. Family means a lot when you are getting on a bit."

So Joy was not that surprised when, at about three that afternoon, the Major Ambleside-Smith rather huffily called her, to ask her to arrange a reconciliatory meeting, and to talk about a Church wedding... "After all, the boy is doing the right thing, eh."

"Oh I think he is," Joy was able to answer in truth and with a clear conscience.

Later, Joy said to Mary, who had come in to copy some new hymn sheets: "I agreed. I gave him a long lecture about the wisdom of being nice to Madeleine. And the kiddies are both willing enough to mend fences. But really, Maddy's a better Christian and she's never been to a church service."

"Well, don't you always say God moves in mysterious ways?" said Mary.

***

The service the next day was fuller than usual, even if Tom was amused at the postmistress's absence. Maddy, Tom's daughter, and Arthur were there. They didn't share a pew with the Major and his wife, but they did sit in the one in front of them.

During the first hymn, Joy noticed that two people had slipped into the back of the church. One was a somewhat cleaned up fisherman. The other was Donald van den Vaestermark. Joy looked at her sermon, at the cross on the altar, and crumpled up her prepared sermon. Sometimes you had to go with faith and faith alone.

She looked directly at the back of the church. "Christians across the world gather on Sunday to worship God together. We are commanded to so. But our God does not need to be wound up on Sunday. Our God is omnipotent, limitlessly wise, and limitlessly powerful, so far beyond our mortal understanding that we must fail to grasp even the tiniest fragment of his wonder. If we believe, we accept that. He never ever needs winding up. With us or without us, he is. His name is I AM, as was told to Moses in Exodus 3:14. I AM the alpha and the omega. I AM every thing that ever was, or will be. Not a sparrow falls, let alone a man or woman dies that I AM does not know of their passing, and the whys, wherefores and how it happened. We... we are not powerful, or wise. We are fallible, we see the worst in each other. God sees not just the best, but everything." She paused, looking at all of them, her little flock, black sheep, and whiter ones, old rams with curling mustachios.

"We are not winding God up on Sunday. We are showing we are willing to let him wind us up again instead, because we are weak and mortal. We cannot see what he can see. We fail often, both ourselves and those we love. He forgives us for that, and asks us to forgive each other. He gives us the strength and courage to try anew. To let the power of his love flow into us again. Our little spring of faith runs down very quickly, and we fail at the new and great commandment, as set out in John 13:34 that we should love one another as God loves us."

She opened her arms and heart to them. "God is Love. And we can celebrate today, that his love has triumphed. I am overjoyed to tell all of you that Madeleine and Arthur have become affianced and are to be married here in our church on Saturday in three weeks from now."

That, considering the time the congratulations took, was quite long enough for a sermon. Besides, what more could she say? A sermon didn't need to be eternal to be immortal.

After the service Donald said, at the doorway. "You needn't think I came for the challenge of your sermon, although I'll grant that you did it better than I thought you would. I came because this reprobate," he jerked his thumb at Madeleine's father, "came out to my farm yesterday afternoon to ask me where he could find his daughter. I said I had no idea but she'd probably be here with the sky fairy glee club in the morning. He said he couldn't come here. I said if I could, he'd survive. I told him to be up, sober and dressed at his boat this morning, and we'd come together."

"Thank you," said Joy. She understood, a little, what the man was trying to do, and what it meant for him to do this.

"Call it a little pay forward."

Joe Denton greeted her perfunctorily, and hung about to speak to his daughter. In this he had some difficulty as she was being rather effectively surrounded. Eventually he came to Joy, who was drinking tea, standing next to Tom, and said, slightly belligerently. "She's seen me but won't come and talk to me! I need to tell her she's my daughter, and it's also my home, as much as Zenobia's. She's welcome to come home and stay there."

"What she needs isn't a roof where she'll get yelled at, and mocked, and given a hard time," said Tom. "She's got a place to stay right now until the wedding, Katie is looking after her like a mother hen. But, Joe, what she needs is her father, not stoned out of his head, but sober, washed and brushed, dressed up and ready to walk her down that aisle on the day. That'll mean more to her than anything else. You think you can do that, or are you too weak?"

Joe Denton looked an interesting combination between angry and cowed. But he nodded.

Joy said: "I'll bring Arthur and Madeleine over to talk to you. I think, for what it is worth, that Mr. Truman is right."

"A first!" said Tom, cheerfully.

EPILOGUE

For there is nothing covered, that shall not be revealed: nor hidden, that shall not be known. For whatsoever things you have spoken in darkness, shall be published in the light: and that which you have spoken in the ear in the chambers, shall be preached on the housetops. - Luke 12:2-3

"Now," said Joy, to the Detective-Inspector, reflecting that the Bishop still had some influence, even these days, to get the man down to Felixtown on a Monday, looking rather irritated to see her, and Sergeant Grogan at the local police station. "As I've replaced Reverend Peter Hallam, and come to know a little about his parish and the man himself. I think I can help you to establish what killed him."

"Ah, the amateur lady detective from the novel," said the Inspector, lifting his eyes to heaven. "Look..."

Joy interrupted him. "He died of anaphylactic shock. He had lupus and suffered from a range of allergies. He was highly allergic to seafood, and accidentally ate quite a lot of it in a pie, which was not intended for him. The baker had come to meet with him – and had brought the pie for her intended husband – to talk about their impending marriage. I think you can see that killing him would have been as far from her best interests as possible. She wasn't there when he helped himself to what he may have thought was a gift aimed at him – priests get a lot of presents of this kind. She had gone to throw up, as she had morning-sickness, and I have a good witness to testify to the state of the toilet. Peter Hallam reacted to the seafood, his throat constricted, his tongue swelled, and when he realized what was happening, he tried to force open his airway with a piece of stick from a flower bowl in the church, while trying to get to his epi-pen or call for help."

The detective blinked. "I was about to say we'd concluded it was probably an accident. His prints were the only ones on the piece of oleander, and yes, he died of anaphylactic shock. According to the pathologist his airway constricted and then his heart gave in. I take my comment back. How do you know all of this?"

"I can tell you the necessary people to interview if you like, but let me tell you the story as I know it," said Joy. "And I suggest you check the menu at the Chamomile Natural Foods Café. The only pie they produce is a steak, kidney and oyster pie."

"It er, sounds dreadful."

"Oh, it's really good, Sir," said Sergeant Grogan. "I don't eat oysters, normally, but you wouldn't know these were oysters."

"And, as Sergeant Grogan can confirm, Reverend Peter Hallam would not have been welcome there, and would not have known that the pie contained seafood. It was, as happens every now and again, just an unfortunate accident. It was as much the police's fault for stopping the bridegroom-to-be rushing to the church, as it was Reverend Peter's fault for helping himself to a warm delicious smelling pie."

Joy had to explain the full story, of course, but it did help a great deal to have the local policeman, with all his local knowledge, right there.

At the end of it, the Inspector nodded. "A typical small town situation. I grew up in one. I'll have to check these witnesses out, but it all fits together very well. I can tell you, off the record, but I also know how that works out here, that I think a verdict of accidental death will be returned."

And so it was. Being a non-medical community, they latched onto the choking followed by a heart attack, and Maddy having called the Ambos – which, after all was what they would have done. No one – as everyone knew Zenobia – blamed her for not sticking around.

The funeral, a few days later, brought Felixtown to a halt, as they laid to rest one of their own, a man that they had not realized in life, was one of them. It was an unusual service, bringing together people who didn't see the inside of a church from one year to the next, and a few, like the Junk shop proprietor, and the assistant postmaster, who had never been seen there before.

It was also unusual in that the town atheist stood up to give a eulogy, his hand on his son's shoulder. A eulogy that began: "Sometimes we say men become good when they're dead. I didn't find out how good this man was, until he was dead. That was my loss, and I now regret it."

Joy walked home, after the last tea-cup had been washed, the last cake remains packed up, the last goodbyes said. Back at the rectory door, she looked at her floral gumboots on the doorstep, and then in at the framed pencil sketch of Reverend Peter Hallam on the far wall. He was smiling, gentle and whimsical. Smiling at her and anyone who entered, smiling out at the little white country church beyond, whose people were still the beating heart of this community.

The phone started to ring. The heart didn't get to stop beating because she was tired after a funeral.

She picked it up. "Reverend Joy listening."